V. Mahanenko

CONDEMNED

Lord Valevsky: Last of the Line

Books are the lives
we don't have
time to live,

Vasily Mahanenko

A Progression Fantasy Series
Book 6

Magic Dome Books

Condemned Book 6: A Progression Fantasy Series
(Lord Valevsky: Last of the Line)
Copyright © V. Mahanenko 2024
Cover Art © Lunar 2024
Cover Design V. Manyukhin
English translation copyright © Taylor Elise Margvelashvili 2024
Published by Magic Dome Books, 2024
All Rights Reserved
ISBN: 978-80-7693-607-2

This book is entirely a work of fiction.
Any correlation with real people or events
is coincidental.

All Series
by Vasily Mahanenko:

The Way of the Shaman LitRPG Series

Dark Paladin LitRPG Series

Galactogon LitRPG Series

Invasion LitRPG Series

World of the Changed LitRPG Series

The Alchemist LitRPG Series

The Bear Clan LitRPG Series

Starting Point LitRPG Series

The Bard from Barliona LitRPG series
(with Eugenia Dmitrieva)

Condemned
(Lord Valevsky: Last of The Line)
a Progression Fantasy series

Law of the Jungle
A Wuxia Progression Fantasy Adventure Series

Table of Contents:

Chapter 1

"ARCHDUKE VALEVSKY, this is a non-negotiable condition! Without it, the waypoint loses all meaning!"

"I'm starting to get the feeling that we're speaking different languages." I remained surprisingly calm. My lessons with Magister Tarra Loyd had not been in vain. "The dark ones who come to Hearth won't be able to leave. The portal will only work for trade. If bloodhounds come here, they will be killed. If the seekers appear, they will be killed. If anyone comes here for anything but negotiations or trade, he will be killed. And I won't care at all what clan the lawbreakers belong to. The law is the same for everyone."

"Perhaps there is still some way to resolve this issue?" A beautifully decorated box appeared in the dark one's hands. The kind that normally held gallo. The box was made of an unknown material that neither steel nor vyrma could pierce. I had my suspicions that it was made of mithril, but over the month and a half since my official recognition as Archduke Valevsky, I'd had no time to figure it out. More and more often the thought had crossed my mind that if I could turn back the clock, I would never in my life have agreed to manage the madness that is an "autonomous city." If not for Eleanore and Viscount Kurpatsky, things would be a complete mess. I just had no time to do anything. It would be nice if I'd been in Hearth this whole time — but no! I'd had to tromp around the entire empire closing three Pharapho dungeons. Sure, the loot was nice — I obtained ten units of bone armor, twenty cutting stones and three level-fifteen altars, but they all went to the "common fund" of the owners of the pie known as the Zarak Empire. Despite the fact that I was the one who had extracted everything, the only thing I received in return was two bone armors and the prospect of turning them into mithril sometime in the foreseeable future. The altars went to Count Shub, under whose personal supervision the treasury was built in Hearth. Considering the artifacts and resources involved, this treasury would soon be the most secure place in the empire, both for the valuables stored inside and the visitors. But this would only happen after the city was rebuilt and running smoothly. Which, from the looks of it, would be never. Count Nikitin, who'd had his title restored, was returned to the capital. Kimal Sarento acted as a mediator in negotiations between the head of the opposition and the emperor, somehow managing to resolve the conflict. Count Nikitin had once again become Duke of Turb and had set off to restore the region with great fervor. I only managed to retain one person in my service: Viscount Kurpatsky. Being head of security for an autonomous city still provided much more room to maneuver than being an assistant to the Duke of Turb.

"Why don't I pretend that I didn't see anything and that you didn't offer me anything." I didn't take my eyes off the negotiator and never lowered them to the box. "You know my conditions and they're not going to change. Either you agree, or build a portal somewhere else. Hearth will not settle for less. I won't keep you any longer."

The dark man's cheek twitched, but he did not dare contradict an Archduke. Bowing, he left to discuss our conditions with the council of the highest hierarchs of Skron. The portal was built, and the minotaurs stood ready to activate it. But without a signed agreement reflecting all my conditions, I would not allow it to become operational. I had no desire to increase the already considerable number of dark ones roaming freely throughout the Zarak Empire. So I was ready to defend the Citadel's demand, which had become mine as well, to the last.

"Sir Archduke, some letters for you." A maid peered into the office, bringing me three envelopes on a tray. I closed my eyes, remembering all the aristocrats of the Zarak Empire, among other people, and silently swearing. Eleanore and I had agreed that all matters related to the restoration of Hearth, except perhaps the portal and the dark ones, would be taken over by my manager. She knew how, was capable, and she enjoyed the work. The perfect combination. But Eleanore had never lifted a finger to pen a single letter to me. Because the bachelor Archduke must deal with these matters on his own.

The envelopes the maid handed over to me contained party invitations. They all said essentially the same thing: Archduke Valevsky, blah blah blah, we're throwing a ball, come and be our honored guest. Written between the lines was the fact that this family had a noble, educated, pure and immaculate maiden who would happily keep me company at the ball, or even throughout the entire length of my difficult but exhilarating life. For the first two weeks after the emperor's decision had been announced, the aristocrats still cast a wary eye on me, believing it to be a joke, but gradually one family after the other began to invite the high-flying young archduke to pay them a visit. And, naturally, everyone was trying to casually introduce me to their daughters. At first these invitations amused me, and I even attended a few, but I soon tired of the nonsense. I couldn't stand the attention — rift beasts were much easier to communicate with than these annoying, timid, cold, hot — and a thousand other epithets — girls. When we were introduced, what they all longed for was a moment of revelation or action on my part, some confession that I had loved only them all my adult life and I couldn't even imagine how to continue to exist without such beauty. Magister Tarra Loyd explained this to me after my first visit to the gala event. Alia flatly refused to accompany me, citing the fact that it was harmful for our unborn child to be in the aura of embittered girls, so I was forced to take my eldest mentor as my companion. It was funny how knowing someone's true age changed your attitude towards them. Tarra's sensuality had not diminished. The woman still evoked hundreds of admiring glances from those around her, but I saw this as nothing but a beautiful facade and had no desire for anything more. At first, the master was amused by this, she even made some efforts to seduce me, just for fun, but gradually, our relationship became purely work oriented. I was taught manners and how to behave in the company of aristocrats, I dragged her to all sorts of balls, where she acted not only as my companion, but also as a second for any duels.

And where would I be without them? Duels! I had five such encounters. Five duels. One for each event. The fact that I was officially recognized as the winner of the imperial tournament haunted many. They used every opportunity to try to insult me. Everyone wanted to demonstrate that they were more worthy fighters than me. Moreover, I had no right to refuse even petty barons of the most remote lands. So, despite my title of archduke, I had to fight. And how did they turn out? All five fights ended the same way: while they tried to break through my defenses with swords or magic, I came close and punched them in the jaw. I beat them with my knowledge of the opponent, as Gustav had taught. My opponent fell unconscious on the floor and there was no longer any talk of continuing the stupid duel. Except that I would take the opponent's sword and allow the family of fools to buy it back. Basically, very little sense and a whole lot of noise. For the past three weeks I had managed to avoid appearing in public places, but now I didn't know how to react.

Because the authors of the letters turned out to be such iconic figures that my heart began to beat wildly. Count Vyazemsky Sr., Count George Vyazemsky and Countess Serlena Przhedetskaya. But who was I lying to? My heart started pounding at the sight of the last name. Serlena...a forgotten feeling of warmth surfaced in my chest. I had met this girl only once, at some ball in the Southeast region. I, then still a humble baron of the outskirts, had the audacity to ask the girl to dance, and she, despite the constant attention of others with the title of count, agreed. The happiest five minutes of my life! Serlena acted aloof, as was befitting of a countess, but she still flashed me two smiles. This was almost a year ago, and I still remember every feature of her beautiful face. The dimples on her cheeks, her yellow-green eyes, her straight aristocratic nose...

"Sir Maximilian, are you okay?" The maid became worried when I disappeared into my memories. Shaking my head to drive away the obsession, I was surprised by myself. When had I gone so soft? Echoes of a past life? When was this past life? It was as if it had never existed, as my new one had captured me so completely. Not even five months had passed since I was made a doomed soldier, and it felt as if I'd already lived two or three lives. Opening the envelope, I delved into reading, but with every second my smile grew smaller and smaller until it finally vanished.

"Dear Archduke Valevsky! Allow us to cordially invite you to a ball on the occasion of my upcoming wedding with Count George Vyazemsky, which will take place..."

The girl explained that she had taken the liberty of inviting me without the consent of her future husband, because she remembered perfectly well "the young Baron Valevsky, who showed her signs of attention...". Although George Vyazemsky would also be pleased to see me at the event. Following our duel, all he had done was admire my strength and nobility. After all, even defeat in the competition between academies did not harm the count's honor, thanks to my actions. So basically, 'You, Archduke Valevsky, are such a wonderful person, so come watch me, the subject of all your childhood nighttime fantasies, marry someone else.'

Opening George's letter, I had a rough idea of what it would contain. 'Archduke, I'm getting married, come visit.' Of course, all this was written in a beautiful and eloquent style that took up almost a whole page, and yet I managed to fit all the verbiage into one sentence. The younger Vyazemsky wanted to see me at his wedding and had no idea who Serlena Przhedetskaya was to me.

And, of course, a third letter. From the head of the Vyazemsky family himself. Once again cutting to the chase, the count had invited me to his son's wedding. Because it was only right.

Three different letters, three different authors, one message. Most unpleasant of all was that even if I could ignore Serlena and George's letters, I had no right to decline an invitation from Vyazemsky Sr. We had already discussed many interesting projects that would turn Hearth into a fairytale city. Renovated hotels and streets, a new stormwater system, a new water supply and sewage system, expanded boulevards, new shops, an entire neighborhood of craft workshops and, of course, homes for everyone who would participate in all this. The emperor had not only allocated me the city, but also fifteen kilometers around it, and now, a month and a half later, this territory had been marked out for future buildings. Moreover, in order to indicate the individuality and uniqueness of Hearth, the construction of a huge wall stretching along the entire perimeter of my lands had already begun. Even the capital of the Zarak Empire didn't have this amenity. Only Al-Khorezm, where I was going to go in a week and a half, had a single wall around the main city.

Long story short, like it or not, in a week's time, I was supposed to show up at Count

Vyazemsky's estate in Turb with a whole mountain of gifts. Both for the newlyweds and for each letter writer separately, as a thank-you for the invitation. Moreover, these gifts must correspond with my status as archduke. Considering that I was not just the only one in the Zarak Empire, but in the entire Light world, these gifts must be exclusive. Magister Tarra had already taught me this. Now I just had to figure out where to get these gifts and how not to kill all the guests in a fit of jealousy?

"Sir, Adeline Sarento is here to see you," the maid knocked on the door once again. As I said, I had no time left to indulge in idle chat. Someone always wanted something, and it was incredibly infuriating. Instead of conquering the rifts, the Fog of Pharapho, or simply studying, I was holding useless meetings and agreeing to unnecessary ceremonies.

"That's not how things are done, cabbage!" Kimal Sarento's wife burst into the office. Outstanding spouse. As far as I knew, after the marriage ceremony and the obligatory wedding night, these two did not cross paths. Adeline was firmly entrenched in Hearth, despite the opportunity she had to go out into the big world. I can't even imagine how Kimal Sarento managed to get such a status for his dark wife. Nevertheless, she did not use it: she had a lot of things to do even without traveling around the Zarak Empire. She was dealing with the portal and, what pleased me most, teaching me the language of the dark ones.

"What now?" I asked in the language of the city of Kerux. Practice never hurts, and within a month I began to make some progress in learning the language. I'd already been able to read almost a whole page from the textbooks that Adeline brought.

"The dark ones will not sign this agreement!" The girl accepted the rules of the game and spoke to me in the dark language.

"If there is no agreement, there will be no portal. Hearth is a waypoint for trade. If you want a travel point, build it yourself. We will destroy it. Even despite Magister Elor."

Over the past month I had heard the name of this dark one more often than any other. Except for my own, of course. The highest hierarch of Skron across several dark clans traveled through the lands of the Light as if it were his home. Magister Elor was considered one of the strongest among the dark ones, and he was engaged in such routine and simple work that I had reason to doubt the true motives of his actions. The dark ones could not be so wasteful that they would assign a figure of such magnitude to the task of negotiating trade with the light ones. Magister Elor was clearly performing additional tasks in our lands that were hidden from the laypeople, while managing to remain unnoticed. The church would gladly finish off this bastard if it could, as most of the recent catastrophes it had faced had been caused by Magister Elor. However, despite all their connections, neither the Fortress, nor the Citadel, nor the Stronghold could catch the dark one. But we needed his signature on the agreement that Adeline so zealously rushed to defend. Another indicator of his status.

Having received the surname Sarento, Adeline finally rid herself of her terrible burn. The new head of her clan…former clan…or was it? This point was not entirely clear to me, but the general gist was that the new head of the clan, Bartolomeo, saved Adeline from an unpleasant burn. Having united with the Gourfans, Bartolomeo dealt a sensitive blow to the Valdez clan. In general, there was so much turmoil among the dark ones that all our issues seemed somehow insignificant to them. If it weren't for the portal and the construction process, Adeline would have returned home long ago to take part in the clan wars.

"Don't piss me off, Cabbage!" Adeline was losing her temper.

"Listen, I've had enough!" I barked, tired of smiling wide for anyone and everyone. "If you don't like it, just throw in the towel and get out of here! I've got enough problems without you. The monitor from the Citadel will kill me soon. If not physically, then mentally, and now you on top of this! The terms of the agreement will not change. The dark ones will use Hearth only as a trading point."

"My mother told me: never get involved with the light ones. They are worse than even the orthodox! "Adeline pouted dramatically, but immediately stopped her theatrical performance.

"Okay, I have other business with you, you spicy little Cabbage. The scholars want to meet you."

"Judging by the significant pause, you were clearly counting on some kind of reaction?" I asked when Adeline fell silent.

"Scholars, Cabbage! From one of the leading dark clans!"

"Must I repeat my question?"

"The ruins in the light lands have been explored far and wide. Nothing valuable can be found in them. If there is anything, it's only in the Pharapho dungeons. And even then they try to destroy them instantly. Real explorers travel through ruins that have never been touched by humans! Ancient secrets, artifacts, monsters, resources — they extract everything that allows us to remain the leaders of this world!"

"Adeline, you're wasting my time. If one of the dark ones wants to see me, he can come to Hearth. Or did you think that as soon as I heard the word 'scholar,' I'd put all my other affairs on the back burner and rush to them with my tongue out like an obedient dog? What did you expect by giving me this information?"

"I was counting on you sticking out your tongue," Adeline winced with displeasure. "Okay, let's be honest. There are ancient ruins in the lands of my clan that we have not been able to explore for two hundred years. The best of the best went there, but they did not return. We hired scholars from other clans, but to no avail. As a result, the ruins of the Bartolomeo Clan were recognized as cursed and no one else will agree to conquer them. Our scholars believe that you will succeed."

"Succeed where the best dark mages failed? No need to overestimate me. You know very well that I'm not a particularly skilled mage."

Not a particularly skilled mage indeed! Kimal Sarento had clearly demonstrated to me the difference between the levels of magic stones, without even using his maximum power.

When I handed the chancellor of the magic academy an amulet that blocked the *Analyze* ability, I persuaded him to spar with me. I really wanted to test the limits of my capabilities before the competition in the Shurgan Empire. After all, the best of the best will be there. And I'd be there too.

Kimal Sarento agreed and struck me with just one bolt of lightning. One! My *Golden Dome of Protection* had fallen as if it wasn't there. Even with all the support stones!

The bolt hit so hard that I was walking around twitching for several days like an epileptic. My stones proved so insignificant in the face of the chancellor's greatness that I felt it was time to throw in the towel.

For at the upcoming tournament, as Kimal Sarento explained, there would be no one with any stones below level twenty. There would be real monstrosities there that may even be too much for him, the chancellor of the magic academy of the Zarak Empire, to handle.

However, he believed in me and wished me success. He was prepared to provide elixirs to increase my stones by three or four levels in exchange for all the resources in my inventory. We didn't end up settling on a final price.

"As for being a mage, I'd go so far as to say that you're not just unskilled, you're barely a mage at all, but this isn't an issue of magic. We have enough mages without you. I'm talking about the Fog. About the insane number of soldiers and sergeants of Pharapho. It has gotten to the point that the clan is seriously considering destroying the ruins by using a rift, but this would greatly damage our rating and reputation. We would like to avoid this, and then we remembered you. Help us, we'll help you. Not only will you get excellent practice in the dark tongue, but the clan also agrees to allot a tenth of all the artifacts obtained to you."

"Artifacts? I'm going to need a little more detail," I said. "What exactly are they and why can't they be extracted after the Fog is cleared from the ruins? Isn't that the logical move?"

"The Fog of Pharapho is not just a dungeon. In fact, the dungeon plays such a trivial role that most clans don't even cast a glance in its direction. Before, they wouldn't consider it because few were prepared to lose half of their warriors for the sake of a six- or eight-level altar. It's dangerous, and my father is proof of that...But I'm getting off track. Anyway, when the ruins are hidden by the Fog of Pharapho, there are lots of exciting things that can be found inside. Fatal damage blocking amulets, for example."

"Amulet blanks can be extracted from ordinary rifts," I reminded her.

"Only one in every hundred blanks becomes the amulet you want," she snorted. "And even then, it may not turn out properly. I'm talking about a one-hundred-percent guarantee of obtaining such an amulet. Or any amulet, really. Because we're not searching for the blanks themselves, but a device for processing them. An ancient artifact that only appears under the Fog of Pharapho. The devices are one of the many artifacts found in the ruins. Weapons, armor, those little boxes you carry around constantly, recipes — all this is mined in ruins."

"Recipes?" I said, intrigued.

"Magical scrolls that can only be used a certain number of times. They allow you to create various elixirs and other things without having to rely on a device. Quite a useful thing and as rare as your good mood. Well, maybe not that rare. Ten percent, Cabbage. They are ready to give you a tenth of everything you get from our ruins. And these ruins, I hasten to remind you, are two hundred years old! They're not just old — they are ancient. Something could have appeared over the past two hundred years that even we don't know about. Something that will make our clan even stronger."

"Are there only Pharapho spawn in the fog, or is there something else?"

"Well..."

"Adeline!"

"There are Pharapho spawn lurking in the fog. They are the main source of power, but each artifact is guarded by a mutated spawn."

"A what?" My heart fluttered. I'd heard this word before. I even had a map of the central region marking the locations of the mutated creatures. Upon studying the map that immediately popped up before my eyes, there were three of them. Moreover, one was already gray — that bushy grass creature that I'd finished off when I found *Praxis*. If these mutated ones guarded not stones, but artifacts...I definitely needed to check. But where would I find the time?

"Spawn that have been altered. The artifacts have warped them beyond recognition, and they're the main challenge the scholars face. We've learned to avoid the Pharapho spawn, but it's difficult to avoid a mountain of stone that springs to life or carnivorous earth. This is why they want you."

"Half," I said without even thinking. "I won't agree to anything less. Plus, everything I get from the Pharapho spawn is mine."

"Aside from the development crystals and cutting stones," Adeline said — she had clearly come prepared — "and we know that you get them from every monster you kill, we want our full share. Twenty percent, Cabbage, is the maximum I was allowed to concede to you."

"Half, Adeline. Exactly half. Otherwise, give

my highest regards to your scholars, activate the rift in the hope that at least something survives. The mutated spawn must have been gaining strength over all these years. I won't walk straight into the jaws of the beast for anything less."

"A quarter!" Adeline cried out after a long pause. The girl looked as if she had been tortured for months and had finally been forced to betray her own people.

"Next time I'm going up to sixty," I said with a shrug. "So better not say anything rash. You know my requirements, I'm not agreeing to less, even if you get your husband to come out here."

"He said I had to deal with you on my own," Adeline muttered. She was in constant communication with Kimal — my wedding gift had been remote communication sigils, which both parties were delighted to accept.

"Because he understands perfectly how dangerous it is. I need to be in Turb in a week, so you don't have much time to negotiate my terms with your scholars. I won't change them."

"Are you going to the Vyazemskys' wedding? I'll have to go too...Why don't we go after the ceremony?"

"Because then I'm off to Al-Khorezm. Magister Meram is already tired of waiting for his student."

Dropping the gray runescribe's name did the trick. Adeline grimaced with displeasure, realizing that she wouldn't be able to tear me away from my training.

"Alright, Cabbage! Fifty it is! It's better than

nothing, if we'll have to make a rift anyway. The Bartolomeo Clan will ensure your protection and bring you back on time. Tell me when you're ready, I'll activate the portal."

"The portal will be activated as soon as we sign the agreement." I wasn't going to be distracted from the main point. If I used the portal without an agreement, where was my guarantee that the dark ones wouldn't just act as if I'd agreed to their terms anyway?

"You're an evil little cabbage and your leaves are bitter." Adeline opened the folder and pulled out three thick bound documents. Each of them had my signature on them to ensure that no pages were later switched out. But even this would not stop me from checking the documents with a notary. Both in terms of the text and in terms of the legitimacy of the signature that appeared next to mine. Magister Elor, representing the interests of the dark ones, signed an agreement to transform Hearth into a trading point. All that was left to do was to check everything to make sure there was no forgery, find a representative of the Citadel dressed in a light green robe, and get his signature on the document as well. Only after this would Hearth receive the status of a "free economic zone permitted to trade with the dark ones."

"Will a couple of hours suffice? We can't put this matter off for another week. These ruins are really snapping at our throats."

"Alia, I need your help," I said, touching my

shoulder to call my personal attendant. "I need to draw up an agreement here. Call Bagration, there's work for him too. The dark ones agreed to our terms. There's going to be a portal in Hearth!"

Chapter 2

"WELCOME TO MY CLAN'S family home, Cabbage. Try not to break anything and don't get into any fights or I'll kill you."

I followed after Adeline Sarento, trying not to glance around too much. No, that was a lie — I was trying to keep my jaw off the floor as I shamelessly stared at everything we passed. There was nothing wrong with examining things that one had never encountered before. The main thing was making it look like you have the exact same thing in your own backyard. But I couldn't help noting some of the interesting solutions they had come up with. It was a shame that the minotaurs, who were almost the direct descendants of Skron, were responsible for the portals. Personally, I would not refuse a convenient means of transportation between Hearth and our capital. Who would?

The portal belonging to the Bartolomeo Clan

was located a distance away from the house so that its inhabitants had time to prepare to fight back in case any potential enemy appeared. There was a perfectly tended garden between the house and the arch, and I couldn't help but grin as a gaggle of broxies ran past us. They paid us no mind — Adeline had a family ring that hid the girl from dark beasts, and I simply put my mirror up and didn't spare another thought for the omnivorous monsters. The dark one sniffled in displeasure when the gardeners and guardians of the estate disappeared among the trees.

"What a troubling little cabbage you are," Adeline muttered. "How are we supposed to defend the estate if a whole crowd of people like you comes close?"

"I think just one of me will be more than enough to stir up some trouble."

"Are you so sure of yourself, young man? Maybe you should back up those words with action." The air a few meters from me suddenly became dense and a man appeared out of thin air. They say first impressions are especially important in building relationships with people, and the man who stepped out of the shadows certainly managed to make an impression. Majestic was the word that first popped into my head. Outwardly, he looked like Adeline — the same high cheekbones, the brows that obscured the eyes — although Adeline was a fair sight prettier. His long, thick, black hair was tied back into a ponytail so that it didn't interfere with his movements, making him look like a Shurganite. But he certainly wasn't. His normal brown eyes spoke of the fact that he was a gray magister, able to conceal himself from Skron, and his tight, sturdy garments were perfect for running through the forest or climbing a mountain, but not for entertaining guests. And worst of all, *Analyze* again sadly shrugged its invisible shoulders, acknowledging its complete uselessness. It was unable to break through the amulet. I was starting to feel like *Analyze* was only useful to me in the initial stages of my new life. The longer I lived, the more I realized how powerless this ability stone really was. It was only good for seeking out converts among the aristocrats. In a month and a half, I'd managed to find twenty puppets in Hearth and hand them over to the Fortress. I had an event ahead that the cream of the crop would be attending, so I planned to get my kicks there — the Zarak Empire needed to be cleansed of the dark infection.

"Uncle!" Adeline jumped out of her seat and rushed to hug the man, as if she hadn't seen him for half her life. The man allowed himself a meager smile and even hugged his niece, while not taking his eyes off me.

"I don't need to prove or explain anything," I answered calmly. "I've already said everything I wanted. I'm not here to test your security system, but to get my fifty percent of the artifacts."

"Max!" Adeline was indignant. "Stop pretending to be somebody! Uncle, let me introduce you to Archduke Maximilian Valevsky, the one I wrote to you about. Maximilian, this is my uncle, the head of the scholars, the highest hierarch of Skron of the Bartolomeo Clan, Theodore Jode."

"Welcome to the lands of the Bartolomeo Clan, Maximilian," Theodore lowered my title, showing that here it meant nothing. Despite the fact that the dark ones themselves did not deign to assign titles as such, there was still a certain hierarchy within each specific clan. Ordinary members, masters, high hierarchs, scholars. This was not a strict vertical of power; Elor was both a magister and the highest hierarch of several clans. Rather, these divisions could be called interest groups.

"Thank you for the invitation, and I have a request — I'd like to get straight to the point of why you called me. In four days I have to return home, and the ruins we're all so eager to deal with aren't exactly behind the nearest grove of trees, as I understand it. I'll need some time to figure out the logistics."

"The ruins are located a week's journey from our house," Theodore replied. "The portal will be opened tonight. At this moment, all those who will be participating in the expedition have already gathered. Now I would like to invite you into my home. We're having a celebration today."

"Celebration?" Adeline frowned. "What are we suddenly celebrating?"

"Today, dear niece, is my daughter's birthday. If you weren't so busy, you would certainly remember the invitation you received two months ago. Naira Jode turns eighteen today.”

Adeline's face stretched into a strained expression, as if she was desperately begging her uncle to refute his words. But Theodore made no move to save his niece. Deciding that all the necessary invitations had been handed out, he turned around and strode off toward the house. We probably should have followed him, but Adeline, who had fallen into a stupor, slowed down the whole process. She muttered something in the dark tongue and I could pick out a few swears here and there, and as I was already a connoisseur of all dirty words. Her final words were scolding herself for forgetting such an important date for her cousin.

“Can you explain what's got you in such a tizzy?” I asked, trying to bring Adeline to her senses. She looked through me, as if she didn't see, but then her gaze focused on me and hope appeared on her face.

“Max! Cabbage to the rescue! Naira needs a gift!”

“And? How do I factor in here? What exactly is going on? Are there specific gifts you're supposed to give dark ones on their eighteenth birthday?”

“It's practically the most important day in any mage's life, and not just for us dark ones. Today, my cousin opens her development model! She will be allowed to approach the altar and given the opportunity to use it. This will determine her fate once and for all, because her entire future life will depend on the direction she chooses. I remembered her birthday, I even prepared a gift, but your portal completely distracted me!"

"The portal is still there, as far as I can see. And the minotaurs are very dutiful at answering your call. What's stopping you from flying off to Hearth and picking up a gift?"

"Maybe the fact that it's in Turb? Kimal prepared a gift and I was supposed to pick it up. But I got all wrapped up in this portal business and forgot, and you, the light ones, with your prejudices towards portals, ruined the whole day for me!"

"And how are we to blame here?"

"Who else?! Alright, Cabbage, stay right there. Kimal, I have a problem..."

Adeline quickly explained the essence of the problem, as well as where we were and where we were heading.

"Maximilian, I have a request for you. Help my wife get through this event," I heard the chancellor say. The huge distance between us was no problem for remote communication. "I don't want to lose face just because of a certain someone's girlish memory. We planned to give Naira two gallos. As far as I know, you have two of the red crystals yourself. Help Adeline, and you will not only get both stones back, but also something else useful. And don't forget — you're supposed to be in Turb in a week. A ceremony on such a grand scale as those organized by Count Vyazemsky happens once a decade. The gift must be commensurate."

"Alright," I replied, regretting establishing a remote connection with him, and not for the first time. I didn't like it when people enlisted my services knowing full well that I had no right to refuse. Looking up, I saw a satisfied, smiling Adeline, demandingly extending her palm to me.

"The fact that I promised to help Kimal Sarento doesn't mean that you don't owe me," I said, pulling out two red crystals. "You do owe me, and a big one at that. Remember this, dark one."

"Okay, enough!" Adeline waved me off, hiding the treasure in her pockets. "We'll settle up. "Let's get going, we need to pick you out some clothes. You didn't think that you could show up to a party looking like that, did you? And it wouldn't hurt to change my own clothes either. Come on, Cabbage! Enough time-wasting!"

The more I learned about Adeline, the less I liked her. She was a twenty-two-year-old menace with no moral values whatsoever. I couldn't even imagine how she had managed to land a position as a junior teacher at a magic academy teaching students logic, with her disposition. Seemed like she could use a lesson in logic herself.

We never caught up with Theodore. When we emerged from the forest, a luxurious estate lay ahead. Almost an exact copy of the one I'd destroyed — heaps and mounds of everything and anything that could be considered a "luxury." Marble columns, stucco moldings, statues, some bas-reliefs, gold — the Bartolomeo Clan spared no expense in furnishing their home. As we walked towards the porch, I could see several dozen supreme converts guarding the estate. The puppets moved silently, like shadows, but still fell under the influence of my *Analyze.* This time it did not disappoint, but still made me sigh heavily. Not a single stone below level fifteen. And these guys were ordinary security guards! I probably shouldn't have quarreled with the chancellor. Previously, I had considered myself invulnerable and had rushed boldly forward with no consideration for the consequences. Now, as I assessed potential opponents, the thought arose more and more frequently that a tactical retreat wouldn't be such a dishonorable choice. The most important thing was surviving — the rest was secondary.

The inside matched the outside. Rich and luxurious. When you first step into a room like that, you start to feel very small, but now that I knew what was on the top floor of the building, all the charm of the expensive furnishings faded away. A Rift Master! The one who protected the house from encroaching strangers and produced broxies on an industrial scale. My soul felt repulsed because I remembered how the Master maintained its own life. Through human sacrifice. Numerous victims. At least a hundred people a year, preferably more to keep the beast strong. And this didn't bother anyone. Think what wretched creatures they must be. But the fair ones would just produce more.

"Must I really attend your private family event?" I asked, not finding the strength within myself to move any further. For some reason, this had hit me hard. It was disgusting to see how everyone was walking around and smiling, not thinking about the fact that three floors above, ordinary people were dying. But I also had no right to interfere with the established order of the dark ones. I knew very well that they were kidnapping the inhabitants of light empires. The fact that I hadn't realized earlier about the presence of the Rift Master in the estate was my own problem.

"Has something changed?" Adeline frowned. She'd picked up on my change in emotional state immediately.

"The Rift Master. I don't like being in the same house with it."

"In the same house?" Adeline said. "What are you talking about?"

"My dear niece, I think you should hurry up and change your clothes. The event is about to start in an hour. I'll take care of our guest," Theodore Jode appeared again, as if out of nowhere. It was as if Adeline was an entirely different person — she perked up, yelped and, uttering some phrase that could be regarded as an apology, ran away. She literally ran away — the girl did not want to waste a second.

"You should watch your tongue, Hunter of Darkness," said Theodore. "You may have noticed that a defensive field has formed around us.

Evidently something like the canopy Alia has."

"You invited me here — I didn't ask to come. The fact that you did not bother to explain to me the rules of this society is your mistake. The fact that Adeline doesn't know about the Master should have been conveyed to me in advance."

The look Theodore Jode shot me could have killed me on the spot.

"Your status as our guest is the only reason you are still breathing."

"So, maybe there's no need to pretend to be hospitable hosts? I'm perfectly happy waiting for the portal to open somewhere off the premises. I have no desire to spoil your holiday with my sour face. It's your day, not mine."

"Your clothes are already waiting for you, they will help you get dressed. A limited number of residents know that there is a Rift Master in the house. This is classified information. If you start shouting about it left and right, even your status as a guest will not prevent me from stopping your tongue. Your task is to deal with the ruins. If the new head of the clan did not personally want to see the one whose life Adeline's father saved, you would not even be allowed across the threshold of this house. Herod, my brother, died because of you."

"He was killed by the Valdez Clan," I reminded him.

"Because of your altar!" Theodore nearly barked, but managed to control himself. "If it weren't for you, my brother would have returned from this Light-forsaken campaign alive and well! An infected rift is not so rare a thing that the heads of three clans should die trying to close it!"

"And the commander of the Citadel, for that matter. There is no need to push human greed onto me, Theodore. No need to shield your brother by making him a hero. My personal opinion is that if Valdez hadn't attacked first, Herod Jode would have. I did not show this letter to Adeline, so as not to traumatize her already wounded soul. You know your brother's handwriting, right? So what do you want to accuse me of? The fact that I, until the very last moment, tried to get through to the head of the Bartolomeo Clan!"

I laid down one of the pieces of paper I'd received from the sixteenth level of the Pharapho Dungeon. Kimal Sarento's genius had to be admired. It was as if he knew that I would need the receipts of every dark one I'd killed!'

Theodore's cheek twitched — he hadn't known this information before. According to the official report, the Valdez clan and the Citadel had dragged us into the depths of the rift. The rest were considered casualties. But, as it turns out, not all the victims were actually victims.

"The presence of a Master on the estate is classified information. Those who are not in the highest hierarchy of the clan have no right to know about it. It is not widely discussed," Theodore looked at the paper for a long time and finally came to some sort of conclusion. Having removed the canopy, he motioned to the servant who had been waiting for us nearby the entire time.

"Find some suitable attire for Maximilian Valevsky to attend the event. He is our guest. The new clan head wants to meet the man my brother sacrificed his life for in person."

There was no talk of returning Herod's receipt to me. Fine by me, I had my own copy. I diligently collected such receipts at each level. And not in vain, as it turned out. I think if the Valdez Clan was given a corresponding piece of paper signed by, say, the Gourfan Clan, this would add further fuel to the Clan Wars.

A suit was chosen for me relatively quickly. The clan had a whole wardrobe for all occasions and sizes. Having donned the beautiful dark suit that fit me as if it had been tailored, I evaluated myself in the mirror. Another high-born aristocrat, of whom there are a dime a dozen in the world. No individuality, just chic, shine and beauty. The uniform of a magic academy would look much more appropriate now. It would stand out from the uniform masses.

When I was taken to the large hall, my suspicions were only confirmed — all the men in the clan wore a similar suit to mine. It was as if everyone had the same tailor. And I clearly saw representatives of other clans among them, so the assumption that this was the uniform of the Bartolomeo Clan was disproven. It was just customary for dark people to wear monotonous attire. A plain dark suit, a white shirt, an awkward bow tie, patent leather shoes, polished to a mirror.

Everything was supposed to be perfect.

The female assembly was more diverse. Lavish dresses that could easily hide two people, in various styles and colors. At last, a pop of color! The monotony was tiring. And the supreme converts' dress sense suddenly clicked into place. It wasn't because they were so comfortable or easy to wear, but because that was the accepted style! Nothing more.

My presence did not go unnoticed. The guests already knew who I was and had begun to whisper, discussing my appearance and demeanor. Nothing new. Light, dark — everyone behaved the same. I calmly walked over to the hors d'oeuvres table and grabbed some nicely decorated small sandwiches stuck together with toothpicks. I'd never seen anything like this, so it was an interesting experience. From what I could tell, all the ingredients were things I'd normally eat, so there was no need to swallow something absolutely repulsive to be polite.

"So you can look halfway human after all, Cabbage? Unimaginable!" I heard Adeline's voice. Turning around, I saw Kimal Sarento's wife and was sincerely happy for the chancellor. Even though his marriage was political in nature, Adeline was a gorgeous woman. Beautiful, curvy, attractive.

"Got your fill? Then follow me, I'll introduce you to the cream of the crop! All the best of the Bartolomeo Clan have gathered here today!"

It was pointless to resist — Adeline had

become a tsunami, sweeping away everything and everyone in her path. Names were spoken, my hand was constantly being shaken, and someone even tried to grip test me, but turned pale when my skin suddenly became harder than stone. No one knew that I was wearing mithril. Or the fact that my weapon was always with me.

Adeline dragged me to the last group, which stood a little further from the rest. Several puppets gestured to particularly zealous guests that they should not approach the highest hierarchs of the clan, but we bypassed this security outfit. For some reason, Adeline was permitted to do a lot. The answer as to why, as always, proved quite banal:

"Gentlemen, allow me to introduce you to Maximilian Valevsky, a dark hunter who was invited to solve our problem with the ruins. Maximilian, you've already met my uncle, but I ask you to extend your warmest greetings to my eldest brother, who also happens to be the head of the Bartolomeo Clan, Cedric Jode."

A slightly aged male version of Adeline stared back at me. The man looked to be about thirty-five, but I assumed he was much older. His athletic physique was able to hide his age very well. Like Adeline, Cedric had snow-white hair that fell like a silken waterfall onto his shoulders. On his head was a crown of white metal, adorned with huge precious stones, on his hand were two rings emitting a red aura, and on his neck hung several amulets, one of which also glowed red. Naturally, there was no question of using *Analyze.* My ability was blocked again.

"Welcome to my home, Maximilian Valevsky," Cedric said in a pleasant velvety voice, finally forming the image of Adeline's brother. A second Kimal Sarento! Handsome, powerful, and with enough charisma to draw others in.

"Thank you for the invitation, Cedric Jode," I replied, deciding to keep quiet, crouching below the grassline. Right now, I was here to wait for my portal and earn a whole mountain of artifacts. Even if I didn't need them, the very fact that I possessed dark artifacts would significantly affect my status in the section of the pie called the Zarak Empire. The larger the piece I managed to bite off, the easier it would be to deal with the Fardi family. If anyone thought that I'd forgotten about them, they would be deeply mistaken. Kimal Sarento was right — there was no point in killing them with my own hands or, Light forbid, hiring assassins from the Nocturnal Guild for this task. Everything must be arranged so that I could overthrow the Fardi family, toppling them to the bottom of the aristocratic pit, or perhaps even completely depriving them of their status. The emperor would never agree to this now — the Duke of Odoevsky brought him a lot of benefits. But, if I suggested something that completely negated this benefit, it would be possible to discuss such a far-fetched idea with Zurgan the First. Kimal Sarento promised to aid me in my negotiations as soon as I had the strength.

They didn't keep me long. A few meaningless phrases, a conversation about nothing, and finally I was left to my own devices. Adeline disappeared into the company of the other girls, and they paid less and less attention to me. It got to the point where people stopped whispering about the fact that there was a Hunter of Darkness among them. This suited me, and I had already begun to think about how to quietly escape from this celebration of life when the doors of the hall opened and the loud voice of the herald attracted everyone's attention:

"Ladies and gentlemen, the star of today's event, Naira Jode!"

The crowd rushed to the doors to greet the birthday girl, and no matter how much I resisted, I was borne along on the wave. Somehow, I managed to end up in the first two rows. The rhythmic click of heels was heard, and an eighteen-year-old girl appeared at the door, preparing herself to stand in front of the altar of development.

My heart skipped a beat and the world ceased to exist for me. The space darkened, but a single ray of light remained, keeping me from the final darkness. This ray of light slowly entered the hall and smiled at everyone gathered, waving her arms. Our glances crossed for just a moment, but my treacherous heart skipped another beat — in place of Naira's eyes, there was nothing but an absolute and all-consuming darkness. But this wasn't enough to make me tear my gaze from the woman who shattered my own inner scale of attraction with her first step into the hall, forever occupying first place. Naira Jode was perfection!

Chapter 3

THE GIRL FLOATED INTO THE CENTER of the hall as people began to congratulate her on this momentous occasion. My ears were still buzzing, my legs weren't moving and I could barely breathe, so I didn't really hear what the people surrounding Naira were saying.

"What an interesting reaction you're having, Cabbage," Adeline said, appearing nearby. "How do you find my cousin?"

"Very beautiful," I replied without pretense.

"Oh, come on! Beautiful? The entire dark world pursues her! If only you knew how many clans we had to turn away from this event. It's only those who are closest to the family. And you. You'd better appreciate it!"

"I do." I closed my eyes and took a few deep breaths, trying to regulate my body. Whatever was happening to it now was something I did not like at all. Yes, Naira was stunning, but was I, already accustomed to lessons with Magister Tarra, really so soft-bellied and weak-willed as to go completely numb just from being in the proximity of a beautiful girl my age?

"You want me to introduce you? But I warn you — you'll need a gift. You can't just approach the birthday girl empty handed."

"A gift?" I thought. I had nothing on me, except perhaps my rings, weapons and mithril gloves. And I couldn't give those to her, could I?

"Naturally. Something that demonstrates your sincere feelings for Naira. And I'm telling you now, don't even think about offering gold. Our clan is up to our ears in gold. Oh, and one more thing — Naira doesn't speak the language of the Light at all. So you'll need a translator. I'm willing to offer my assistance, for a fee…"

"Maximilian Valevsky, Hunter of Darkness!" the herald's voice rang out, and everyone's attention turned to me.

"Oh, you're in trouble now. Your cabbage is cooked," Adeline whispered, giving me a shove. "The Clan Head wants to introduce you as a guest of honor. Think about your gift. You can't go without a gift, or the doors of the clan will be forever closed for you."

Adeline grabbed me by the arm and led me to the birthday girl, whose interest was piqued. Bartolomeo, the clan head, already stood next to her, as well as several other senior hierarchs of Skron. Including Naira's father.

"Unfortunately, my command of the dark language is deplorable," I said, turning to the girl. I spoke in dark, albeit very broken. Our language really was easier on the tongue.

"That's no problem, I understand the language of the light ones perfectly well," Naira smiled, and muffled laughter was heard from Adeline. That witch had pulled one over on me again! Although, I must admit, I was glad to take full advantage of those moments when everyone's attention was on her, using the time to center my breathing. Yes, Naira was beautiful. Dazzlingly beautiful. Her voice was both enchanting and captivating. But she was an ordinary human, and I had to behave as I would with any other ordinary human, and not as with a deity.

"In that case, I must congratulate you on your eighteenth birthday and admit that I am somewhat at a loss. A certain jokester, who's having a little fun, warned me that if I did not give a gift corresponding to the beauty of the birthday girl, I would never again be allowed to pass over the threshold of the Bartolomeo Clan. But how can one give the gift of the sun? Only that would be able to outshine your radiant beauty for even a moment."

I succeeded in my main goal, which was to force everyone to turn towards Adeline again, who had fallen silent. What, dark one, not so fun anymore? Did you think that since I fell for one of your tricks, I would fall for the second?

"Some people have a little too much fun, as

you so rightly put it, and should receive a good lashing for it," said the clan head. Adeline suddenly remembered that she had urgent business somewhere on the other side of the palace, and was about to leave, but suddenly froze without taking a step. The clan's supreme converts were blocking her path, acting on a gesture from their master. Adeline frowned, turned to her brother and was about to say something, but then I took the floor once more:

"Nevertheless, she's right — it's improper to leave the birthday girl giftless, especially when she is about to encounter the altar of development for the very first time. Perhaps I do know what gift could be considered worthy of such a girl."

With these words, a development crystal appeared in my hands. I enjoyed the process of materializing immaterial objects. There was something enchanting about it. Magical. It had a similar effect on the people around me — they froze, gazing in awe at the magic of the incarnation.

"A development crystal? Cabbage, don't tell me it's a good one." Adeline changed her mind about trying to escape, coming closer and leaning over my shoulder, peering at the gift. "What's in there? Probably *Adaptation*, right off the bat?"

Mischievous chuckles were heard — apparently Adeline had made some sort of local inside joke. Even Naira smiled, which made me almost smile myself. It was good that Magister Tarra taught me to keep a straight face. I didn't really want to look like a lovesick idiot who had forgotten all else in the world.

"Out with it, Cabbage. What's there? I'd never believe you brought something run of the mill."

"Am I even permitted to talk about this?" I answered her question with another. "Didn't you say that information about human development models is personal and trusting it to anyone, even a cousin, is not the best idea? Especially a cousin such as yourself."

"That doesn't apply to development crystals," Naira laughed, accepting my gift. "So there will be no fatal consequence for everyone knowing the true value of your gift."

"As the birthday girl says," I nodded. "This crystal contains *Magic Speed*, *Magic Power*, *Vampirism*, *Dark Indifference* and *Adaptation*. According to Adeline Jode, these are quite important parameters for any dark person.

A deafening silence fell over the hall. People even seemed to take a few steps back, as if they were afraid to be in the presence of such a gift. Naira turned pale and looked at the crystal as if it were something dangerous. And I didn't like the looks the higher hierarchs were giving me at all.

"You certainly know how to make enemies, Cabbage," Adeline said pensively. "One at a time's not enough, you've got to make them *en masse!*"

"Return the crystal!" Theodore demanded, but everyone was distracted by a new player on this strange stage. An unusual man approached us. More like a beast shrouded in darkness that resembled a man. I tried to pierce through it with *Analyze*, but to no avail. No, he didn't have an amulet, my ability simply had nothing to grab on to! For the stone, the human hidden within this dense fog didn't even exist. The surrounding crowd recoiled even further from us, and it was unclear which had inspired a stronger reaction, the crystal or this strange being.

"May I?" His voice was an unpleasant hiss. The startled Naira held out my gift, which immediately vanished into the fog. A few seconds later, it was once again found in the hands of the birthday girl.

"Hunter of Darkness, Rift Conqueror and Dark Mirror Archduke Maximilian Valevsky does not lie. This crystal really does have the parameters he stated. We will be waiting for you at the Temple, Naira Jode. Translate my words for the light one. He must be aware of what is happening."

"That's a member of the Temple of Skron," Adeline whispered after she translated the being's words for me.

"The Bartolomeo Clan will send the acolyte to the Temple of Skron in two weeks," Cedric bowed his head.

"Tomorrow a group is leaving for the Derval rift," replied the dark mist. "The new acolyte should be with them. This is Skron's will."

"The Bartolomeo Clan will submit to the Temple's demands," Cedric nodded. "Naira Jode will report to Kerux tomorrow morning for training."

"I won't let my daughter follow Herod's path! It leads only to death!" Theodore exclaimed indignantly. The mist-being raised its head, staring at the scholar, and I recognized the strength Naira's father had. He would not back down and held the dark being's gaze.

"Is this the official position of the clan or the opinion of one scholar?" the being asked, turning to Cedric.

"The clan's position has been voiced, henchman."

"She's your cousin!" Theodore was indignant.

"She is of the Bartolomeo Clan! And she has a chance to reach greatness! The law is the same for everyone, Uncle, for ordinary servant and daughter of the clan's chief scholar alike! Naira will become a rift conqueror!"

Adeline translated as much as she could. Judging by how serious she had become, something out of the ordinary was happening, so I decided to intervene. Since it was my gift, it was my responsibility to mend the situation.

"If I may?" I took the development crystal from Naira. "Gentlemen, do I understand correctly that the main problem of this crystal is that it has *Adaptation*? That is, if I change this parameter right now, and make it something ordinary, instead of *Adaptation,* all issues will be resolved?"

"Cabbage, what are you doing?" Adeline said cautiously when a frightening silence fell over the hall again. Even Skron's misty henchman's focus was carefully trained on me, and I admit it made me feel a little uneasy.

"I think I spoke quite clearly. I could try again, of course, but I'm not sure what good it will do. I can remove *Adaptation,* right here and now."

"Can you only remove *Adaptation,* or can you add it to another crystal," the unpleasant voice hissed.

"I chose all five parameters that are on this crystal myself. Initially, the crystal was entirely different."

"I understand, but this is no longer necessary. If you remove *Adaptation,* Naira Jode will die in the rift tomorrow. From here on out, she is an acolyte of the Temple of Skron."

"To insert a crystal, you need a socket in the development model. What kind of altar does the Bartolomeo Clan have? Fifth or sixth level? What if there is no nest six steps away and Naira chooses the wrong path? Will the temple provide access to a thirteenth level altar to ensure the nest is found?"

"Only the highest hierarchs have access to the altar," answered Skron's henchman after a pause. "Naira Jode is not one of them."

"So the Temple of Skro openly states that if Naira Jode is unlucky with her development model and choice of direction, she will die? Give her four days."

"What will change during this time? She will become a rift conqueror in any case. This is Skron's will."

"In four days, the Bartolomeo Clan will have a level fifteen development altar."

And again the hall plunged into deadly silence.

"Cabbage, what are you talking about?" whispered the frightened Adeline. "What is this about a fifteen-level altar? Where will we find it?"

I was compelled to elaborate.

"Tonight, I go to the ruins immersed in the Fog of Pharapho. We will spend two days searching for artifacts, after which I will destroy the fog and obtain the altar. Using this altar, Naira will find the nest and insert the development crystal."

"The Temple of Skron has patience," the man replied after a pause. "Clan Head, we will be waiting for Naira in four days. She will go into the rift. Return the crystal, dark mirror. Without it, Naira will die."

The terrified girl extended her hand, which was visibly shaking. I had no choice but to return the development crystal to her. Swallowing, Naira hid it in her pocket and, turning away, rushed into her father's arms. A moment later, sobs were heard. The representative of the Temple of Skron stepped aside, considering his mission completed.

"Maximilian Valevsky, leave my home," said Cedric Jode, drawing everyone's attention to me. "The guard will escort you to the portal. After you complete the task for which you were summoned, the Bartolomeo Clan will declare you..."

"Brother, don't be hasty to say something that will cause the whole clan to suffer!" Adeline interrupted. "By declaring war on Maximilian Valevsky, you will lose access to the portal in the light lands. Think about it, Head of the Bartolomeo Clan, are your emotions worth it? Or do you want to dishonor the agreement we signed to protect the portal?"

Cedric's stony face showed no emotion. Now it was clear that he was much older than thirty-five. Even his athletic figure could not hide his age. According to the agreement, the portal that led to our lands opened only from one point — the very portal through which I arrived in the dark lands. It was impossible to get here from any other route. The Bartolomeo Clan would act not only as guards, but also as customs officers, collecting duties for the transit of goods. The enterprise promised to be beneficial to everyone, so Cedric simply had no right to refuse.

"The Bartolomeo Clan will fulfill its obligations," Cedric answered after a pause. "Maximilian will be declared an undesirable person with the opportunity to use the portal. That's my word. See this...light one off immediately!"

Two converts appeared next to me.

"Brother, I hardly recognize you. When did you become so emotional? Do you intend to drive the Hunter of Darkness out in this suit? Without returning his clothing? There's no need to get caught up in the heat. I will accompany Maximilian myself. If you want to find the culprit for what just happened, look in the mirror. You knew why we invited the Hunter of Darkness to our lands. Tell me, why did you decide to drag him to this event? One who not only does not know our language, but also has no idea about our customs and laws? You are the head of the clan, but you act like a baby! Father would never do this! Maximilian, follow me! You are no longer welcome in this house."

Glancing back at Naira, who continued to sob, her face buried in her father's shoulder, I followed Adeline. It didn't take long to change my clothes, and soon we were heading towards the portal.

"Can you explain what just happened?" It was only when we left the security zone and broxies were running between us that I decided to figure out exactly what I had done.

"Oh, Cabbage, how do I even explain?" Adeline sighed heavily. "You have just declared war on at least five dark clans, including the Valdez and Gourfans. How many clans will actually want to finish you off is a good question. I would even say, an extremely pressing one because everyone had their eyes on Naira. Beautiful, rich, smart, daughter of a scholar. An ideal member for any clan. But then Cabbage comes around and, revealing its next layer of leaves, ruins everyone's plans."

"So no details?" I asked

"What detail?" Adeline asked, exasperated. "*Adaptation* is such a rare parameter that anyone who possesses it is considered inviolable. Any clan that hides the fact that they possess a stone with this parameter loses much status and privilege. They might even be expelled from the clan council. There are precedents. If someone receives a crystal with *Adaptation,* by accident or due to the evil intent of another, then they have no right to refuse. It is believed to be a gift from Skron. So Naira simply has no choice but to become a rift conqueror. Same as my father. When I disappeared...Well, disappeared — when I got stuck in Seretino with Alejandro, my father got scared and called the Interrogator. This..."

"I know who he is. We're already well acquainted."

"The Temple has exacted a monstrous price for such a calling — it demands all clan rift conquerors, save for the head. The clan lost twenty people in whom they had invested ten years. They were the strongest fighters, capable of closing rifts of the twentieth level. But they are gone now. When Father died, the Bartolomeo Clan unexpectedly lost its place in the rankings. We didn't have any rift conquerors, and this took a big toll on our reputation. Attempts to attract people from the outside were unsuccessful, so we lost more and more status. It got to the point that the Bartolomeo Clan was not invited to the clan council this month. Because we have become weaker! The presence of even one rift conqueror will correct this situation, but I did not think that it would be Naira. Poor girl...now she will have to undergo grueling studies, forgetting all her suitors. The rules of the Temple of Skron are strict — no relationships during study."

"Suitors?" I said, rolling the unpleasant word around in my mouth.

"Naturally. Did you really think that such a beautiful girl wouldn't have a boyfriend? A couple of favorites? With my own eyes, I have seen five marriage proposal letters from five different clans. Those who will now consider you their enemy. Because you deprived them of such beauty."

"And who was that misty fellow? What gives him the right to give orders within the clan?"

"A servant of the Temple of Skron. We, the dark ones, have a slightly different governmental structure than you. There are a bunch of clans that are independent or dependent on each other. Nobody even knows how many there really are. Clans unite into a clan council that governs Kerux and determines the general policy in our area. Somewhere far away, there are other dark territories with their own capitals, but we have practically no interaction with them. The distances are too great, and the cost that the minotaurs demand to travel is simply exorbitant. Actually, our capital is the common city shared by all regional clans. Everything that is in it, and this includes shops, production and academies, belongs to the council of clans. It is also involved in the development of the city. But then there is the Temple of Skron. The domain of the orthodox and those who have followed the path of darkness. They are responsible for rifts, the Fog of Pharapho, and the mutated. They provide training and restoration for all converts. The influence of the Temple is limitless. Their word is taken as Skron's word. If someone begins to oppose the Temple, all other clans take up arms against him. Together, forgetting any strife they may have. For anyone who does not speak out against the violator will himself be recognized as a violator of the law. Remaining neutral is impossible. The only thing I don't understand is why the servant of Skron appeared at Naira's birthday party? Could they really have an oracle?"

"What are you on about?"

"There are rumors that one of the beastmen can predict the future. That's why Skron's servants appear whenever they are least expected. As he did today. There is, of course, no real evidence of this."

"So Naira has a fiancé?"

"Don't even think about it, Cabbage. They've been together for more than three years, it's all very serious. There's no need to stick your nose where it's not welcome. Better if you just tell me how you managed to change the facets on your development stone. When did you become a magical jeweler?"

I didn't reply. My mind was back in Hearth — a place I suddenly had no desire to return to. The news Adeline reported was clearly not good. She still tried to goad me into talking, but soon fell silent, lost in thought.

The portal appeared late that evening. A

delegation of gloomy people, including Theodore, approached us. Judging by the way the scholar looked at me, he had already cursed himself several times over for deciding to invite me to the lands of the Bartolomeo Clan. I behaved coolly. Things happened like they happened. Next time they would think twice about inviting people over who were unfamiliar with the basic rules of dark etiquette.

I immediately noticed that this was no ordinary Fog of Pharapho. I'd only seen so many spawn in one place once before — when they were devoured by an infected rift. They stood so close to each other that they formed an impenetrable wall. I even raised my eyebrows in surprise, no idea where I'd hold all the loot I was about to receive. I didn't have enough space in my inventory! There had to be a hundred sergeants here, no less!

"Do I need to kill them all?" I asked. Theodore looked at me with approximately the same look as Count Kuzminsky did when I announced that I was declaring open season on the fog monsters. Simply incredulous.

"If you can," Naira's father answered forcefully. He was disgusted that he had to speak to me.

"Stand back. This might take a while," I warned. Speeding up, I took a deep breath and, using *Dash,* I got right up next to them. Removing the lid from the level eighteen ousel box, I flew into the crowd of creatures with another *Dash* and began the important, though tedious work of gaining loot. Cutting stones, as practice has shown, were too valuable a prize to be ignored. Soldiers died in dozens, but I didn't dwell on them too much. My target was ahead — the sergeant. It took me no more than thirty seconds to scoop the carcass from the bone armor! Ripping out the development crystal, allowing the creature to explode, I threw the bone armor to where I expected the scholars to be. Another sergeant. Several dozen more soldiers. Another sergeant...After some time, I had to maintain my condition with *Heal* — the speed with which I moved from one creature to another was beyond my capabilities. However, I didn't stop for a second. I was given only four days, two of which would have to be spent on the Pharapho dungeon.

I stopped only after I had maxed out the number of cutting stones my inventory could hold. Three hundred!

Looking around, I couldn't help but grin — behind me was a strip devoid of fog. It was slowly filling once more, but I still managed to catch a glance of the bare land that hadn't seen the sun for two hundred years.

Picking up three bone armor shields that were lying nearby, I trudged back. I had to unload them in order to continue my deadly speed run. If the dark ones didn't give me all the bone armor, as we agreed, this would be the first and last time I worked with them. I'd lose any faith I had in these bastards.

I saw a flickering in the fog several meters

before I got to it. I had to clear the area of soldiers in order to get to the right spot, throwing the cutting stones into my pocket. Bending down, I pulled out an oblong stick emitting a blue aura. *Analyze* did not bring any clarity:

Magic artifact. Identification required.

The item wouldn't go in my inventory, so I had no choice but to tuck it under my arm, hoping it wouldn't fall out.

Emerging from the fog, I stopped when I saw a huge procession standing not far from the border. There were not only the scholars with whom I had traveled to the ruins, but also all the top brass in the clan, including the head. I threw the bone armor and strange stick to one side, then retreated just in case, not understanding what was happening. *Dash* could take me back into the fog, but first I'd have to survive the attack. Maybe it wasn't worth the risk and I should just run away now?

The dark ones were clearly up to something bad. Why were they here? And they even brought Naira! If my vision served me right, it was the birthday girl standing there!

"Cabbage, what you did..." Adeline began, which made me take a few more steps back. Yes, I definitely needed to run! They were clearly intent on revenge!

"Hunter of Darkness, Rift Conqueror and Dark Mirror Archduke Maximilian Valevsky," said

Cedric Jode, for some reason addressing me as formally as possible. 'As the head of the Bartolomeo Clan, I invite you to join the clan. You will become the highest hierarch of Skron.'"

Chapter 4

"I CERTAINLY DON'T NEED that," I replied, deciding not to hide my true feelings behind pretty sugar-coated epithets. "What I really need is a container into which I can offload three hundred cutting stones."

"Cabbage, how can you refuse? An offer like this happens once in a lifetime!" Adeline was astonished. Whispers began to flow through the dark ranks. They clearly did not expect this reaction. Apparently, the offer was very valuable. For the average person.

"Well, I don't need it," I responded calmly. One of the seekers brought something that looked like a basin. I put my hand into my bag and began to embody the stones into it from my inventory. I had to put on this show, since I nearly screwed up badly when I materialized the development crystal for Naira in front of a huge crowd of dark ones. I couldn't make the same mistake again. As if the dark ones knowing about *Devour* wasn't bad enough.

"If you become part of the Bartolomeo Clan, especially the highest hierarch, great prospects will open up for you," Adeline began to explain. Apparently, this girl never got anything right the first time. And she taught logic! But she wouldn't back down, continuing to bribe me:

"You will be able to enter our magic academy, you will have access to our resources, opportunities, and connections. You will gain access to our artifacts, rifts, ruins. You will have everything!"

"Alright, let's waste a little time and state the obvious. Cedric Jode, I am grateful to you and your clan for such a generous offer, but I cannot accept. Neither on moral, nor physical grounds. You are dark, I am a hunter of darkness. My job is to kill people like you. And yes, Theodore Jode, I am confident in my words and, if necessary, am ready to prove them with action. If one of you comes to the lands of Light and breaks the treaty, or if I meet someone outside Hearth without a good reason, they will be killed. Then we'll see what my words are worth. And furthermore. You steal children from our lands and turn them into willess converts. You protect your homes in such a terrible way that, if I were not bound by the agreement, I would try to destroy your estate. Yes, I would have most likely died doing so, but I would have at least put up a fight. I don't see any point in saying that not even a day has passed since I was expelled in disgrace from the house of the Bartolomeo Clan, and in the company of other clans and a representative of the Temple of Skron. Only a person devoid of even the slightest concept of honor and self-respect would forget this fact. It seems to me that everything I have just voiced was clear from my initial phrase — I don't need it."

"The servant of the Temple who came to our holiday brought news of the appearance of an infected rift. If the Bartolomeo Clan does not send a representative, he will lose his place on the clan council. Tomorrow a group will leave from Kerux to destroy the infected rift. Our representative will have to be there, otherwise the consequences for the clan will be catastrophic. Up to and including complete dissolution."

"Send whoever you like, Magister Meram will close the rift without any outside help. The presence of clans in this process is nominal. I know for certain — I saw it with my own eyes."

"Magister Meram will not come to this rift. The territory where it has appeared belongs to the Derval Clan. The clan that many years ago expelled the gray magister from its ranks. The rift will have to be completely destroyed. The Gourfan Clan is already on location, but the rift is gaining strength too quickly. Two levels per day. Today it was only level six, the Gourfans were able to lower it to level four, but a full reboot took place. And part of the group that easily copes with twenty-level faults suffered losses. Therefore, the Temple servants are gathering all the other clans. Time is running out."

"Reboot? What's that?" I frowned. I'd never heard such a word before.

"When an infected rift absorbs a normal one, it not only gains its levels, but also completely restores the entire population of dark beasts. The Gourfans did not have time to regroup and were attacked from several sides at once."

"Cabbage, a convert will be sent to Turb. He will open the portal in exactly seven days. You and I will have time to get to this stupid and useless wedding. Don't forget, I need to appear there too."

"Excellent news," I couldn't refrain from sarcasm. "So you're just openly stating that you are going to violate the agreement we signed?"

"This is an issue of more than compliance with some contract," Cedric answered. "It's an issue of existence itself. At least five clans will happily crush us if we lose our positions and retreat. If we cannot ensure the protection of the portal, the Orthodoxy will rush to the light lands and the portal will have to be blocked off. This will cause damage to your city — without a point of trade with the dark ones, Hearth will turn into any other city."

"I've already lost count of how many times I repeat this, so I'll just say it again: I don't need this. If there is no portal for trade with the dark ones, Hearth, of course, will lose a lot, but will also gain no less. The representative of the Citadel will finally leave me in peace. I am here only at the request of this eccentric girl who managed to persuade me to help her clan with the Fog of Pharapho. And instead of filling my pockets with all sorts of goodies, I'm engaging in conversation. Actually I don't even understand the essence of the problem. You just need to send someone into the rift, right? So let me make you a few development crystals with *Adaptation* at a reasonable price, choose some doomed soldiers who will gladly lay down their lives for their clan. You are not tasked with destroying the rift, are you? This will be done by the Gourfan clan. It is important for your people to enter the rift and show that they are truly rift conquerors. Just think, they will die not on the first, but on the second level. This happens sometimes. But it's better not to count on me in this matter. Thanks to you, dark ones, I'm stuck with Magister Meram's rift limit — no more than three per year. And for the next ten months I only have the opportunity to enter one more rift. Then I'll die. Which I'd rather not do."

"Master Meram has promised to increase this limit to five," Adeline said, but immediately fell silent as the entire clan stared at her.

"You knew about this and remained silent? Made me come here, humiliate myself before the light one, knowing that he would refuse in any case?"

"But he still has one rift left!" Adeline tried to defend herself, but all her defenses fell when Cedric slapped the girl in the face. Her shield coped with the blow, but it was the fact that he struck her at all, and not the strength of the blow, that was important.

"I don't want to see you in my house for an entire year, sister," Cedric said, barely containing his anger. "Your behavior has crossed all boundaries! Light one, how many crystals can you make and how quickly? I need to choose a team. Theodore, we'll also need some of yours."

"If there are crystals on the table, I'll find a group," replied the head of the scholar research team, and then added: "I'll go myself."

"No!" Naira's pained cry was heard, nearly causing another pang to go through my heart. Only this time I was ready. My heart had gone soft, and I needed to take it in a steel grip and force it to continue pumping without being distracted by external circumstances.

"Cabbage, they will all die!" Adeline tried to appeal to my sense of compassion. But how can you appeal to something that doesn't exist? Compassion for a dark one? Never heard of it.

"Take my sister away. It's time for her to return to her husband," Cedric ordered, and two converts appeared next to Adeline. Only now I realized that there are very few of these converts left. It wasn't that the opening of a new portal wasn't a momentous enough occasion to warrant their presence. It was just that they had started running out.

"How many crystals can you make and what do you want for them?" asked Cedric, ignoring the befuddled Adeline.

"First, the crystals must be made. As for what I want for them, I know my price: the artifacts that your clan has. Adeline once mentioned such a thing as a recipe. These are what I need. I want to see what they are."

Cedric looked toward his sister once more. This time, there was fury in his gaze. She had clearly hit a nerve.

"Agreed. We'll decide on the quantity later. Theodore, start forming a group."

"Stop!" Naira cried suddenly and walked over to me. I had to put the lid back on the ousel box and be glad that I had finished off all the Pharapho spawn within a hundred-meter radius. The fog had already recovered, but the creatures never showed up. The girl came close to me and winced slightly from the bright light of the crystal that shone on my head. This gave me the opportunity to notice Naira's unusually yellow eyes. Just like a snake's. Wait a minute! Yellow eyes?! Had she already integrated my gift and become a gray master? *Analyze* confirmed my suspicions, demonstrating that since our last meeting, the girl had received seventy additional enhancements. Damn, it was good to be the daughter of the head of the leading clan's scholars! No one had given me seven gallo stones on my eighteenth birthday!

"My father is all I have left of my family. My real family. My mother and brother were killed," said Naira. My heart tried to flutter, but I managed to keep it under control. "Tell me, Maximilian, wouldn't you do everything possible to save the life of the people you love? I think you would sacrifice everything you have to do it. In your opinion, what is the probability of surviving in an infected rift for a person who has just received *Adaptation*?

"Zero," I replied after a pause. "Anyone who is sent there will die. That's why I said right off the bat that you need doomed soldiers. Those who understand what they are doing and why."

"Now I know your limitations. I know that tomorrow such a rift may appear next to Hearth, and you will have to think about how to destroy it. But now I could lose my father, so I have to give everything I have to save him. Uncle, can Maximilian join our clan for just a little while?"

"That's not an option, Naira. Once we close this rift, we could get an order to close another one tomorrow. There's no use in a Hunter of Darkness solving one local issue. My father paid too high a price to learn this lesson with that...with my sister."

"What is the likelihood that another infected rift will appear in the lands of the Derval Clan? Zero! After some time, I will become a rift conqueror and will be able to represent the clan until a full-fledged cleanup group appears!" Naira exclaimed hotly. "We just need time, which we don't have right now."

"Temporary clan membership..." Cedric said thoughtfully. "The practice does exist, but not for the highest hierarchs of Skron."

"The first crystal," a stone with five rays appeared in my hand. Making it had taken sixty-five cutting stones in total. It took a long time for the required parameter to appear. While the dark ones were arguing and making decisions, I was going about my business, trying not to think about how many resources I was wasting. Because none of this concerned me. I needed recipes and I would get them. Everything else, including Naira's emotional speech, rolled right off my back.

"Maximilian Valevsky, do you agree to temporarily become a member of the Bartolomeo Clan in order to destroy the infected rift? As a reward...you can have me! I will be your wife!"

The area was blanketed in silence. Even the Pharapho spawn stopped moving, as if they, too, were shocked by her words. The Bartolomeo Clan clearly did not expect such an act from their sparkling diamond. But it wasn't going to be bamboozled so easily by her proposal. Magister Tarra, how grateful I am to you for trying to seduce me for a whole month! Although far from absolute, I had acquired some kind of immunity to such things. Some part of me was entirely ready to prostrate myself in front of her and accept, but it was too small a voice to drown out the rest.

"That one who's trying to inch toward the portal right now explained very clearly why I shouldn't even look in your direction, my dear Naira Jode. You have been dating the young man who is fated to be your husband for three years now. Please answer a simple question: why do I need a wife who will hate me all her life?"

"Oh Cabbage, oh idiot!" a muffled

exclamation was heard, followed by a ringing blow of a palm to the forehead. Adeline Sarento stopped resisting and even ran towards the portal, but then Cedric's order was heard, forcing the supreme converts to speed up.

"Stop her!"

Adeline begrudgingly stopped and turned around. Judging by her expression, the dark one was overwhelmed with unprecedented fury. Toward herself? No, of course not! Toward me! Because I blabbed about what she'd said! Great Light, could this lady be trusted at all?

"Explain yourself, niece!" Theodore Jode demanded. "What young man has my daughter been dating for three years?"

Naira herself looked at her cousin with round eyes from shock, completely clueless.

"And you would have the Hunter of Darkness start courting her? I told this lie for the sake of the clan!" Adeline said. "Cabbage wasn't supposed to blab about it! These things aren't discussed in polite society, by the way!"

"Two years, sister," Cedric could barely restrain himself from strangling Adeline with his own two hands. "I banish you from the clan for two years! And I'll add another year if anything else like this happens! Leave!"

Amid continued indignation, Adeline was escorted to the portal. The convert that formed it collapsed to the ground — it had reached the maximum number of passages. The dark one could not return, even if she really wanted to.

"I don't have a young man I've been dating for three years," Naira answered when the passions subsided. "Laws prohibit dating before initiation. I won't hate you, Maximilian Valevsky. I will sincerely fulfill my duties as a wife if you protect the Bartolomeo Clan and save my father. I suppose that you may already have a wife, so I'm ready to be a simple concubine. I understand that you will have to give up your last chance to enter a rift for the year. I understand how difficult it is to become part of a clan that publicly expelled you, but...I can't lose my father as well. Please, Maximilian."

Skron drag me to the Light by my ankles! While at the beginning of Naira's fiery speech, I had been ready to say "no" to her face, by the end I had difficulty restraining myself from rushing to the girl, who had tears flowing down her cheeks, and hugging her to me. The rest of the clan stood with gloomy faces, not daring to interfere and awaiting my decision.

"I don't have a wife, nor do I have any obligations to anyone, but I don't need a wife under duress," I said, trying to keep my breathing even. For some reason my head had become hazy, but I tried to stay the course.

"We can do things differently," came Theodore's voice. "You don't need to tie the knot here and now. Naira will become your bride and after, say, a year, if you both decide to continue this relationship, you can make it official."

"Then what's the point at all?"

"So that during this year everyone knows that

Maximilian Valevsky represents the interests of the Bartolomeo Clan. Even if he's not a full-fledged member."

I looked to Naira again. She looked as if she was ready to rush headlong into a pool just to save her father. I even thought about helping the clan for free, but I immediately drove away this treacherous thought. I didn't work for free anymore! Stop! Brain, come back, I'll forgive you for everything!

"In four days, Naira Jode must report to the Temple of Skron for training. One particularly mouthy person we all know very well said that she'll be there for two years, during which time she can have no relationships. Is this true? If so, why are we even discussing marriage?"

"You are of the Light," Cedric answered after a pause. "If Naira becomes your bride or wife, she will no longer have the right to study in the Temple. The responsibility of raising her to be a rift conqueror will fall on you."

The way Naira's eyes widened indicated that she had not yet been made privy to this information. Two bright ambers stared at Theodore, demanding confirmation. The scholar nodded and explained:

"It's true, daughter. You will not be sent to the Temple. But the path home to you will be closed as well. You'll have to remain with your suitor in the lands of the Light."

The ambers flicked from Theodore to me, and I saw a prayer in them. Apparently, the Temple of

Skron was not the most desirable place, since the dark ones tried not to go there.

"Fine. Naira Jode will become my bride, and I will represent the Bartolomeo Clan at the closing of the infected rift. But what should we do about these ruins?"

"You have the whole night ahead of you. All the loot you can obtain today is yours. You have the word of the clan head. We'll leave the dungeon for the future, the main thing now is to clear the area of Pharapho spawn. The scholars will help you find and identify artifacts. A convert will open a portal for you in the morning. All the papers and the clan ring will be waiting for you in Kerux. Welcome to the Bartolomeo Clan, Highest Hierarch of Skron Maximilian Valevsky."

* * *

The main estate of the Bartolomeo Clan
Two hours earlier

"It's no use," Cedric's fist hit the table. "It's all useless! The Temple will not refuse her! Naira is too tasty a morsel for them to pass by!"

"I've consulted with my husband," said Adeline. The girl, whom everyone was accustomed to considering eccentric, was now unusually serious. "He believes that the only way to get Naira out of this situation is to give her to Maximilian. The Temple is incapable of allowing someone into its ranks who is associated with the Light, and the

Hunter of Darkness survived his meeting with the Inquisitor. What could be a greater confirmation of Lightness if not this?"

"This cannot happen!" Theodore barked. "I will not give my daughter to this rift conqueror!"

"Either that, or in four days she will be given to some other higher hierarch," Adeline calmly noted. "Do you think her age will stop them? She's over eighteen? That's enough. She's ready for a relationship. In addition, the infected rift must be closed in any case. Negotiators, including my husband, have gone to Magister Meram, but there's no guarantee that the runescribe will even open the door for them."

"How can you give Naira over to the man who made her a rift conqueror?"

"That means he should be responsible for her fate," Adeline stood firmly in her position. "That's what Skron decided, uncle. If Naira is destined to live in the lands of Light, so be it."

"But the light one..." Cedric grimaced with displeasure.

"Formally, he's dark," Adeline reminded him. "He's been officially recognized by the church as dark. I don't like the idea either, but I don't see any other way out. I'd rather give Naira to Valevsky than send her to the Temple of Skron. And lose another one of our own. Brother, you'll have to banish me for a couple of years. I now have a family, I want to spend more time with them. I have no desire to constantly go to clan meetings, which due to the current situation will be almost a daily occurrence. Are we all in agreement? Then I'll tell you the best way to proceed. Uncle, you'll have to play along with me. This is the only way your daughter will do what we need her to…"

* * *

Magister Meram's residence
Al-Khorezm, Shurgan Empire

"Wine?" Kimal Sarento positioned himself opposite the disgruntled runescribe and made no attempt to conceal his satisfied grin. The scenario, which at first glance seemed unrealistic and unfeasible, had played out perfectly, and without having to resolve the issue of leaving the clan later. Adeline, a smart girl, had done everything required of a quality pupil. From her hints about a gift to Valevsky, ending with her expulsion from the clan. Now Maximilian would have a legal wife, and with her would come a whole host of new problems. The particularly zealous clan heads would not forgive the insult — the most beautiful girl of the last twenty years chose a light one, and not one of them. And the light ones would do everything to attract the attention of such an outstanding person. If he were forty years younger, perhaps he would also be interested, but as the Evil Engineer says, they were small fry. Now he was much more interested in seeing how Maximilian got out of this situation. The young man would need to be tested in all domains before he moved on to the next stage.

"I'm not going back to Derval! Let them all die there!" Magister Meram answered angrily.

"Who said I'm here to deal with that trifle? Magister, the infected rifts will now be closed by Valevsky, and you won't be able to do anything about it. Sooner or later he will close them all and your era of greatness will come to an end. Get ready. I'm not here to persuade you."

"Then why did you come?"

"What, I can't pay a visit to an old friend?"

"We were never friends, Kimal! We're anything but friends. Tell me why you came."

"Karina Fardi. A week ago you refused her, but that was a big mistake. This year she must become your student. Along with Maximilian Valevsky. I'm not asking for any favors. On the contrary, you'll need to drive them as hard as possible. If they can't cope, you can banish them in disgrace. But it is imperative that you take them both on."

"She's one of Magister Elor's people. Why do you need this?"

"He was the one who asked me for the favor. And you'll heed my words much more willingly than you will his. As for what I stand to gain...Let's just say I have lofty plans for these two."

Chapter 5

"THE BONE ARMOR AND CUTTING STONES will be delivered to Hearth," Theodore assured me when my harvest had come to an end. "All artifacts will also be sent there after identification."

"How many converts will you need?" I asked, assessing the result of that night's marathon. I had to lean on my knees to catch my breath a little. I'd stopped breathing a few hours ago. Despite all my supposedly inhuman endurance, I had to work hard to get as much done as possible. And my *Body Fortification* stat had increased by half a percent overnight! With my parameters, this was a lot. A monstrous amount.

"The minotaurs will be responsible for delivering the objects. The travel restriction only applies to humans," said Theodore. There was no trace of the Fog of Pharapho — I'd cleared the whole thing! A group of dungeon conquerors had already descended to resolve the issue with the ruins once and for all, but I had no intention of joining them. Since Naira managed to install a development crystal, there was no longer any need to give the Bartolomeo Clan a level-fifteen altar. If my temporary clan wanted to possess such a treasure, they'd have to participate in the auction like everyone else. Overall, the night was a great success. I'd gotten my hands on sixty-two pieces of bone armor alone! And an equal number of development amulets. To say nothing of cutting stones — I had to empty my inventory, which was jammed to capacity, four times. I urgently needed to increase the level of my *Devour*, but the lack of any credible information on how to rearrange the stones on my magic field once they'd already been placed stopped me. On top of that, Cedric Jode refused to divulge any information about increasing the size of my magic field. As the head of the clan stated, this knowledge was intended only for the permanent highest hierarchs of Skron. If I wished to know...essentially, I'd have to go without this vital information. But that was fine, life is long and our paths would cross again. And now I knew exactly what my next demand would be.

Another interesting find was a bunch of blue objects that shimmered with a blue, and sometimes even a gold light. Artifacts of the ancients, the scope and range of which was absolutely incomprehensible. As was any way of identifying them. Cedric had made a mistake when, with a sweeping gesture, he'd given me all the loot from these ruins. Theodore's long face spoke volumes when I began to consolidate all my loot into one pile. In fact, there would have been more, but it took a while to understand the main principle of obtaining artifacts — they could only be obtained from the fog. If I killed a sufficient number of Pharapho spawn and completely cleared the space of fog, the flickering objects would go dull and they'd lose their properties. But as soon as this dawned on me...I basically made out like a bandit, pulling more than fifty different artifacts from the fog. Starting with sheets of paper similar to recipes, ending with a small statue. All these things needed to be identified, but this proved impossible to do on the spot. The identification device was located on the clan estate and was almost more heavily guarded than the treasury. I needed to give the dark ones their due — they were smart about how they went about things, providing me with a complete list of the things they had obtained with their descriptions. To rule out the possibility of forgery, as Theodore explained.

But the most valuable acquisition, which I didn't even know what to do with, were the fragments of *Fog Stalker*. Of course, I didn't combine them to form a key that could take me to some far off location, but the fact that I now had five of these keys warmed my soul. Surely they could be traded. I just had to make sure not to sell myself short. Better yet, I could find out what exactly it was and how it walked. What if the reward that falls from this rare type of Fog is so magnificent that I wouldn't want to give it to anyone? And I should have sorted out all my *Amplify* shards a long time ago too. I also had a ton of shards from this stone. It was time to level up my stones, and not just hang around with a first-level *Amplify*, complaining that everyone was insulting the poor dark hunter. After I was done dealing with this infected rift, I'd get to work on these red gems.

It took a whole hour to scrub myself clean. I was taken to Kerux, but I had no opportunity to appreciate the beauty of the dark capital, as the portal was located directly in the hotel where they had rented a room for me. There were more than a hundred portals in Kerux, as they explained to me, and those that were closest to the desired point were used. The minotaurs still turned their bullish eyes toward me in displeasure, but they performed their duties without complaint. The maids helped wipe off the dried dark crust left behind by the Pharapho spawn, after which I was given a set of rift conqueror clothing. The local tailors demonstrated their skill, altering the garments to fit me like a glove. The symbol of the Bartolomeo Clan shone on my chest, the ring of the highest hierarch Skron on my finger, and in my backpack were papers giving me the right to represent the Bartolomeo Clan and informing the Temple of Skron that from now on, Naira Jode was my bride. Incidentally, I hadn't seen her since our encounter at the ruins.

Apparently, one does not simply walk into the Temple of Skron. The building was located in the very center of Kerux and was a giant onyx pyramid, but there were no doors or windows. The only path inside was through the portal near the front, where minotaurs performed their eternal service. The beastmen carefully studied my accompanying documents, discussed something amongst themselves, and then one of them disappeared into the portal. About ten minutes passed before the minotaur returned and I was allowed to enter the portal. For a few moments, the space around me shimmered and became a desolate, windswept steppe. The Temple servants didn't even consider it necessary to let me inside and threw me directly into the infected rift. There were a bunch of tents around, the dark ones and their puppets were scurrying about everywhere, and the variety of clan symbols that flashed above the tents dazzled the eyes.

"State your name!" came the unpleasant hissing voice. Next to the portal there was a table at which sat a misty servant of Skron. *Analyze* once again had nothing to grab onto, so I had to be content with just a visual inspection. A man. Maybe. Judging by the voice. Or a very hoarse woman. Two arms, two legs, one head, and that's all I could glean.

"Maximilian Valevsky, highest hierarch of Skron of the Bartolomeo Clan."

"The dark mirror?" the head of the mist beast

changed position, as if it only now had turned to look at me. Apparently, every servant of the Temple of Skron knew who I was and what I could do. And I didn't really like that.

"The very same. What level has the rift reached?"

"Infected rift," the mist man corrected me. "Twelve. Wait here, someone will come for you now."

Sure enough, a few minutes later another mist man approached me. Considering that the clerk sitting at the portal did not use remote communication, there was some other method of communication between these creatures. I'd remember that for the future. I was taken to a large tent, over which a completely black banner fluttered. Evidently the flag of the Temple of Skron. The inside was full of people, and only the dark ones were present, without puppets. My appearance did not go unnoticed — the eyes of all those gathered turned to me. Because a strong wind entered the tent with me, scattering several papers.

"Maximilian of the Bartomoleo Clan," the hissing voice introduced me and the tent flap closed, blocking the wind. In the center of the tent there was a huge table, around which an impressive team of dark ones had gathered. My gaze fell on familiar symbols — Valdez and Gourfan, but representatives of at least ten more different clans were present here. The meeting was led by another vague representative of the Temple of Skron.

"How much did they pay you, Light One, that you dared to come here?" judging by the tone, the mist being clearly did not like me. Strange, considering that I hadn't done anything to insult the Temple yet. Or had I?

"Enough to become an official representative of the clan for the next year," I said as I approached the table. The looks I received indicated that I was clearly not welcome here. "Do you need help? Or can you handle such a small rift on your own?"

"Who is this, Seven? Why is he here?" asked a woman of about thirty. Gourfan Clan, if I interpreted the symbol on her chest correctly. It was full and attractive, but her chest was the only thing that was attractive about her. The lady turned out to be extremely ugly. The facial features were all in the right place, but they seemed somehow...superfluous, or something. Crafted. Unnatural.

"This is a hunter of the dark ones from the light lands," explained Seven. "A dark mirror who can ignore Skron's influence. His safe passage is guaranteed for the duration of this mission. The Temple of Skron will punish any clan whose members try to attack him. This rift conqueror came here to close the infected rift. How long will it take you, Light One?"

"From what I understand, this rift has already reached level twelve. It will take me about four hours to reach that depth. When's the next reboot?"

"In five hours," replied Seven.

"Excellent. Then only one more vital question remains: how will the winnings be distributed? How much goes to the Bartolomeo Clan?"

"Four hours to close a twelve-level infected rift? What kind of nonsense are you peddling, Light One?" asked the Gourfan representative. "That's barely enough time to reach the Master!"

"If the Gourfan Clan doubts my abilities, then they can close the rift themselves and take as much time as they think is appropriate. The Bartolomeo Clan is willing to wait as long as necessary. The only limitation is that for each level above the twelfth you will have to spend about thirty minutes. My personal opinion is that it would be a good idea to wait for the metamorph to appear and allow the infected rift to reach level seventeen, but it's up to you."

"Level Seventeen?" They looked at me like I was crazy.

"Half an hour for each level after the twelfth?" Seven said, to which I just shrugged, indicating that the conversation was beginning to tire me. "Let's say the Temple of Skron is interested in getting in on this. What are your terms?"

"Half of everything that is mined from this infected rift will go to the Bartolomeo Clan. I will receive the ring from the metamorph for my own personal use, and that's actually all I demand. Oh yeah — I'll have to kill all the exclusive monsters. They react badly to me."

"The infected rift will open up in six hours," said Seven after much thought. "By this time it will have reached level fourteen. I have heard your demands, Light One. The Temple of Skron will discuss them and make an offer to the Bartolomeo Clan, but it will not be today. Today we just need to close the rift. You will have five hours. If you fail, the Bartolomeo Clan will lose its place in the clan council. Are you satisfied with these conditions?"

"I didn't hear anything about how the winnings will be distributed." The news that I had to hurry was not particularly encouraging. I really didn't want to let the red creatures through, since they dropped essences. If only I knew exactly what essences were…Maybe I should take a chance and expose the krona essence now? For one thing, their reactions would tell me exactly what it was and whether it was really worth anything. Second, I could find out its practical use. What if it came in handy for me as well? Who knew…Of course, there was another scenario holding me back. Perhaps essences were banned and anyone found in possession of them would be immediately executed. Having no information was hard. Should I take a risk? Probably not worth it. Not now.

"The Bartolomeo Clan will receive fifty percent of everything mined from this rift if you can close it in five hours."

"In that case, let's stipulate the conditions for my passage right here and now. Five hours from now, I will descend to the fourteenth level and destroy the Master of the infected rift. At this moment, all creatures that inhabit the rift will lose mobility. You can do whatever you want with them. It will take me some more time to return to the surface, and I'm afraid the total time will be much longer than five hours. But the rift will be destroyed in time."

"The Temple of Skron can track the life cycle of an infected rift," Seven assured me, but still clarified: "Will all the rift beasts lose mobility?"

"All the ones I don't kill. The exclusive beasts, as I already said, I will have to destroy. At least, any who get in my way. I won't run from cave to cave, seeking them out."

"The Temple of Skron wants you to preserve as many of the exclusive creatures of the infected rift as possible," Seven said a little too quickly, betraying his own desires.

"Will you try to extract essences from them?" I took a risk and, judging by the way those gathered reacted to my words, I hit the nail on the head. Some even held their breath, afraid to miss even the slightest word.

"Do you know something about that?" asked Seven.

"About essences? Only that they exist. When I closed the infected eighteen-level rift, I was lucky enough to become the owner of a krona essence. Now this little orb is guarded in a safe place, awaiting its fate. I think I might surrender it to the Church of the Light. What if they know what it is and what it is used for?"

"The Temple of Skron has heard you, Hunter

of Darkness. Yes, we want to obtain the essences. This is why we want you to leave as many exclusive monsters as possible."

"Agreed," I could only shrug. "If I suddenly manage to obtain an essence now, what should I do with it? Why do the dark ones need them?"

"This is not information that we are ready to share with the Light Ones," answered Seven. "If you obtain the essence of a krona or any other creature, you must transfer it to the Temple of Skron."

"Free of charge?" I said. "No, servant of the temple, I will not give anything to anyone for free. So I will do everything I can to ensure that this essence does not fall into my hands."

"Do you know how to improve the drop rate?" Seven had caught on quickly.

"This is not information I'm willing to share with dark ones. I'm just here to close the infected rift."

"The Temple of Skron has heard you. You have five hours to rest. You can use any tent in this camp. The Temple of Skron gives you this right. I hope the clans won't object?"

The mist beasts evidently were high up in the hierarchy, since no one dared to resist the order. Looking around, I noticed a lone chair.

"I'll just take the chair, Seven. If you don't mind, I'd like to prepare. The descent ahead of me will not be an easy one. Make sure I have a document in my hands in five hours, outlining the agreement we just made."

"You do not trust the Temple of Skron?" The hiss was filled with ire and the others instinctively recoiled from the mist being.

"Why should I?" I said. "All my experience with dark ones has demonstrated that your word alone is not sufficient. It must always be backed up with some sort of contract. Or is the Temple of Skrona trying to claim that it has never deceived the light ones?"

"You are currently representing the Bartolomeo Clan, not the world of the Light."

"And yet, you presented me as a light one, and not a representative of the Bartolomeo clan. I need it on paper, Seven. Alright, perhaps not, then. I'll go down, kill the Master, and you may even fulfill all of your verbal obligations. But the Temple of Skron aren't the only ones that know how to draw conclusions."

There was no reply to this statement, so after a minute, I sat back in the comfortable armchair. Finally, I had time to collect my thoughts.

"Alia, hello! Have you already heard the latest news?"

The conversation with my personal attendant didn't go very well, to say the least. She was categorically against me visiting the last rift of the year. Because, "No one knows what could happen tomorrow, or the next day!" I needed to keep one in reserve so that I had time to react. I left the Zarak Empire, and indeed the entire world of the Light, with no protection for the sake of my own personal interests. And when Alia found out about the more personal of these interests...I never knew she could swear like that. So our little chat didn't end on good terms.

"Is that remote communication, or have you lost your mind and started talking to yourself?" Three Gourfans appeared next to me. At the head was an unpleasant...I wanted to call her a matron, but I'll just say "woman" and leave it at that. Judging by the tone, I was clearly being provoked, but I didn't want to play into such a stupid ploy and decided to just close the issue.

"Remote communication. A gift from Magister Meram."

I knew not every clan was able to get their hands on remote communication, for the gray runescribe was an extremely exclusive person. No one knew why he refused some and agreed to help make connections for others. The fact that I was one of the "chosen ones" greatly increased my value. Of course, I didn't mention the fact that I could make this connection myself.

"I'll go with you," the woman said.

"Are you familiar with the way a mirror operates?" I asked. "I just walk right up next to the rift beasts and they don't pay me any mind. They'll also have to be killed, in addition to the exclusive ones. Can you make yourself invisible among beasts on level fourteen so that they don't attack you?"

I already knew the answer — no, she couldn't. This clearly wasn't the head of the clan standing in front of me. She didn't have an amulet to block my *Analyze*. Just as she didn't have *Phantom*. But the rest of her stats made my head spin. A real goliath, perhaps stronger than even Count Vyazemsky himself! First off was her magic field, which extended eight squares in both directions. An eight by eight! If I had a field like that, all my issues with *Devour* would be resolved! I would increase it to level ten, and then all the resources in the infected rifts would be mine! This woman's ability and support stones were also impressive — not a single one below level twenty. She specialized in fire, suppression auras and healing. The only thing I considered myself better at was defense. She had the classic *Magic Armor*. In my opinion, *Golden Dome of Defense* was much more exciting. But wait — all above level twenty...how many elixirs did she have to drink to pump her stones up so much? Or was there another way of increasing stone levels without drinking tens of thousands of vials? This was a point I absolutely needed to clarify. My defense and attack were level six, and these numbers were catastrophically insufficient for living a long, safe life.

"They told me who you are, Maximilian Valevsky. Head of Hearth. A city in the Light where the portal authorized by the Church of the Light is located. You are a merchant. This means you understand that you have a product that you cannot use. I want to buy the krona essence from you.

"Most decent folk would introduce themselves before they started bargaining." I made no move to get up from my chair. The three representatives of the Gourfan Clan had clearly come seeking an audience with me, but such trifles did not interest me.

"My name is Nayna Moises," the lady answered, grimacing in displeasure. Apparently, every dog in the street should know her name. Although, to be honest, it did ring a bell.

"Nice to meet you, Nayna Moises. Yes, I have a krona essence. But at this point, it is an unidentified item worth all of Kerux to me. I can't state a sufficient price when I don't even know what it's used for. I'd be happy to hear your offer."

"Our offer?"

"Certainly. Believing the dark ones is the last thing on my mind. I'll hear offers from all the clans, the Temple of Skron, and the Church of the Light, and only after that I will be able to say for certain the value of this item."

"The Gourfan Clan will send you an official proposal," Nayna answered after a pause. "If you don't agree with it, you will be put on their black list."

"Is this some kind of convoluted way of committing suicide?" I asked and smiled when all three took a step closer, as if wanting to crush me like the pathetic insect I was. Which, I have to say, was not unintimidating — each one had stats far exceeding my own. Nayna in some ways resembled Magister Meram. I didn't even try to count the number of open parameters. She had invested significantly in her development. Indeed, she was the best rift conqueror of this world. Or that's what she'd fancied herself, at least, until some light one had waltzed over. I wasn't worried though — I was under the protection of the Temple of Skron, and even the Gourfans did not dare challenge that.

Soon the three of them left, and I was even able to get some shut eye. I didn't bother asking Kimal Sarento about why the dark ones valued essences so highly. First I'd try to ask Cedric or Theodore. That the dark ones were interested in this was an irrefutable fact. It doesn't seem as if essences are prohibited items, but for some reason everyone got extremely excited when they were mentioned. Kimal was on our side, of course, but it was always useful to hear several opinions before forming your own.

"Time, Maximilian of the Bartolomeo Clan. The infected rift will open in ten minutes." I was awoken by one of the misty servants of the Temple of Skron, but definitely not Seven.

"Has it gotten deeper?" I asked, stretching my stiff muscles. Sleeping in a chair was not my brightest idea.

"It's level fourteen. The next level up is in eight hours."

"Why is it so regular? Are all your rifts located the same distance away from one another?"

"This infected rift is still too shallow to drag any neighboring rifts into it. That starts at level twenty. For now, it's just growing on its own, draining power from the surrounding environment. Now, if it reaches level thirty, then we're in trouble."

"Has that happened before?" I asked and from the reaction I realized that it had, of course, but that no one would talk about it with me. That's okay, I had my own informant. Adeline wasn't going anywhere, and she'd be compelled to give me answers.

An impressive crowd had already gathered near the entrance, headed by Nayna. I had to drink a mana elixir, which I haven't done for a long time. My constant use of *Analyze* sapped my mana faster than the *Drain* curse.

"Your contract." Seven was also standing near the entrance. "We need to perform an inspection before you descend. The Temple of Skron is not in the habit of trusting the light ones. We need a complete list of your assets before you enter the infected rift. So that later there won't be any problems allocating the goods later."

The requirement was logical, but a little out of place. It would have been a lot better if they had checked me in the tent, and not in front of this crowd. However, I did not resist. Handing over the backpack to the mist man, I began to undress, not at all embarrassed by the surrounding eyes. They examined me with all seriousness. When I was left in only my underwear, one of the dark ones began to pat me down, as if I could have anything important hidden.

"Get dressed," ordered Seven. He seemed disappointed, as if he had been hoping to find the source of my power. The reason why the rift beasts wouldn't touch me. But he found nothing of the sort. Not even a ring. Nayna, for instance, had eight. Svirella — the one I'd killed — had one. It turned out that the dark ones had been farming metamorphs for a long time. Red rings are not a luxury here, but an everyday occurrence. It wasn't too nice to feel like the resident of an empire with such limited means.

What can I say about the passage itself? Only that I walked and walked until finally, I arrived. Behind me lay only mountains of flesh that were once exclusive monsters. So the servant of the Temple of Skron wanted me to leave as many red creatures as possible? What a pity that I didn't succeed. When I killed the Master, all the monsters in the rift would become the same color anyway. Their aura would disappear, so how could they sort out which was an elite and which was exclusive anyway? The number of essences in my inventory had increased significantly, as had my *Amplify* fragments. But I still wanted to use them as soon as possible. And, of course, *Devour* automatically collected high-level resources from each level. Why should I share with the dark ones what could simply and elegantly remain mine? If they hadn't examined me so carefully, perhaps I would have left something to be extracted, but now...well, they brought it on themselves.

Once again, I didn't dare to try extracting essences from the guards. I'd only do so in a two-level rift with the support of other mages, just to ensure that the beasts wouldn't rush me. For now,

I just passed by and reached the ugly little Master. The impact of the mithril gauntlet ripped out the essence of this wretched creature, and when I destroyed the remaining hearts, a notification appeared before my eyes that the infected rift had been destroyed. Three hours and twenty minutes. Who was the best? I was done!

Location map obtained...

The Master didn't drop anything particularly special, so I returned to the cave with the guards. These fourteen carcasses on legs could give me one hundred and ninety-six units of yem, but I couldn't fit them in my inventory. It had been clogged up since my last trip, and I simply had nowhere to unload such valuable resources. What a drag it was to have a level-one *Devour*...I had to make the gut-wrenching decision to leave the guards behind. Let them rejoice. At the same time, this was a foundation for the future. They can learn that it was profitable to hire me to close rifts, instead of some Gourfan. I didn't like Nayna at all.

Once I made my ascent, they inspected me again. Representatives of the Temple of Skron took away all the magic stones. Although I tried not to get too greedy, I did manage to extract some stones along with the essences. One good thing — there wasn't a single exclusive among them. I didn't want to give something of such value to the dark ones. I was lucky.

"The Bartolomeo Clan destroyed the infected

fourteen-level rift, fulfilling its obligations. Their position in the clan rankings has been fortified, and the head of the clan will preside over the next clan council," Seven proclaimed when they allowed me to get dressed and even brought me water to wash off the dirt. Judging by Nayna's look, I had a new fangirl — a clan that specialized in destroying rifts would not forgive such a blow to its reputation. Some light one from the Bartolomeo Clan just rolled into town and instantly destroyed what the best of the best could not cope with. And did it in three and a half hours!

"The portal will return you to Kerux," said Seven, indicating that I had to go. On this I completely agreed with the misty minister of Skron. The sooner I returned to Hearth, the sooner I would meet Naira. Although she was a little too hot-headed when she said it, Alia reported that the girl was already in the city. Together with Adeline.

The space around me swam, but instead of the usual lush decoration of any of the hotels of Kerux, I found myself in absolute darkness. For a moment I was overcome with panic, but I managed to quickly extinguish it. Taking out the lighting crystal, I looked around. I was transported to a large room. I found no doors or windows here. All the walls were framed by the arches of portal passages, which now turned out to be inactive. Turning around, I saw the same dead passage behind me. The minotaurs were gone. I didn't know how to call them to get out of this place. Opening the map in the vain hope of understanding where I'd ended up, I was amazed to see that this area was already known to me. Before heading to the rift, I'd teleported to the Temple of Skron. It appeared on my map, only last time the point indicating my position was outside the building. Now the map showed that I'd gotten myself into trouble. I was inside the Temple of Skron. A place the vast majority of the dark ones I knew avoided like the plague. Placing my hand on my shoulder, I said, trying to speak as calmly as possible:

"Sir Chancellor, I have a small problem. The Temple of Skron kidnapped me."

Chapter 6

"FOLLOW ME. Nothing will harm you here. The Temple of Skron wishes to speak to you."

The door through which the misty servant of the Temple entered the room appeared out of nowhere. Part of the wall simply moved aside, revealing a wide opening. I did not resist — Kimal Sarento told me to comply with any demands of the Temple, even if they forced me to hop on one leg and perform a whole song and dance for them. He wouldn't be in touch with his connections for another day. At the moment, he was not far from Hearth, coming back from Al-Khorezm, where he had held his pointless negotiations with Magister Meram.

Unlike the room with the portals, the corridor was illuminated, so I took off my light crystal. We walked for quite a while, going down, then back up, constantly twisting and turning down different branches. There were a surprising number of people in the Temple of Skron. The passages to several rooms were open, and I had a chance to see the dark ones training. A large group of future rift conquerors sat around a cage with kronas. Some of the dark ones were already lying on the floor, some were staggering, but the especially persistent ones managed to stay upright. It looked like the training grounds at the academy, except that the creature sitting in the cage was clearly not from the third level of the rift. Because exclusive monsters start at level five, and the monster in the cage exuded a red aura. There were many such rooms. The misty servant of the Temple of Skron did not react in any way to the aura of the dark creatures. Despite the fact that when I walked past one room, this aura even weighed on me. Not much, as if the monster had been taken out of level sixteen, but still, it stung a little. Next to this monster, there were only two rift conquerors. Evidently third-year students who had already spent some time getting to know the beasts.

We turned again, leaving the corridor with the students, and went up to the next level. A few more turns and we finally stopped near a closed door. The Temple servant pressed a button and the door slid up. Interesting mechanisms here. I wouldn't mind implementing these in my own place. The space where I was taken looked like a small conference room. Windowless, with a small round table, at which were already the three highest hierarchs of the Temple. Or so I thought — it was unlikely that they brought me to a gathering of janitors.

"Archduke Maximilian Valevsky of the Bartolomeo Clan, Hunter of Darkness, Rift Conqueror, Dark Mirror, delivered by your order," said my escort, and the doors closed behind me.

"Sit down, Light One," a voice said. It's not particularly pleasant when you can't see the faces of your conversation partners. I couldn't tell which one of them was speaking. There was only one empty chair at the table, so there was no question about where I was supposed to sit. But the fact that they called me "Light One" raised several questions. I knew there was no hope of a friendly chat.

"I am Four," said the mist-being sitting between the other two. "This is Six and Seven. You have the essence of krona. We need it."

Just like that, no prefaces, overtures or small talk. Well done! Alright, two could play this game.

"You have knowledge of what this essence is used for. I need it."

"The Temple of Skron knew you would demand this. The essence is needed to create a monster torn from Skron. Capable of existing under the sun without losing its aura. Submissive to its owner. It is a pet that can be used as a fighting force in its own right."

"What level will the krona you create be, and can its level be increased?"

"The creature created will be the same level as its source essence was. It can level up by absorbing other essences, but from other beasts. Not kronas."

A shiver ran down my spine as I realized what a deadly monster this could make. A krona on a leash that would allow you to outfit it in steel armor, like the one we encountered in the capital, and with an aura that kills anyone who was not a rift conqueror on the spot...an ultimate weapon in the constant clashes between clans that even the best rift conquerors wouldn't be able to cope with right away. What if there were several such kronas — let's say ten of them — that behaved not like frenzied flesh-hungry monsters, but like trained fighters carrying out the orders of their commander? Then no army in the world would be able to counter them. Although no, the army can handle it. One or two hundred crossbow-men...What if the armor was made of vyrma, which steel bolts cannot pierce? An army is only effective at a distance; if a dozen kronas ranging from levels thirteen to sixteen approached the soldiers, they would become mincemeat immediately. Now I understood why the clans were so alarmed when they heard about the essences. Nobody wanted to miss out on a weapon of such power.

"You want me to sell an essence to the Temple of Skron, which you will then use to make a weapon and send it to the lands of Light?"

"Not sell — give," said Four. "You will transfer the essence to the Temple of Skron without any conditions. The creatures that are created in this way are not intended for your empires."

"For what, then?"

"This information is not available to light ones."

"You want to get the essence for free. Let's say I'm willing to do this — I need to clearly understand that by giving it to you, I won't be dooming the world of the Light to ruin. In this case, it would be easier to destroy the essence than to give it to you. The Temple of Skron will have to share information with this particular light one."

"You are not light," Seven said, for some reason. "You are a dark human who has been recognized by the Church of the Light."

"I'm a human who has survived an encounter with the Inquisitor. No dark one is capable of this. Or is the Temple of Skron not aware of this information?"

I didn't like that this mist man was trying to classify me as dark. In this case, it would be possible for them to force Naira to go to the Temple. After all, her fiancé was dark, not light. Even if our relationship didn't work out and tomorrow I realized that despite all her external beauty, she was just a beast, I still didn't want her to be forced to come here.

"The Temple of Skron knows about this," admitted Four reluctantly. "We are ready to agree on your alliance with Naira Jode and deprive her of her status as a rift conqueror if you transfer the essence to us."

"I will give you the essence only when you tell me where you'll use the krona you create," I returned to our main topic of conversation. "How are you using your pets? I need this information because my city is the only official transport hub for the darkness. If a krona suddenly pops up in Turb or Al-Khorezm that exudes a dark aura and is also able to ignore the effects of the sun, I won't be able to justify my decision. The portal will close, I will be executed, and all trade, which has not even had time to improve, will be destroyed. Is this what the Temple of Skron wants?"

"The creature we create will not be used in the lands of Light," said Four. "It will go to the border with the offworlders."

"Offworlders? Like beings from another world?" I asked, hearing the word for the first time but gleaning the meaning perfectly.

"The territory of Kerux is expansive, but it has clearly defined borders. Some of the neighboring lands are inhabited by other dark humans, but others are home to offworlders. Beings from other worlds. In those areas, magic ceases to work, objects acquire strange properties, and the only effective way to protect our lands from the encroachments of offworlders is to use creatures freed from their dependence on Skron. Offworlders cannot survive the dark aura. Each such creature is put to special use, because essences are dropped too rarely. I have answered your question, Sir Maximilian. The essence is ours. Now we'd like to know how you got your hands on it."

I was really tempted to offer my services to the Temple of Skron. If offworlders couldn't tolerate rift auras, then a dark mirror from the eighteenth level would create a huge bang. But did I really need all that? Definitely not now. Looking at Four, who was hiding behind his misty veil, I couldn't resist a note of sarcasm:

"And you expect me to give up this information for free as well?"

Sure, the position I was in wasn't the most enviable, but it had opened my eyes to many things. All dark portals were controlled by minotaurs or, if you turned your gaze a little higher, by the Temple of Skron. If the Temple didn't like someone, it simply transferred the unwanted person to its pyramid, and everyone forgot about them forever. They simply disappeared. The thought of never using a portal again...I didn't even know — before, the idea of opening a new portal seemed quite sound. Now that I realized who controlled them and what powers they have, maybe I didn't need such a thing. After I returned to Hearth, I would never use this means of transportation again. Better to drive a dozen horses, and have at least the illusion of freedom than to give myself up to the waiting hands of the Temple of Skron.

"What do you want for it?" Four replied after a pause.

"More information. I can make a list, if you'd like. I'm interested in a broad range of things. How can you increase the size of your magic field? How do you level up your stones without gulping down thousands of elixirs? What is *Fog Stalker*? How can you pull exclusive stones from your magic field? I also recently learned that there are recipes — I need at least five different ones. This is what I want in exchange for information on how I obtained the krona essence.”

“The Temple of Skron has heard your wishes. We will think about how we can improve our cooperation. There are several more infected rifts in our lands. Now they are sealed, but every year the seals become thinner. Soon they will disappear completely. The Temple of Skron wishes to involve the Bartolomeo Clan in solving this problem.”

“Thanks to the Valdez Clan, I have a limit to the number of rifts I can visit. No more than three per year. Today was the third. If I enter a rift in the next nine months, I will die. Which is something I’d like to avoid.”

“The Temple of Skron has seen the runes Magister Meram placed on you,” said Four. “We’ll offer you a deal, Light One. We will cleanse you of all runes and you will destroy one of the oldest infected rifts, the seal on which could break at any moment.”

“Can the Temple of Skron cleanse me of what Magister Meram has cast on me?” I was surprised.

“Magister Meram became a runescribe in the Temple of Skron. Now he is following his own path, but initially, he studied with us. We know how to cleanse runes from bodies.”

“One rift in exchange for wiping the slate clean?” I tried to keep my breathing even, although excitement made my heart beat mercilessly in my chest. "What's the catch? No, that's the wrong question. What level is this infected rift now?"

"Twenty-three."

"That's too deep for me." All the joy of the impending cleansing disappeared. "My current maximum level is eighteen. A twenty-three level would flatten me out like a pad of butter on warm bread."

"The Temple of Skron believes that there will be a metamorph in the infected rift. You will receive a ring."

"The ring will allow me to descend one more level, no more. Will you give me five more rings? I'd need a maximum dark aura reduction. Only then could I agree to this madness. Without six rings, going into that rift would be suicide. Or, as an option, you can stock up on food for several years and slowly move from level to level, allowing the body to adapt to the influence of darkness. I don't see any other options."

"The Temple of Skron will consider your demands," Four answered reflexively. Translated into ordinary language, did this mean that I and my demands could screw off back to Hearth? But I wasn't going to allow myself to lag behind.

"I have a counteroffer. The Temple of Skron will remove my rift restriction, give me some kind of amulet so that Magister Meram can no longer put symbols on me, give me access to two or three ordinary level-twenty rifts or an infected one no deeper than level twenty, confirm that all resources from the rifts will belong to the

Bartolomeo Clan, in which case, if I am lucky again, I will be able to provide you with another essence."

"You mean you can acquire them with some degree of probability?" Four immediately seized my offer.

"I have already voiced my requirements for exchanging this information."

"The Temple of Skron knows how to wait and is ready to invest in a future partnership first. We can free you from your restrictions and provide protection from the runescribe. In exchange, we wish to enlist your services to destroy the infected rifts on our lands. You will have to appear at our first beck and call, and we'll set up a form of remote communication with you. You will have to pass through the first two infected rifts without your required payment. The Temple of Skron now has information on your level limitations as far as how deep you can go, as well as the requirements for increasing the depth."

"How many infected rifts are there in your lands? I need to understand the amount of work ahead of me. You'll want to get rid of them all, right?"

"The Temple of Skron believes that giving out this information will do no harm. Currently, we have forty-two sealed rifts reaching as far down as level twenty five, as well as one infected rift that we did not manage to seal. It has currently reached a depth of seventy three levels and adds a new one every six months. The clans that lived in that territory have all gone to Skron, and we are losing kilometer after kilometer every year. Even if there is a desert between us and the rift, sooner or later this problem will also have to be solved."

Seventy three...I didn't even know what to say. Sure, giving out this information wouldn't do any harm, unless you counted the sleepless nights ahead of me. I couldn't even imagine what beasts might dwell in these depths. The metamorph that was the scourge of the light lands would look like a helpless puppy in comparison.

Drag me to Skron — imagine what loot they must drop! I looked down at my palms and squeezed my fingers forcefully several times. If mithril takes on the properties that its owner requires, wouldn't it have the ability to completely ignore the dark influence? Where could I find four mages who wouldn't try to grab the mithril themselves and could keep their mouths shut? I didn't really want to use the four counts and have to give up a quarter of everything to them.

"The Temple of Skron would like to know how many shards of *Fog Stalker* you have," Four said unexpectedly.

"This is personal information," I was surprised at this line of questioning. "I have quite a few. It's hard not to amass them when you're mowing down Pharapho spawn in huge quantities. I would like to understand what it is and what will happen if I collect the required amount. The light ones have no knowledge about this."

"The Temple of Skron would like the key if you

collect it," the Fourth stated simply, and that was when I realized that my patience was starting to run out. These creatures communicate with me as if with one of their subjects! Do this, give us that, the essences are all ours, urgently transfer the *Fog Walker* key to home base...As soon as I got out of the Temple and returned to Hearth, I would never use portals again in my life! Let the dark ones deal with their problems themselves!

Evidently, my thoughts were written on my face, as Four suddenly said:

"The Temple of Skron believes that we no longer have any reason to hold you. Everything mined from the infected rift will be sent to the Bartolomeo Clan. We express our gratitude, Rift Conqueror, that you took the time to communicate with us. The Temple of Skron needs time to discuss how our further working relationship should proceed. A representative will go to Hearth with you. Give him the krona essence. You will be contacted shortly and we will voice our proposal."

The door opened and the attendant entered the room. I still hadn't figured out how to distinguish between the mist beings during the meeting. If they were to play musical chairs, I'd never be able to guess which was Four, Six or Seven. It could easily turn out that my escort was actually Five or One. The Temple was not particularly inventive with its naming procedures.

I was taken to a familiar room with portal arches, and this time there were minotaurs. We jumped to the territory of the Bartolomeo Clan, and then a moment later, to Hearth. My chaperone followed me as if glued to me. I had to pretend that I was entering my personal office, asking the Temple servant to wait for me outside, after which I embodied one of the essences and returned to the uninvited guest. He accepted the krona essence as something incredibly precious and, without saying another word, retreated to the portal. All this time, the city guards followed directly on our heels, keeping the guest in the sights of their crossbows. In agreement with Viscount Kurpatsky, one of the crossbows was loaded with a vyrma bolt. To be sure to finish off any beast that entered our lands without permission.

It was only when the portal's flickering faded and I returned to my personal office that my emotions overwhelmed me. I was shaking as if I was standing in negative forty degree windchill in only my skivvies. The fact that I managed to buy off the Temple of Skron at the cost of just one essence, of which I had more than two hundred in my inventory, was incredible luck. What could I say, even Kimal Sarento said that I should fulfill all the demands of the dark ones. What irked me most was that I knew perfectly well that the Temple would not just leave me alone. Even if I shattered the portal arch right now, they would find a way to come visit me and make their demands. Now I was incredibly weak relative to the dark ones who had taken an interest in me. And they decided to take advantage of this.

"Max, you don't look like yourself. What

happened?" Alia asked as she stepped into my office. She sat down opposite me and threw up a canopy so that the invisible people, of which there must be many in Hearth, would not hear my stuttering. I continued to shake for quite some time. Even when they brought me a cup of hot tea and carefully covered me with a blanket.

"We should have expected that everything would turn out exactly like this," Alia sighed heavily. "I already have two full books of information that should not be shared with the public or the Fortress. And this is just after a couple of months of work. A year or two, and our archives will become more extensive than those of the church. We need a treasury. One that Count Shub does not have access to. Do you even realize that your bride is a dark human? If even one seeker of darkness gets to her and checks her, you'll be in it deep. She must not be allowed out of Hearth. At least until you get permission from the Fortress."

"We need Father Nor," I agreed. "First of all, we must check Naira's commitment to Skron."

"He's already on his way. He'll arrive by evening. Max, answer just one question: why do you need all this? You are light, why tie your fate to the dark? To one who could turn out to be truly dark?"

"I simply didn't have another choice," I sighed. "I turned her into a rift conqueror, and I am responsible for that. Where is she, by the way?"

"She was given a room on the floor above,"

Alia said, stroking her own stomach. The purple robe hid the girl's figure, but I knew that her belly was already rounded. A few days ago, I had stroked it myself. Unlike Eleanore, Alia constantly visited me at night. Pregnancy did not affect her passion. Sex with my personal attendant was passionate and stormy. I didn't even think about the twins anymore. Why did I need anyone else when I had Alia?

The doors opened and Kimal Sarento burst into the office. He noticed the canopy and knocked on it, demanding to be allowed inside. When Alia deactivated it, Kimal looked at the ceiling and said:

"You have ten seconds to leave the premises. If you disgrace my sight again, you will die. Your time is up."

As I had predicted, my office was full of invisible people. Three *Phantom*s instantly peeled off the wall and left without even casting a glance in our direction. The doors closed, and Kimal Sarento stood for some time, listening to something. Finally, sitting down in a chair, he nodded to Alia, and she threw the canopy back up.

"Have you had your little chat?" A familiar grin crept across the chancellor's face. "How much did your escape from the Temple of Skron cost?"

"An *Essence of Krona*." There was no point in hiding this information.

"Did you find out what they are for?"

"Yes." I stared at the satisfied chancellor for a while and sighed heavily. An unpleasant thought dawned on me. "You had no idea what they were used for."

"How would I know? It is available only to the highest hierarchs of the clans and the Temple of Skron. Us ordinary chancellors of magic academies are not made privy to this information. Alia, will you give me a fresh copy of your notes later? I've already read all the old ones. You've got a good archive, I want to tell you. Although it wouldn't hurt you to learn the basics of office work. Records need to be structured and kept in binders so that you can add dividing sheets. The way you keep your books now is a shame and disgrace to the Fortress and its teachers."

"You..." Alia became indignant, but fell silent when she saw Kimal Sarento's warning gesture.

"I have shown you that your supposed secret is already possessed by many. We need to take more care of such things. I had to make big efforts to ensure that only I caught sight of your two books. Moreover, they brought them to me at the academy, then returned them back, but you didn't notice anything. Alright, before you start arguing, I want to show you one piece of paper. When I was trying to get permission from the Citadel for Adeline to have official permission to travel across our three empires, I managed to obtain something else. This form. Similar to the one Adeline has, with only one difference — it's blank, no name is indicated. I believe that even if Father Nor, who is now driving the horses, identifies darkness in Naira Jode, she will have the right to accompany you wherever you go."

A paper with the seal of the Citadel appeared on the table. I couldn't resist, I read the text and gulped. Kimal Sarento's connections were frightening. What had he offered the Citadel to obtain a blank form? I had no doubt that this was an original and not a product of the chancellor's own machinations. No one in their right mind would forge Citadel documents.

"And it could be yours, in exchange for a good story about your journey to the dark lands. Starting from the list of loot you obtained, ending with any agreements you made with the Temple. I know you too well, Maximilian Valevsky, not to understand that you must have made some sort of agreement with them. I want to know exactly what it is, how it can benefit me and, perhaps, you as well. And, of course, why is everyone after these essences? Maybe some wine? I remember I gave you two bottles. As far as I know, they are still in the box. Second from the top on the left side. Please start the story with how much bone armor you decided to hide from us and how you decided to activate them without the help of our mages?"

Chapter 7

"NO," I REPLIED after a long pause.

"No?" Kimal's brows raised sky high.

"No."

"Persuade me."

"What for? You've stated your terms, and I don't agree to them. Why should I explain myself? Alia, take the canopy down, we're done here. Sir Chancellor, did you come straight here from your long journey? Would you like a bath drawn? Freshen up a bit? Are you hungry? Our chefs aren't bad. I won't offer you wine — the bottles in the second drawer from the top on the left-hand side are as dear to me as a memory. The one who gave them to me categorically forbade me from using them for any ordinary occasion. Only for moments of true joy or sorrow."

"So you don't need Naira Jode's permission to leave Hearth?"

"If Father Nor confirms that she is susceptible to Skron's influence, my temporary bride will live happily within the walls for a year, then return back to her clan. I'm not going to hide behind some bureaucratic loophole and let a dark one susceptible to Skron into the world. Even if this dark one has turned gray. By the way, this also applies to Adeline. Has she already been inspected?"

"Maximilian, there's something you don't seem to understand." The broad smile on Kimal Sarento's face became a wry grin, and his voice became like the grinding of steel. "You are not an independent agent. You are mine. And if I tell you to jump, you jump. Otherwise, you will simply disappear, like so much refuse."

"And I did jump, up until I got into the Temple of Skron." I held his gaze and decided to go for broke. It was now or never. "Moreover, I did everything just as you asked. I had to do a whole song and dance to convince the Temple servants to release me. There's just one small problem, my dear Chancellor, and it's that essences proved too valuable to the Temple of Skron. Just half an hour ago, Hearth played host to a misty Temple servant who confirmed their interests in our mutual cooperation. I knew that you would show up and, instead of negotiating, start demanding. Maybe even threaten, which I see has already happened. So, anticipating all this, I made a deal with the Temple of Skron. They will receive five essences in exchange for my protection. Moreover, the Temple knows perfectly well that if something suddenly happens to me, or I suddenly become upset because one of my people has disappeared or died, the culprit will surely be Kimal Sarento, the chancellor of the magical academy of the Zarak Empire. You know very well how important essences are for the dark ones, but you do not understand why they are needed. Continue to insist, threaten, and you will experience first-hand the true intensity of the Temple of Skron's interest. And one more important clarification, so that you don't even cast a thought in this direction. The Temple of Skron taught me how to bind exclusive stones to a magical field so that my killer could not remove them. We were discussing *Amplify*s at the time, but this method also works for other stones. So you won't be able to kill me and take the essences for yourself."

"Has Archduke Valevsky decided to declare war on me?" Kimal's face showed nothing. Even his smile had vanished.

"Not war, Count Sarento. I will gladly continue to cooperate both with you and the other slices of the pie, but only on mutually beneficial terms. Where you do not tell me, 'You are mine,' or 'You will vanish like refuse.' You need bone armor — let's discuss it. If you need information, I will be happy to share it for a fee. If you need cutting stones, you know where to go. Even if you need artifacts, I will be ready to discuss their transfer to your possession."

"There are the artifacts as well," Kimal said

thoughtfully.

"Those as well. I am open to cooperation in all areas, Count Sarento."

"Bravo, Maximilian, I'll remember your attempt to stand your ground," he replied, losing all seriousness and cracking a smile. "Continue in that vein and it might eventually work out for you. But not today. In order to bluff like that, you need at least some reason. Attracting the Temple of Skron...Maximilian, I could believe the Bartolomeo Clan, but the Temple...This is too much. But it was worth a try. Now stop talking nonsense about your agreements with the dark ones and answer my questions. I don't have enough time to listen to your baby talk."

At the end of his speech, Kimal once again became deadly serious. I was going to defend my freedom to the last. I wouldn't get a better chance again. Now I had at least some power in the form of information that Kimal needed. In the future I'd have no such leverage. I'd become a regular bargaining chip that the chancellor would use at will. And then he'd throw me away like refuse.

I just couldn't convey this idea to Kimal Sarento. There was a knock on the door and a chalk-white maid came in, distracting us from this "heart-to-heart."

"Sir Archduke, you have...a guest."

Without waiting for my answer, a misty servant of the Temple of Skron entered the office. I looked at the dark one in surprise. My escort had left quite recently, not even an hour had passed.

Although perhaps it had — telling Alia about my journey in the dark lands took a lot of time. The chancellor's face stretched out in surprise for a moment, but immediately returned to its usual appearance. He, like me, did not expect to see Temple servants in Hearth. This meant that I needed to do everything to show that this was the meeting I had been waiting for my entire adult life. Without giving my guest a chance to speak first, I asked:

Have you discussed my terms so quickly?"

"The Temple of Skron knows how to make decisions quickly, Rift Conqueror. We agree to your terms. We require…"

"I apologize for interrupting, but there are those present here who are not allowed to have this information. Sir Chancellor, would you wait for me in the guest room? I need to discuss my joint projects with the Temple of Skron."

The chancellor managed to take the blow on the chin, but his cheek twitched several times. Kimal Sarento was clearly infuriated by what was happening, but even he was unable to ignore the power of the Temple of Skron.

"Kimal Sarento isn't your master?" There was surprise in his voice. I clenched my fist to release some of the emotion this evoked, then answered coolly:

"Sir Chancellor and I are partners working on mutually beneficial terms. He is not my master."

"Is this true?" the Temple servant turned towards Kimal Sarento. An evil grin appeared on the man's face.

"Archduke Valevsky has never been my servant, if that's what the Temple of Skron is interested in. I really should leave you two alone. I'll return later to discuss the acquisition of several hundred essences of kronas, rapeseeds, ousels lurges and even two Masters that are within our dear rift conqueror's possession. A mutually beneficial partner, right? Good luck with your negotiations, gentlemen."

This final blow dealt by this vengeful bastard was well below the belt. Kimal knew where to hit the hardest and clearly demonstrated what would happen if I decided to rock the boat against his will. The Temple servant turned in my direction so sharply that it seemed like he was about to rush towards me and finish me off right there, just to get what he wanted. Only the fact that he had no idea where the essences were stopped him. The chancellor left my office, and the dark one installed some kind of figurine next to us, judging by the field that appeared around us — an analogue of Alia's protective canopy, only without the need to use a magic stone. An artifact? Definitely.

"Is the representative of the church's presence required here?" he asked, gesturing toward the silent Alia.

"She is my personal attendant. Everything that I know, she knows. But not the church. I trust her as I trust myself."

"The Temple of Skron accepts your terms,

Light One." He sat in the chair where Kimal had been sitting just moments prior. "A few hundred essences. What was he talking about?"

"That is not what you came here to determine. First let's resolve the previous point, then we'll move on to the next."

"The Temple of Skron does not wish to put any matter related to the essences off until later. You must surrender them to us."

"Why, all of the sudden?" I asked, sincerely surprised. "I'm not your servant. I left the Bartolomeo Clan as soon as I finished destroying the infected rift, you saw the written evidence. Why does a servant of the Temple of Skron dare to break into my house and, without even introducing himself, begin to make demands? We are on the territory of the Zarak Empire, a light state that obeys the Light, not Skron. Maybe we should call a representative of the Citadel? There's one on his way. Is the Temple of Skron looking for cooperation? Then let's cooperate, not demand."

"I am Seven," he presented himself. "Our previous agreements are meaningless. Now we can only speak of essences. You must give them to us."

"I don't owe the Temple of Skron anything." His demanding manner of speaking was starting to aggravate me. I was getting it from all sides at once! The chancellor, the dark one, Adeline, and even Alia were demanding things of me. For some reason, everyone always needed something from me, while few considered my own interests. Didn't anyone take my heart and soul into account?

"The Temple of Skron wants to know the exact number of essences."

"That you can have. Here's a list." Alia handed me a sheet of paper, where I quickly scribbled down about half of what I had in my inventory, with the exception of a few items.

"There are no Riftmaster essences listed here," he noted.

"But you know about them, and that's enough. This is a list of the items I am willing to trade with the Temple of Skron right here and now. I think this should suffice to keep the border with the offworlders safe for a little while. By the way, why haven't the dark ones destroyed them yet? You send ordinary beasts to the Wall."

Seven was quiet a long time. He just stood there, silent as a statue. I even began to worry that my list had caused him to short circuit, but logic suggested he was actually just communicating with other servants. Someone in the top six. If it was a remote connection, then I liked it. I wanted it for myself.

"The Temple of Skron believes that we can find a common ground. You have what we need, we have what you need. Artifacts. Knowledge. You are dark, although you act like you are light. The questions that you asked at the meeting with Four show that you do lack the full education that all dark ones receive, without exception."

"I have a wife who has received this education," I said, but this comment had hit a nerve. I really was willing to give up a lot in exchange for some information. "I'll learn everything I need to know from her."

"You'll learn part of what Naira Jode knows, no more. But that will not make you a master. The Temple of Skron can grant you the ability to give light ones access to their status bar."

"And transform them into dark ones?" I couldn't refrain from asking.

"The presence of a status bar does not make a person dark. It is simply a tool. Just like this pencil. You can use it to write, or you can stab someone with it. How the tool is applied is determined by the person wielding it. Not their allegiance to god. It just makes their job easier. Or do you disagree, Light One who has survived the Inquisitor?"

I had to admit that Seven was right. The status bar was a valuable commodity. I couldn't even imagine how others got by without one. They just closed their eyes, imagined a magic field, their abilities…It all seemed like complete nonsense to me. The status bar made it much more convenient, more efficient and much faster. Alia, despite all the Light she contained, would be the first one I gave this to if I got the opportunity.

"I would like to examine the Temple of Skron's offer in full," I said. "What you will receive is written on the paper. True, there is no *Essence of Riftmaster,* but I'm not willing to part with that yet. First, I'd like to know whether it makes sense for me to work with the Temple of Skron, or if it's better to hand over everything to the Citadel? I'm sure they'd be happy to take these essences off my hands, and they'll also probably give me some sort of rank or accolade. I'll become a commander. Within the light empire hierarchy, this is a fairly honorable and influential role. Prove that it is more effective to cooperate with you. Is the Temple of Skron ready to make its offer now or does it need time?"

"We need time," answered Seven after a pause. "When preparing for this meeting, we did not count on such a large number of essences."

"When you're ready to give your offer, don't forget that I still need to be cleansed from Magister Meram's sigils," I reminded him, just in case. "When should I expect your response?"

"The Temple of Skron will not keep you waiting," Seven assured me and stood up. "As a gesture of goodwill to show how interested we are in our relationship, you will be taught to work with artifacts. Come with me."

I didn't hesitate for a second. Anything that included the word "teach" was a tasty morsel for me. What I didn't receive in childhood, I tried to make up for at every opportunity. Approaching the misty servant, I almost recoiled when his hands grabbed my head and his forehead touched mine. Exactly as the Evil Engineer did to me. With one small exception — this time he transferred not a map, but something more. Something that almost made my body convulse as if I was at level twenty of the rift! Everything swam before my eyes, but the reason for this could have been the dark mist into which I had been plunged. Something unnaturally white flashed before my eyes and, without even realizing it, I used *Analyze*! Hold on! The mist was dissipating!

Seven. Highest Hierarch of the Temple of Skron. Beastman.

The thing shrouded in mist was not human. It was...I couldn't even find the right word for it. Something white, anthropomorphic, faceless. I once saw a mannequin in one of the stores. The misty Temple servant looked exactly like this mannequin. Most surprising was that this monster's stats were practically zero. He had five enhancements in total that unlocked basic options. That was it! At the same time, he knew how to transfer knowledge — when he let go of my head, a message appeared before my eyes:

New functionality unlocked: Artifact storage

A new pictogram appeared on the status bar, and once I opened it, I saw some kind of inventory. Except it was quite simplified.

"Currently, there are already seventy-two people in the world with a similar gift," said Seven. "The Skron Temple knows how to be generous. From now on you have the ability to work with ancient artifacts. Starting from their definition, description, and ending with storage. If you die, all artifacts will automatically fall out of your intangible inventory. Consider this if you decide to die. The Temple of Skron will take a brief interlude and come to you soon with an offer."

"A gesture of goodwill can come from two sides at once," I replied. Pretending that I was rummaging through a desk drawer, I embodied three krona essences at once. The Temple of Skron's gift to me was quite valuable. That mountain of artifacts that I found while clearing the ruins for the Bartolomeo Clan could now be in my possession, and not my bride's clan. Seven accepted the essences calmly, as if he had been counting on something like this. Without saying a word, the misty dark one took the artifact and left, taking the heavy aura with him. Communicating with this creature was proving complicated.

A maid immediately peeked into the office.

"Sir, Count Sarento has left Hearth. Before leaving the estate, he left you this paper."

The blank form from the Citadel was placed on the desk. Alia and I looked at each other in bewilderment. Why suddenly such generosity from Kimal and such a strange escape from the city? Did the chancellor really deign to be offended? Then why did he leave the paper?

"Invite Naira Jode to my office," I asked the maid and, when she ran off, I looked at Alia. "There are invisible ears all around us. You need to protect yourself. There's no need to add to the archive yet. Until we come up with a guaranteed way to preserve information, sharing anything with Count Sarento is unnecessary."

"Max." Alia looked at the sheet of paper as if it were a vial of poison. "Why do you need the dark girl? Aren't I enough?"

The question was so unexpected that I didn't immediately find an answer. The sincere gaze of my personal attendant penetrated into the very depths of my troubled soul. What could I say? That Naira was just an incredibly beautiful girl? Who made me swoon and turned my legs into jelly? I didn't think that was the appropriate response right now.

"Information," I said, groping for an answer. "Seven just said that all dark ones are taught to work with status bars and magic fields. I need to be as prepared as possible for my meeting with the Temple of Skron so that they don't pass off common knowledge as something rare and unique. As for our legal relations...What you don't know yet is that I managed to avoid an elopement. This is the only way the girl can be pulled out from under the influence of the Temple of Skron."

"And is that really worth doing?" Alia posed the provocative question.

"When Father Nor arrives, we'll know. If he admits that she is susceptible to Skron, we will not let her out of Hearth, even despite this paper, and in a year Naira will go back to her clan."

"And if not?"

"If not...then within the next year I'll have a bride."

"With whom you, as an Archduke, will have

to appear at the wedding ceremony organized by Count Vyazemsky."

"What's all that for?" I asked, surprised.

"Because those are the rules, Max. If you show up alone, and someone later finds out that you have a fiancée, it will be a direct insult to the Vyazemsky lineage. You did not consider them worthy to meet your wife or fiancée. And if you think that no one will find out... How many invisible people were there in this room? How many are there now? I think that tomorrow the entire Zarak Empire will know that Archduke Valevsky has become engaged to a dark one. Even if she is gray."

I pursed my lips in displeasure — I had never thought of such a thing. Naira and I really would have to travel to Turb. Wasn't that why the paper had appeared on my desk? So that Kimal Sarento had the opportunity to prepare some nasty surprise, only on his own territory? That sounded like something he'd do. What a vengeful bastard he was!

"You wanted to see me?" a melodious voice rang out, and my chest sank. For some reason, in Naira's company, I became a different person.

"Alia, put up a canopy, please," I said. "Naira, please, take a seat. We have to decide how we're going to proceed."

"I recognize your right..." Naira began reflexively, but I interrupted her:

"Let's not start with that, alright?" I decided to drop any pretense of formality. "Everything with your clan has been decided. You don't owe me anything, and if in a year you decide to return home, no one will force you to stay. Now the situation is as follows: a member of the dark inquisition is coming here. If he decides that you belong to Skron, you will have to stay in Hearth all year, without leaving its borders. If he doesn't find darkness in you, you, as my fiancée, will have to accompany me to all sorts of events. So let's get straight to the point. This is Alia, my personal attendant. I don't even know how to describe her function so that you can understand it. She is my most trusted confidant. Everything that I know, she knows. And vice versa. According to the laws of the Zarak Empire, I am dark. Through Alia I communicate with the church."

"You...you're dark?" Naira asked, astonished. "Not gray?"

"Yes, I'm dark. Let's not go into detail, just accept this as a fact. It is true. Naira, I need your help. I have problems with the dark language, and your cousin, who taught me, escaped safely. Not only from your clan, but also from my city."

"Okay," the girl agreed easily. "I'll only speak to you in the dark tongue. This will be good practice. If you say something completely unintelligible, I'll make a suggestion or correct it."

"I need more than just speech practice. I have three textbooks from the Kerux Magic Academy. The goal of learning is to be able to read them yourself. The textbooks were provided to me by Adeline."

I had to clarify, since Naira's yellow eyes narrowed, as if I was leading her towards treason.

"Further. In addition to learning the language of the dark ones, you and I will have to undergo a somewhat unpleasant procedure to adapt to the influence of darkness. You will have to spend at least two to three hours a day on this, no matter how bad it is. It is important. And lastly, the exchange of knowledge will be mutual. I will teach you how to adapt, and you will teach me how to work with the status bar and the magic field. There are no light teachers who can discuss these topics calmly with me. Usually any conversation ends with appeals to send me to the stake."

"I agree," the girl answered in the dark tongue after thinking a moment. "I also have a question. According to our laws, the groom cannot compel the bride to share a bed with him. You refused to have me as your legal wife, ready to fulfill my obligations, now I want to know the boundaries of our relationship. What are you planning to spend this year doing?"

Naira had to repeat this phrase twice. Once in Dark and once in Light, because the first time I didn't understand anything.

"I don't want to see you in my bed by force or against your will," I answered. "For now, our relationship is purely business. I need to prepare you for going to the rift so that you don't die on the first level, you need to teach me the basic principles of working with the status bar and the magic field. Everything else depends on the circumstances."

"I'm more than happy with that," the girl smiled, and her shoulders sagged, as if a huge burden had been lifted. Apparently, this topic had been troubling the girl. Sleeping with someone you've just met, and from the opposing faction, was a dilemma. Although this did not stop Adeline.

"In that case, welcome to Hearth, Naira Jode. I hope you enjoy it here."

It was only by miracle that I managed to resist the phrase "and stay here forever and ever." No, I was glad that she was here. I need to learn to behave as calmly as possible in the company of such beauties. I was sure there would be many more Nairas in my life.

* * *

The road between the autonomous city of Hearth and Turb, the capital of the Zarak Empire

Kimal Sarento sat in a carriage rushing to Turb, staring at a single point. Just five months ago, the throne of the Zarak Empire was his grandest dream, the highest goal of his existence. Everything else was considered 'impossible' for him. The man strode slowly towards his goal, pushing Zurgan Shor to seize power and take the first blow. Everything was going so smoothly that it was time to start dreaming about a brighter future. But Kimal was wrong. For almost the first time in twenty years, he was wrong, but now, as he sat in the carriage, he was incredibly happy about it. The throne was not his goal. His sights were on more than just the Zarak Empire. And now, when Maximilian Valevsky appeared in this world, driven by the will of the Light, this something more became closer. This awkward young man was at the beginning of his journey and hadn't yet encountered any truly strong individuals. Those in the Citadel and the Temple of Skron. The real masters of this life. He needed support. And this was Kimal's task for the near future.

A satisfied smile crept across the chancellor's face. Today, the young Archduke had started to snap back. Bare his teeth. This is what Kimal had tried to cultivate in him from the first days of their acquaintance. The fact that the mist men had crawled out of their pyramid spoke of one thing: Valevsky had managed to pique the interest of the dark ones. To say the least. His decision to mention the essences was taken with the utmost caution. Valevsky would feed the Temple one or two stones and remain on the same level as ordinary people. No! He had to stop playing around with trifles — it was time to bring out the big guns. Rouse the Temple from its slumber so that it opens its eyes and pulls its powers out from the depths to examine the fascinating new bug. Kimal knew what this would lead to: Valevsky would either die or rise to such heights that there would be no one equal to him in strength in the Zarak Empire.

There would only be the Citadel, but Karina Fardi would take care of this. Magister Elor was too angry with the church, so he would do everything to cause it harm. No need to disturb him, but he certainly needed to be observed. If Magister Elor forgot his goals and suddenly became ensconced in something else, he'd have to be given to Valevsky. The new and improved Valevsky. The one who survived communication with the Temple of Skron.

Now Maximilian's task was simple. He needed to get rid of the prejudice that he owed something to someone. The young man would have to realize the fact that the whole world would be his. No matter how simple it may sound, Valevsky needed to come around to this point. And he, Kimal Sarento, would definitely guide the young Archduke in the right direction and place a mountain of obstacles on this path. So that what arrived at the finish line was a seasoned wolf, capable of overturning this whole, rotten world.

Why go through all the trouble?

Kimal Sarento felt a warmth in his chest as he thought about his goal. He knew it would all be worth it in the end!

Chapter 8

"READY?"

"Yes!" Naira replied a little too enthusiastically.

"Then let's go."

I moved the latch for the box with the fifth-level ousel to one side. Naira wheezed and fell to her knees, unable to stay on her feet. I looked calmly on at her suffering, in no hurry to remove the aura. The first experience with the darkness generated by the rifts was always very revealing. I didn't have a training ground or steel cages, so I had to use what was at hand. I gave Naira two rings that almost completely eliminated the ousel's influence. But, judging by the way the girl writhed and wheezed, they didn't help much. When the breakfast she'd eaten many hours ago came back up again, I finally came to her aid.

"Listen to my voice. Concentrate on it. Forget

the pain. Forget the fear. There is only my voice and you. Nothing else. You are from the Bartolomeo Clan. You are not some pitiful peasant who falls on her knees in front of an ordinary rift beast. You are above that. There is nothing that can break a member of the Bartolomeo Clan. You will not disgrace your clan. Listen to my voice. Concentrate on it. Remember who you are. You are Bartolomeo!"

Of course, this wasn't the right way to go about it. Father Nor had warned me of this, and I'd found out the hard way. It wasn't good to adapt to darkness by harnessing your anger. It worked well enough in the early stages, but then this coping mechanism began to work against you. But we didn't have a training ground here, Naira didn't belong to the Light, and she wouldn't be able to go into the depths of the rifts alone. This meant that I needed to set her down the same path I had taken, even if it wouldn't work for anyone but me.

My words seemed to help — her wheezing subsided. I continued my train of complete nonsense without removing the aura, and soon my efforts were rewarded. The girl growled and even tried to get up. She only had the strength to get on all fours, but even that was an excellent result. Naira had begun to resist the aura. She'd started to fight.

"Stand up!" I commanded. "You're stronger than this! You are Bartolomeo! If some light one can do it, why can't you, daughter of the clan's head scholar? You can do this!"

It seemed I'd overestimated Naira's capabilities. She growled once again, even assumed a vertical position, but then her eyes rolled back and she fell flat on the floor, unconscious. Did that stop me? Not at all! I didn't even use any healing magic, not wanting to interfere with the adaptation process. When a person was unconscious, the influence of the aura stopped causing them pain. I knew this from practice. Meanwhile, the aura continues to act on the body, forcing it to adapt. Like a sun tan. The main thing was not getting burned.

For the first time I decided to limit myself to thirty minutes. Closing the lid, I used *Heal*, stopping her muscles from eating themselves, removed the rings, after which I carried the girl from the training ground to the house and handed her over to the care of the maids. Naira had to be washed, changed and fed to bursting. True, she had to be brought to her senses first, but that was a minor detail. As long as she was fed. Otherwise, it may negatively affect her figure.

Returning to the office, I once again opened the page with artifacts. The first adaptation procedure, which may have seemed so simple and easy, actually took quite a lot of time. The preparation alone took more than an hour. My muscles ached pleasantly after the morning workout with Gustav, which Naira was also present at, so I decided to spend a couple of hours on myself.

Four days had passed since my last meeting

with the Temple of Skron. Two of them had been spent in Hearth as I awaited a reply, but there was none. Apparently, the mist servants were thinking hard, deciding what could be offered for two hundred essences. Or they were looking for a way to get their hands on them without having to pay. In any case, they were playing for time, and this fact personally made me incredibly happy. Because what was revealed to me once again radically turned my world upside down, and I seriously began to think that giving away the essences was not such a bright idea.

I learned the other use for essences.

I could be considered lucky. When Father Nor declared that there was no darkness in Naira and she could travel freely as my companion throughout the Zarak Empire, the girl went home. Since she had to appear before the highest society of our empire, she wanted to look appropriate. This required her formal attire, which she left at home. I did not object, asking only one thing — that on the way back, Naira would capture all the artifacts that I managed to get from the ruins. And it made no difference whether they had been identified or not yet. Two days later, the girl returned, and the minotaurs dumped a huge pile of objects shining with a blue and yellow aura near the portal. Fifty-three items, of which the Bartolomeo Clan was only able to identify three. One per day. I had exactly the same restriction for learning new artifacts, but at the same time I had an indelible advantage over the dark ones. I had the ability to hide even unidentified artifacts in the intangible world. Naira's relatives were able to identify a small figurine and two identical golden plates. It somehow made the air around it more breathable. Cleansed, cooled, moisturized and ionized, whatever that meant. Setting up the figurine in my office, I realized that it would be a great pity to part with such an item. It really did make the air feel fresher! It was as if I had been transported from the noisy, dusty, filthy city to a high mountain forest. The plates proved to be great resources, and they ended up in both the "artifacts" and "inventory" sections. In fact, the fresh air gave me the idea to identify the golden recipe first. If the dark ones were to be believed, some rare and unique artifacts, including recipes, could appear in the two-hundred-year-old ruins. So I identified the golden leaf, threw it into my inventory, opened it and froze, realizing what I had just read.

Gloves from the Thunderer set. *10 out of 10 available. Ingredients for preparing gloves: 2 golden plates, 2 dorim crystals, 2 kilograms of vyrma, 2 yem, monster essence (the amount varies depending on the rarity of the essence). The number of parameters of the created item depends on the rarity of the essence used. Preparation method: place the ingredients on the work surface and click the "Create" button.*

No blacksmiths, forges or other devices

required for the manufacture of metal armor were required. Artifacts were created in a different way, incompatible with common sense. I placed all the necessary materials in the appropriate field and, after thinking a little, decided to limit myself to the krona essence. More precisely, fifteen krona essences, which were the simplest and most widespread. Before spending rare essences, I needed to understand what the result would be. What if it turned out to be a mere trifle? A couple of moments later, golden gloves shone green in my hands. It was hard to describe how the gold shone with green light, but that was the only way to describe it.

Considering the fact that the recipe for this armor befitting an emperor included vyrma, breaking through it to damage the hands of the wielder would be exceedingly difficult. Taking into account the materials costs, producing these artifacts on an industrial scale wouldn't be feasible, especially since the number of copies available using my ingredients had decreased to nine. My first desire was to make one for myself, but I suppressed my greed. These gloves would be useless to me. Whatever their stats were, they wouldn't hold a flame to my mithril ones. And with krona essences..if I were to make them for myself, I'd need to use the Riftmaster essence, nothing less. I moved the gloves to the "artifacts" section, knowing exactly where to put them to use. I'd give them to George Vyazemsky on his wedding day. Vyazemsky Sr. would have to get the air purifier, unless I found something more interesting among the various artifacts that had not yet been identified. I didn't know what to give Serlena yet. I'd figure it out as I went.

Two days later, without waiting for the servants of the Temple of Skron, we went to Turb. The two days of travel gave Naira mixed feelings. The girl did not understand why the light ones spent so much time moving between two large cities if it was possible to use portals. The answer that the transport network was controlled by the Temple of Skron was not accepted. What difference did it make who controlled what, if it was so much more convenient? Alia remained in Hearth, so no one was there to lecture the dark one on the difference between darkness and light. I was too lazy...

And finally, once we reached the estate, we began training. In the morning, Gustav drove me and Naira into the ground. The girl really held up well, all things considered. And her spear work was pretty decent — I actually had to exert a lot of effort to win. The dark ones taught their people well. But not well enough. In every exercise we performed, I was at least a little better. Naira's tension showed that she was not giving up — her clan pride did not allow her to come to terms with the fact that she was losing to some light one. However, no matter how hard the girl tried, she couldn't do it, and three hours simply flew by. In the end, I had to use *Heal* to transform her from a statue back into a human. She had given it her all.

Then came the first training session with the dark aura, which turned my bride into a wheezing pool of jelly, unable to even rise to her feet. Should I show her pity? They had thrown me into the second level of the rift and let me find my own way out. No one had cared that I hadn't yet adapted to the influence. But then take the Temple of Skron, whose rift conquerors lay on the ground unconscious, and no one bothered to clean them up. Training should continue until the teacher says "enough," not for as long as the student can stand it. Maybe I became a mirror precisely because I had learned to acclimatize to the dark without any help from the academy. Who knows?

Naira regained consciousness relatively quickly. My healing magic had done its job. The maids helped her get ready, and soon she joined me for dinner.

"I don't even know who you'd have to be to volunteer for this kind of work," Naira said and shuddered at the memory of the day's experiences. "Torture yourself to the point of unconsciousness just to descend one more level...I don't know. It's some kind of perverted sadomasochism."

"First of all, it's honorable work. Secondly, it pays well, and thirdly, it's no worse than any other job. Usually the training is a little more gradual, but I don't have a beast from the first or second level. Only the fifth."

"But you have all those lovely little rings, which for some reason you refuse to wear," she said. "Why?"

"Maybe because I don't need them to travel in the rift now?" I responded. I didn't tell her that I was already wearing them.

"The rings help protect against mental attacks and several other unpleasant auras," Naira said, demonstrating that she had carefully studied my temporary gift. "Is that why Adeline calls you Cabbage? Because no one knows what's lurking under your next leaf? Because you're always ready to reveal another surprise?"

"Please try to refrain from using that word, if possible," I said grumpily. "I don't like it, so Adeline tries to shove it in my face whenever she can. For some reason, she finds this amusing, but never bothered to ask the other parties involved how they felt."

"That doesn't sound like my cousin at all," said Naira. "Adeline was always quite clever and sharp, but lately it's as if she's been replaced. And the hysterics she put on when they offered you a spot in the clan were disturbing even to me. This behavior is not befitting of the highest hierarchs."

"Adeline is among the highest hierarchs?" This was news to me.

"Naturally. She was the daughter of the clan head, and now she's the sister. Consider her the second in charge. I am also a highest hierarch, by the way."

I thought about it. If Adeline's behavior even seemed strange to Naira, then that meant that something was fishy here. So fishy that I felt her husband Kimal's hand in it. And the blank form granting Naira the right to appear in the lands of Light had appeared just in time. What if this was all going according to his plans and scenario? No, Adeline didn't say anything that would encourage Naira to offer herself as payment for her father's life. It was more likely that Theodore himself was meddling. Adeline and Theodore? The way she threw her arms around his neck as if they were close, and then suddenly became cold? I was getting a headache from all the stupid scenarios blooming in my mind. I decided to clarify:

"Naira, do you have any guesses as to what threats I might face from the darkness if you become my bride?"

"Several clans may be offended," the girl answered and blushed. Apparently, she found the topic uncomfortable. "I also know that there were some agreements between my clan and the Gourfans that I would be in the company of Xander Moises for some time. We were supposed to study together in the same course at the magic academy. Gourfans never forget insults. It's a matter of principle for them."

"I know that already. I've had several less than pleasant interactions with Naina already. So, the Gourfans. Will they harass your clan or try to get to me? And you don't need to look at me like that — I'm asking you to guess, not say for certain. I need to understand where to expect trouble. So that I can react in time."

"They'll most likely try to get to you directly. There's no point in touching my clan." Naira looked me straight in the eyes. "Is this a problem?"

"Why would it be? This is information that I need to protect my loved ones. And any innocent bystanders. Tomorrow, they will be expecting us at one o'clock in the afternoon. We must leave here at twelve. How much time do you need to prepare?"

"Considering that I don't have my assistants, and your maids have no idea what to do, if I start right now, I should be able to get everything ready by twelve noon tomorrow. But that's not a guarantee. You don't have your own hairdresser or manicurist, from what I gather?"

"I don't have many people. If you make a list and requirements for each position, I'll find a suitable candidate. Not here — in Hearth. We'll only be in the capital for short visits."

"And spend four days on the road each time," Naira sighed sadly.

"Most likely. Another question. Do you need a remote connection with me? We may find ourselves in a variety of different situations where I won't always be there. And you're still dark — in the Zarak Empire, people like us are treated with open malice."

"Remote communication?" Naira asked, surprised. "Actually, that might be nice, but I don't know where you expect to find Magister Meram now and how you'll persuade him to do this. As far as I remember, the previous head of my clan did not have such a connection with anyone."

"Where do you want the sigil, on the left or

right shoulder?"

"Left," Naira replied, dumbfounded and let out a muffled scream when the golden symbol flashed in front of her.

"To use it, all you need to do is place your hand over the symbol, and you can do it through your clothes. Then start talking and I'll hear you."

I had to place my own symbol on my right shoulder, as the left was already occupied. This whole system was really inconvenient. I wanted to communicate like the Temple servants! The magic in our world proved much too cumbersome. There was too much of it, and too many different types.

First of all, there were the magic stones of all different stripes, including amulets. This is the most widespread and familiar system of magic to the common folk. Stones granted certain abilities and allowed them to be modified and enhanced. This magic had been around for as long as Skron had been in our world. That is, a thousand years. And during this time, it seemed to me, the mages had to create some kind of universal and ideal set of stones. Surely somewhere in the secret archives of the Citadel or Temple there were enough magic fields, stones and amplifiers to easily cope with anything life could throw at you. But, of course, no one allowed ordinary archdukes to have access to such information. I'd need to ask the Temple. Communicating with them proved much easier than negotiating with members of the Citadel. All they did was make threats.

The next kind of magic that I had encountered was the magical seals. Symbols, pictograms, runes. Anything not related to magic stones, but which still had the ability to summon magic. Moreover, it often turned out that runic magic was much stronger than the magic conducted through stones, but slower. By the time it takes to draw one rune and bring it to life, you could be killed many times over. I had three books on this type of magic, but my knowledge of the dark tongue was not yet sufficient for me to understand the text. Nevertheless, working with Naira was much more effective than with Adeline. This was due to the fact that I didn't want to lose face in front of the bride. I had to do a crash course.

Next came the artifacts, in their sundry forms. During the time we were moving to Turb, I managed to identify three more objects and now I knew what I would give to Serlena. The fresh air figurine would go to her. Because I'd found another gift for Count Vyazemsky Sr.

Moving on to the magic of the beastmen. This included the minotaur portals, as well as all the abilities possessed by the Temple of Skron. This kind of magic seemed completely unlike any of the other types.

I didn't fully understand whether Light magic could be placed in a separate category, but Pharapho magic was definitely a separate type. The fog spawn existed at the strange will of their master, who had settled in Black Mountain, and had their own unique system of magic. Mithril, with its fantastical properties, belonged in this category as well.

The last type, I only knew from stories — I had never encountered offworlders. But, according to the Temple of Skron, standard magic did not work in their lands, which indicated the uniqueness of these mysterious beings.

What did that give us? Six different types of magic in one world? Wasn't that too much? And I wasn't even sure I had listed them all. Surely there were other types I hadn't yet encountered. So why were there so many different magic systems in our world? Or was this normal, and I, lacking a proper education, was simply staring at a flock of sheep behind the gate and wondering why they were all different colors? I hated uncertainty.

I decided to skip the morning training session with Gustav. Like it or not, I also had to go through the arduous process of preparing for a formal event. Alia, smart girl that she was, had ordered a suit for me back in Hearth, so I didn't have to run around the city looking for tailors. The giggling maids, half-heartedly trying to dodge my light pinches, helped me dress up, and at five minutes to twelve I stood in the hall and waited for Naira. The carriage was cleaned, gifts were selected, flowers were bought. My hands were shaking a little. This was the first event I would attend with my fiancée. Even if our relationship was only temporary.

"Madam Naira," one of the maids announced, and my companion appeared at the top of the staircase. She began to descend, keeping her eyes on mine, and the same thing happened as on the day we met: the world around me faded, losing all color and volume. There was nothing and no one except the goddess descending from heaven to her faithful servants. The dark blue, off-the-shoulder dress seemed incredibly provocative compared to what girls wore in the Zarak Empire. The tight-fitting style emphasized the girl's ideal figure, and the long slit, from which her bare thigh peeked out with every step, caused a storm of emotions in a rush of blood in my chest. Her hair, gathered into a beautiful messy bun, exposed not only her shoulders, but also her long neck, on which hung a dazzling necklace. All this charm was accompanied by a stunning aroma and long gloves that stretched to her elbows. Naira was spectacular!

"You look nice. It's nice to see a man dressed up in something other than the default formal suit," the goddess said, bringing me back to reality. Gulping, as my throat had suddenly gone dry, I smiled:

"We're going to be in trouble tonight. Serlena Przhedetskaya is considered one of the most beautiful girls of the Zarak Empire, but her beauty will look dull in comparison to yours."

"Oh, do you really think so?" Naira blushed. "Do you think I should choose a more casual look?"

"It's too late to pick anything up. Besides, I'd be completely opposed to the idea. Anyone who sees such beauty at least once will not waste their time on any alternative."

"Alia is also beautiful," the color on her cheeks suited Naira very much, making her look even more lively and sweet. "And your manager, Eleanore, in my opinion, is the most beautiful woman I've ever met in my life."

"And yet you stand out, even next to them. Trust me as a connoisseur of beauty. Shall we go?"

"Let's go," Naira sighed picturesquely. She was not at all saddened by the fact that the attention of others would be focused not on the bride, but on her. She was used to basking in everyone's attention and now she consciously chose the most charming and aggressive dress. These narrow-minded light ones, who don't even know how to use portals, must realize that the dark ones can and know how to be beautiful. Naira was well aware of the impact she had on those around her. Both dark and light. My reaction had spoken volumes.

The journey didn't take long. We spent most of the time waiting in the line that stretched from the front of the Vyazemsky Palace. We had to wait for almost half an hour before the carriage drove up to the main entrance. The herald's assistant clarified who we were and rushed to announce us. A few moments later, a loud voice rang out:

"Archduke Maximilian Valevsky and his bride, Naira Jode!"

A stunned gasp passed through the crowd as we entered the main hall. I heard a man not far from us gulp noisily and reach for his neck to loosen his tie. The first reaction to my bride was exactly as I had imagined — Naira had attracted the gaze of everyone present.

"Come on, I'll introduce you to the guests of honor at today's ceremony," I said, catching sight of George Vyazemsky and Serlena Przhedetskaya. The young man did not take his eyes off my bride, while Serlena looked from Naira to her future husband and back. Serlena frowned. She didn't like George's reaction, but she couldn't be openly indignant. The law had not yet granted her such a right. However, there was clearly trouble brewing. George's pupils were far too wide, and Serlena's too narrow as they approached.

But no matter! They still hadn't seen my gifts!

Chapter 9

I HAD TO GIVE IT TO GEORGE — unlike me, who had frozen, mouth agape, during my first meeting with Naira, young Vyazemsky quickly pulled himself together. It only took a few moments before his pupils returned to normal and a smile appeared on his face.

"Archduke Valevsky, I see you've managed to escape the construction site."

Apparently, the entire empire already knew what was happening in Hearth. The renovations were truly all-encompassing: they'd had to demolish the entire city and build a new one in its place, with all the necessary accommodations, which, for some reason, hadn't been there before. Constant noise, the cracking of boards and billowing clouds of dust were daily occurrences for anyone who dared visit Hearth now, of which, I was happy to say, there were still many. Thanks to Count Shub, my city had become a distribution point for goods from the Shurgan Empire, so receiving five or six caravans a day was considered the norm. The fact that George began the conversation with a sarcastic remark set the tone for our discussion. No high-born niceties or flowery words. They had invited me, if not as a friend, then as a good acquaintance. It was a little strange, as young Vyazemsky and I had only crossed paths a couple of times in our lives, but I did not want to refuse such a gift of fate. I hated all the polite exchanges. For me, the simpler the better. Apparently, despite all the efforts of Magister Tarra, my upbringing as a lowly baron still shone through.

"Count Vyazemsky, how could I miss it, when your invitations were so persistent?" I turned to Serlena. In the time since I'd last seen her, the girl had become even more beautiful. Her childish angularity is gone, replaced by a feminine smoothness. Her thick, dark hair fell freely across her shoulders, sky-blue eyes sparkled like stars in the sky, but held a note of contempt. A year and a half ago, I would have given everything I had and much that I didn't just to take George's place, but now, with Naira next to me, the thought didn't even occur. Serlena was wonderful. Dazzlingly beautiful. But Naira was better. And this was a fact that I did not want to argue.

"I am grateful, Countess Przhedetskaya, for the invitation," I said to Serlena, making her blush.

"Where do you know him from?" George looked at his future wife in surprise. The legal wedding ceremony would take place behind closed doors. There would be no guests allowed. In fact, the closing of the ceremonial door was considered the end of the event.

"We were introduced at an event in the southeastern region," Serlena explained. Her voice was still as melodic as before.

"So, you received two invitations at once?" For some reason this news seemed to amuse George.

"Three," I replied, noticing the elder Vyazemsky. He and his wife were nearby, talking to Serlena's parents. "I received invitations from both Counts Vyazemsky at once."

"But you still came?" George frowned. Now I know that he had broken some unspoken rule prohibiting people from sending more than one invitation per guest. If you received three or more, you had the right to refuse with no blow to your reputation or loss of honor. No one was obligated to spend their fortune on gifts for just anyone with a blank piece of paper and an envelope.

"I am an archduke, I have no right to refuse," I said with a smile. "What's your custom here? Are gifts given immediately, or do you have to wait for the official gift-giving ceremony?"

"Either or. You can give it right now, or after the third dance. Up to your discretion."

I looked over to Naira and realized that I had no desire to stand in line with the other gift givers. I'd rather spend the time talking to my new bride.

"I suggest we get the formalities out of the way now, so that we can spend the remaining time celebrating."

"I also see no use in waiting," the elder Vyazemsky called over. My business partner broke away from the guests and came over to us. "Archduke Valevsky, I'm glad you accepted my invitation. We're always happy to welcome you into our home. I cannot say the same for you, Naira Jode of the Bartolomeo Clan."

The hairs on the back of my neck prickled as I felt the attention of all the guests in the room turn toward us. Few in attendance knew that I had a wife, but certainly no one had known that she was dark. And a real dark human, not some kind of marionette.

"She has been verified." I felt the undisguised hatred that Count Vyazemsky had towards my companion. Moreover, this could not be considered an insult — the count's attitude towards the dark ones was known throughout the empire. The fact that two dark humans showed up at the event at once, especially as official companions, did not bring him joy. Which he openly stated. Unlike his son, Naira's appearance did not improve the elder Vyazemsky's mood. He saw into her essence, without confining himself to her superficial shell.

"I know that. Otherwise, the dark one would not have been allowed across the threshold of my house. People from the Neutral Lands are welcome in only one place: on the church pyre."

Now that was openly hostile. Which was quite strange. During the time we worked together, the elder Vyazemsky always knew how to find compromises and showed flexibility. A buzz of whispers could be heard as those gathered discussed the count's words.

"I've heard your words, Count Vyazemsky," I said, mentally bidding farewell to any projects I had planned with the count. "If my bride isn't welcome in this house, then I'm not welcome either. George, Serlena, I wish you two a happy life together, free from adversity! Before we leave the house in which we are no longer welcome, allow us to present our humble gifts. Serlena, the southeastern region is full of fresh forest air with the scent of salt from the sea. You must miss that here, in the capital. Please accept this figurine. The freshness it inspires will remind you of home.

I pretended to reach into the inner pocket of my jacket, embodying the small figurine in my hand. The fact that it couldn't have physically fit there didn't bother me. As long as no one saw it suddenly appear in my hands. The air around us immediately became cool and pleasant. Serlena's eyes widened, accepting the gift, which was faintly glowing gold. Even though she was a countess, not every high-born house had an artifact, especially one that was so useful. Even if someone did have one, it was hidden away in the treasury, and not for personal use. Let the Vyazemskys get a headache trying to figure out how to protect something so valuable.

"George, at one time I was lucky to fight with you one on one and I can declare with certainty that you are one of the most difficult and powerful opponents that I have encountered. I was lucky to win that battle, but I am sure that over time you will become stronger, and the next time the tournament bracket pits us against each other, victory will be on your side. Please accept these gloves from me. They will make you stronger."

Again I reached into my breast pocket and those gathered, who surrounded us in a dense crowd to see the gifts of the incomprehensible Archduke, gasped in amazement. None of them had seen gold with such a bewitching green glow.

"This is an item from a set," Naira whispered in shock. My gift amazed even the dark one, who had been standing tall and proud beside me.

George took the gloves, shooting a dumbfounded glance toward his father, and pulled them on. The metallic armor adjusted to fit the size of the young count's hands. He made several gestures and movements, getting used to the new armor. From the way his fingers moved and palm turned, one would assume that the gloves were made not of golden plates, but of fabric. George could not resist and took out a steel knife. His grip was firm. Running the blade over his gloves, the young man caused a new wave of surprised exclamations — the blade was ground straight off, leaving not the slightest mark on the gloves. And when George turned his palm up, brought his fingers together and lightning formed between them, the crowd began to buzz with excitement.

"They're..." George gulped and looked up at me.

"I was able to obtain these two gifts thanks to my bride's family. And on that note, gentlemen and women, allow us to take our leave. Two dark humans have no place in a home where others dream of burning them."

I decided not to give the elder Vyazemsky his gift. He didn't deserve it. Our relationship was in the toilet anyway, so such a small detail would go by unnoticed. Taking Naira's hand, I turned around and walked towards the exit. I had no intention of saying anything or making any excuses. Naira was my bride, albeit temporary. Anyone who wished harm upon her wished harm upon me. There was no other option. It was unacceptable to be in a house where they so openly expressed their negative attitude towards my companion. Even if I would live to regret it a hundred times, I still could not act otherwise.

We were still detained at the exit — the road was blocked by Kimal Sarento and Adeline Jode.

"What a familiar aroma," Adeline inhaled, and Naira suddenly clung to me, as if seeking protection. "This is from my collection, right? 'First impression,' if my memory serves me correctly. Cousin, who gave you permission to rifle around my room? Or did you decide that since I allowed you to use my perfume on your eighteenth birthday, it is now yours? Give it here!"

Adeline held out her hand demandingly.

Naira threw me a pleading glance, but I didn't want to interfere in the conversation between two cousins. They were adults and had to figure things out for themselves. Especially when it came to potential theft.

"I'm waiting!" Adeline said.

"You left it at home! You wouldn't have been using it anyway!" Naira flared up. Opening her purse, she took out a small bottle, the liquid in which barely covered the bottom.

"How many spritzes did you use?!" Adeline was wildly indignant. She stared in disbelief at the remnants of the perfume.

"I used as much as I needed to!" Naira said.

"'First impression.' What an interesting name," Kimal interrupted. "Is it associated with anything?"

"Oh, is it," Adeline replied.

"Cousin, don't!" Naira tried in vain to stop her.

"If you do something wrong, be prepared to bear the consequences, little sis. This is not home, your father will not get you off here. My dear, as you know, the first impression a girl makes on young men forever determines whether they will pursue her to the ends of the earth, or whether she will remain one in a line of many pretty faces. I think that alone says it all. When Naira entered a closed room with no normal air circulation, and even taking into account the amount of perfume that she spilled on herself, there was not a single man left who did not look at her with admiration.

Because at that moment, for them, the whole world was pushed aside, leaving only the wearer of this magical aroma. Extremely expensive, extremely rare, this perfume only affects men. Moreover, the older they are, the less influence it has. And this effect lasts about ten seconds, no more. Then all that remains is a pleasant memory and the conviction that the wearer is a spectacular person. With no magic, just a good deal of feminine wiles. Everything that makes us so adored."

"Archduke Valevsky, I consider this behavior on the part of your bride to be inappropriate and I demand satisfaction!" I heard someone exclaim. "I, Count Udaltsov, challenge you to a duel to defend my honor and dignity!"

"I, Count Lusinsky, challenge you, Archduke Valevsky, to a duel!" The second call immediately followed. And then a third. Fourth. Seventh. Tenth. Fifteen people volunteered to demonstrate to me that my fiancée had committed an unforgivable crime. If I were in their place, I would have done exactly the same thing. If Adelina was right, Naira's behavior had been ugly. To put it mildly. After all, I, too, had fallen under the spell of this perfume. Both today, when the girl came down the stairs, and on the day we met, when she entered the common room.

"Gentlemen, I accept your challenge. Tomorrow morning I will be waiting for you at the imperial arena, please be sure to rent it out. We will fight until first blood. We will not spoil the newlyweds' celebration today."

"Archduke Valevsky!" The voice of the elder Vyazemsky rang out, silencing the crowd. The stern head of the family approached us, pretending that Naira did not exist. As well as Adeline.

"Did you know about the effect of your bride's perfume?"

"No." I wasn't going to cover for the dark one. "It was an unpleasant surprise for me as well. You have my word!"

"As the owner of this house, as well as the head of the highest aristocratic society, I cancel all duels that were scheduled for tomorrow. The invitation of Archduke Valevsky to this event was initiated by me, and I am responsible for this. If someone still believes that his honor has been hurt, he has the right to challenge me to a duel. I will accept any challenge. There will be one condition: we fight to the death. This is the only way to restore honor. Archduke, today's incident will not affect our future projects."

"The gloves were that impressive?" Kimal said, unable to refrain. Count Vyazemsky turned a heavy gaze toward the chancellor and, after a long pause, replied:

"Impressive is not the right word. But they did make an impression, not just because of their stats and defensive functions, but also for the name of the creator."

"Is that so?" Kimal looked at me with interest. As did the two dark ones. "The current stats, as I understand it, are a secret of the Vyazemsky family?”

“Absolutely. Archduke, we need the full set.”

“As I said, the source of this object is my bride's clan.” I looked to Naira. “Or the clan of Kimal Sarento's wife, if you'd like. There's nothing like it in our lands. Your words have been noted, Count Vyazemsky. I am glad that the incident will not affect our projects. Thank you again for the invitation, but now it's definitely time for us to go.”

The carriage was already waiting at the entrance. We reached the estate in complete silence. Naira tried to explain herself several times, but every time something stopped her tongue. Gustav was surprised to see us so early, but even more surprised when I said:

“We are leaving for Hearth. Get your things ready. You have three hours. Naira, is this enough time for you to change into your traveling outfit?”

The girl, flushed with color, nodded and, again, without saying a word, ran into the house.

“Where are you going?” Gustav was surprised when I returned to the carriage.

“To the academy. I need to pay off some old debts.”

In a month and a half, the academy had improved significantly. The main building was completely rebuilt, and there were even classes being held there. The only active construction site was the arena, which we passed by. Judging by what I saw, there was at least another six months of work left — the builders had finished erecting the walls and had begun laying pipes. Overall, the magic academy was filled with noise, acrid construction dust and the swearing of foremen telling their workers what they needed to do. Nothing new, I had the exact same thing going on in Hearth, only it was the whole city.

The training grounds were also nearly complete. No work was currently going on, and the crystals from the rift under the main building were being dragged to the spot at night. This was because the sun destroyed them. There were no doors yet, so I went inside without any hindrance. The first three entry level caves had been completed. They even installed steel cages for future kronas. From the fourth to the ninth, crystals were being installed, and in the tenth, I finally found the man I'd come to see. The Evil Engineer was giving instructions to the foremen, and I couldn't help but grin. People who were used to giving commands went pale and broke into a sweat in his presence as the dark mist oozed from his body. They were afraid to breathe too loudly and miss their terrible master's orders.

I did not interfere and calmly waited for their conversation to end. The foremen, wiping large drops of sweat on their foreheads, trudged back, and the Evil Engineer finally deigned to turn his attention to me.

"Interesting amulet. I've never heard of such a thing. Why did you come? I have nothing more to teach you."

I silently extended my open palm. It contained a development crystal and four gallos. The Evil

Engineer's cheek twitched. He clearly hadn't expected this from me.

"These are *Dark Indifference, Adapt, Maximum Limit, Double Strength* and *Melee.* You know what gallos are and what they grant you. Father Nor will provide you with access to the altar of development."

"What's all this for?" The Evil Engineer remained unfazed.

"I just wanted to see the color of your eyes," I grinned. "I actually owe you. You made me into who I am. You taught me to move forward even when I had no more strength. Taught me not to give up. I won't offer anything else, I know you'll refuse. But you can't refuse this gift. Because it comes from the heart. The gift of a student who recognizes the greatness of his mentor. And it doesn't matter what heights the student has reached. What matters is whose close supervision guided them during their very first steps. We have chosen very different paths, Evil Engineer. But I don't want to move on without saying thank you."

The pause dragged on. The Evil Engineer looked into my eyes, without lowering his gaze to my gift. I got the feeling that he was trying to work out the caveat. But I was entirely sincere. This dark one really had done more for me than anyone else alive today. It was thanks to him that I had become the man I was today. If given the chance, I would have taken him to Hearth without a second thought, but I understood that students at the magic academy also need to be trained. And no one would do it better than this dangerous, evil old man.

Finally, the Evil Engineer came up to me and did something that seemed somehow against the laws of this world. Even when he'd repaid me for saving his life, he had shown less emotion. The dark one hugged me and pressed me to him with such force that my bones began to crack! I didn't resist. The opposite, actually. I grabbed my mentor and squeezed him until he crunched back. We stood like that for some time, like two wrestlers unable to overcome each other. The dark one released me first. Taking the crystals, he grinned:

"You're no longer such a wimp as you were four months ago. You were just pitiful to look at, then."

"You're also not as scary as you were four months ago," I said. "I used to be too scared to even breathe with you around. Are you still tormenting students?"

"Why would I? Let someone else deal with these small fry. I'll finish the training grounds and get back to work on the mine. They plan to increase the rift to level six; they need a direct path to the Master. Father Nor told me that..."

"Wait," I interrupted. I assumed rather than saw or felt that there were invisible people around us. The fifth-level ousel had no effect on the Evil Engineer, but all the *Phantoms* around us were another story. Two bodies instantaneously collapsed to the floor, shuddering in horror. I tore off the bandages and grinned — an old friend of mine. The assassin from the night guild who turned out to be hired by Kimal.

Switching off the aura, I pointed to the exit and said:

"You are both free to go. Next time, there will be no concessions. I'll snuff you out. Pass this along to your handlers."

Nobody argued. Collecting their belongings, both the invisible people left our artificial cave. After waiting a little, I turned on the fifth level aura again. Nobody else fell. Either there was no one, or they had already adapted. Fine. I'd use the second ousel next time.

"Both?" the Evil Engineer asked with interest. "You have two forces spying on you at once?"

"These two belong to Kimal Sarento and the Emperor. Two others are missing, from the Fortress and from the dark ones. Apparently, they didn't expect my impromptu trip to the academy."

"I see you lead a fun life. Why didn't you finish them off right away?"

"Why? Like it or not, spies can be very useful. I wouldn't mind having a couple myself, but I don't know where to find the right people. Those who I'm certain won't be working for several parties at once."

"You have the *Phantom* stones?"

"This is the least of my issues. I'll get the stones."

"Do you need them at Hearth?"

"Are you saying you know people?"

"I have a couple of acquaintances," the Evil

Engineer answered vaguely. "Your ousel will not work on them."

"Well, I have another one. Do you want to test it out?"

"Yes, let's!" Despite the fact that they were little more than black holes, the Evil Engineer's eyes sparkled. "What level?"

"Eighteen. Are you sure you can handle it? It would instantly destroy anyone who was completely unprepared."

"Turn it on!" he said decisively. All I could do was nod and push back the latch. Despite my rings, convulsions also shook my body. I'd need a lot more time to acclimatize to this level. The Evil Engineer collapsed to the floor where he stood, but he wasn't the only one. A large piece of stone fell off the wall and transformed into a human body. Another one! Returning to my mentor, I almost screamed in shock. He didn't even twitch. He just lay there motionless. Not even breathing. Returning the latch to its place, I used several healing potions at once, bringing him back to life. The evil heart began to beat again, a convulsive breath and a cough were heard — returning to the world of the living was not the most pleasant feeling.

"Skron take them all!" he swore as soon as he could sit up. Looking around with glazed eyes, as if still not quite sure where he was, the mentor stopped at the body that lay nearby. The black holes flicked in my direction, demanding an explanation.

"I warned you that next time I wouldn't make concessions." This invisible man did not heed the voice of reason and remained, considering himself more literate than the rest. His choice. But the fact that they started sending trained spies to me was a little unnerving. Evidently, I'd have to schedule some time in to root them all out. And next time there wouldn't be five — they'd send ten at a time.

"What an exciting life you live," the Evil Engineer grinned. "If I were thirty years younger, I would come guard you myself. But I'm getting too old for this. Level eighteen...and you dropped that low in just four months?

Instead of answering, I took off my mithril glove, revealing three rings at once. The Evil Engineer just gulped when he saw the katars and crossbow that suddenly appeared on my hand. I no longer worried about safety — besides the two of us, there was not a single living creature left within a radius of thirteen meters.

"I have no further questions," he nodded. "I'll give you two spies. Prepare the stones. These guys are coming to you as completely blank slates. They had to give up everything in order to escape the attack of the Fortress and the night guild. If you supply them with everything, you won't find better or more loyal people. You have my word!"

Chapter 10

"MAX, YOU HAVE SOME misty guests."

"Warn them that I won't be there for another ten hours. We're on our way back."

"Why so early?"

"The circumstances have changed."

"Got it, I won't pry. We're waiting for you."

That's why I loved Eleanore — for everything she was. A smart, understanding, wise woman. Just like a good estate manager should be. I looked at Naira, who was gloomily taking in her surroundings. All the charm of this dark one had disappeared into oblivion. When you knew that your feelings were not the result of a fateful coincidence, but the effect of an enchanting perfume, you began to look at things differently. We didn't even really talk. The girl nevertheless mustered up her resolve and even tried to justify something, but I had lost all interest. What difference does it make what motivated her? It was done. I once again replayed the conversation with the elder Vyazemsky in my head and felt a niggling itch deep in my soul. I'd had to bend over backwards, put my pride in a distant box and confirm that our projects still remained intact. Now I had neither the strength nor the resources to resist the count. Yesterday, I got a clear demonstration that, despite any show of acceptance, I was still perceived as a small and inferior boy who had not matured to the level of adults. And the only reason I hadn't been killed yet was the general interest in what I could do. Rifts, resources, and now also armor from the set. For the sake of all this, you coulc tolerate a cocky young upstart, as long as they were constantly put in their place. It was a useful trip. Informative. If I want to be anything more than a source of rare items, I needed to get stronger. Much stronger. And not just me — this also applied to my loved ones.

The carriage moved smoothly, as the road between Turb and Hearth had been repaired first. All holes and ruts were removed and the road was widened in some places. It had been transformed into a real travel artery meant to connect the two iconic cities. To put it nicely, if we were planning for the long term, we'd still need to make some renovations. Raise it a little so that the rain didn't flood it, cover it in a special substance to make it an even smoother ride for the carts, and lay a trail for horseback riding nearby. I had a lot of plans overall, but was facing the same limitations as ever — namely, a lack of time. First, I needed to complete the entire reconstruction of Hearth before moving on to other projects.

The pictogram flashed to alert me that it was ready to identify a new artifact. I scrolled through the list, deciding which one was most interesting. Of the fifty-three objects, thirty-two were plates and rods used to craft other things. There was no point in wasting my daily artifact identification on them, as I had no intention of making gloves. Among the remaining artifacts, there were several golden notebooks, but they were so similar to each other that they were most likely also resources. The rest of the items had a blue aura, indicating that they were of little value. But I was getting greedy, deigning to declare artifacts valuable or not, despite the fact that until quite recently, I didn't even know that artifacts existed.

But I didn't even want to bother with the blue artifacts, so I returned to the golden notebooks. Even if they were just resources, I'd still need to work with them eventually. Why not now? The unidentified object assumed its place in the middle of the special field and was momentarily immersed in white fog, which soon cleared to reveal a description.

Scholar's Notebook. *Number of synchronizations: 0. Allows you to save and systematize information about the appearance, behavior and characteristics of people, monsters* *and other creatures, features of various types of locations, events, objects and artifacts. If necessary, it can be synchronized with the notebooks of other scholars to automatically transfer information. After the synchronization process, the two items become one. Can only be removed in the event of the possessor's death.*

Would you like to integrate *Scholar's Notebook*?

Swallowing hard, not expecting such a gift from fate, I agreed to integrate the notebook, and a new pictogram appeared on my status bar. Opening the notebook, I saw empty sheets, but as soon as I looked at Naira, all the data from my previously conducted analysis moved into the notebook. Several images of the girl appeared. Both full-body and head, from several different angles. The information was displayed concisely, but it was clear who it was. Some of the fields were left blank, such as her behavior and characteristics. Apparently, I'd have to fill that out myself. This had to be done with the help of an artifact that appeared on my belt. It looked like a small notepad that, when opened, manifested into a full-sized blank notebook.

"My father has the same one," Naira said when I stopped messing around and returned the book to my belt. Since Theodore used an artifact like this, it meant it must be quite handy. I had three more books, so I'd need to give one to Alia, the second to Father Nor, and I'd save the third for the future. If I understand the meaning of the word "synchronization" correctly, all knowledge would be gathered in one place. I'd send Alia to the Fortress archives and would slowly download their knowledge. A very worthwhile acquisition, in my opinion.

"Maximilian, what do you plan to do next?"

"What are you talking about?"

"With me."

"I don't have any plans for you. After what happened yesterday, we won't be invited anywhere for the next year at least, and Hearth won't accept guests for a long time to come. So you are free to return to your clan, if you so desire. The Temple of Skron won't demand that you become a rift conqueror."

"I do not wish to return," the girl answered after a pause. "I want to somehow find a way to fix what I've done."

"Unless you can turn back time, there's no point. What's done is done. We move on. I actually have no idea what to do with you. Tomorrow or the day after I'll be leaving on my long trip to the Shurgan Empire. I will go to study with Magister Meram, and I'm not sure how long I will stay. What's the point of you hanging around in Hearth?"

"You're going to be Magister Meram's pupil?" Naira's eyes grew wide. "Who exactly are you?"

"By the way, what do you know about sets? How did you know that the gloves that I gave to

George Vyazemsky were part of one?" I ignored her exclamation.

"In the treasury of the Bartolomeo Clan, there is a breastplate from the *Undaunted* set," she replied reluctantly. "It exudes the same green aura as those gloves. Where did you get them from? How is my family involved in this?"

The notebook icon began to blink. Opening it, I noticed new entries. This time, the artifact had collected all the knowledge that I had on sets, starting with recipes and ending with what sets exist, what they consist of and where they were located. Damn it! Why didn't I research this book first? It was so Skron-damned convenient! No hearsay — only information that I had received personally. Moreover, even the source of this information was indicated. For example, next to the records of the Bartolomeo Clan having body armor from the set, there was a note: "Information received from Naira Jode, verification required."

"Maximilian, don't ignore me!" Naira started to get angry.

"Explain why I have to tell you any information? Because you are my bride? It's just temporary. Because you are beautiful? After yesterday, I'm not sure what's you and what's your perfume. You're smart? Useful? Faithful? What is it about you that I should abandon all my principles and tell you without hiding everything that's going on with me? We have only known each other for a week, and during this time you managed to make sure that I won't be invited to any events for a long time. I'm actually amazed at you. Instead of withdrawing and looking at me from under your brows, you deign to get angry. You have no idea who I am or what makes me tick. Where do you get such reckless courage and confidence in your own safety? Do you think that your strength will be enough to protect you if I were to take you out into the woods and ravage you? Then I'd attribute my temporary insanity to the effects of the perfume. You need to get used to the idea that I don't owe you anything, Naira Jode. And you don't owe me anything. We are just two people, temporarily brought together by the will of fate. Moreover, I seriously suggest you return to the clan. You will have to be alone for a long time."

"I can come with you to Al-Khorezm!"

"Sure, you can come. But what for? So you can ensure that I'm not accepted anywhere?"

"Are you ever going to let me live that one incident down? Everyone makes mistakes!"

"True, everyone makes mistakes. But how do I know that mistakes are not your MO? I didn't like it when Adeline said that your father won't be able to shield you now. That means similar things have already happened before. And will likely happen again."

Naira didn't have anything to say to this. She scowled dramatically and remained silent all the way to Hearth, pointedly not looking in my direction. I was more than happy with this — I'd found something else to occupy me. I was cataloging my property. It was one thing when my resources and artifacts were in my inventory, and another when there was a detailed description for each of them, including the location where I found them and their applications. I even entered data on two of my recipes. But I decided to hold off on the rings for now. Even though I could still remove them, it was impossible to put them back on my hand without removing the mithril glove. The only thing I had to tinker with a lot was combining the map and notebook. When this happened, a separate block appeared in the book called "Location Maps," and I grinned with satisfaction. Now let Kimal Sarento try to steal my knowledge. The only way would be to kill me or Alia. I definitely needed to protect my woman. I'd make her…

Wait! Protect who?

I was surprised to find myself thinking about Alia this way. Not as my personal attendant, but as my woman. The person I felt most comfortable with. The one with whom I could share everything, without skirting around any topics. Serlena and Naira were perhaps superficially more beautiful than Alia, but they were strangers. They weren't my person. Now that I'd spent five days next to a girl who was ideal in all external aspects, I was completely convinced of this.

When we arrived in Hearth, I, inspired by the revelation of my personal attendant's importance in my life, rushed to my office. Alia was usually there, fiddling with papers. I wanted to make her feel good, but as soon as I opened the door, the smile instantly disappeared from my face. There were two people in the office. Covered in dense fog, a servant of the Temple of Skron and one of the hierarchs of the Citadel. An extremely unpleasant type with eyes filled with Light, whose gaze penetrated into the most hidden corners of the soul. The dark one and the light one sat opposite each other and did not move, as if they were playing a game of chicken to see who would budge first. If that was the case, then the dark one lost. When I entered, he turned in my direction, while the light one continued to burn a hole with his eyes.

"The Temple of Skron is ready to make you an offer, Hunter of Darkness. We can't talk in the presence of the Citadel. You will have to visit the Temple."

My cheek involuntarily twitched at the proposal.

"That will be impossible. The last time I was sent to the Temple of Skron without my consent, with no guarantee that I would return alive and in one piece. What would you do if I panicked and started destroying your hall and portal passages? Would you give me a pat on the head? Or use some kind of magic against me? This is out of the question. I'm not willing to go to the Temple anymore. Servant of the Light, I ask you to leave us. What will be discussed here is a trade secret between Archduke Valevsky and the Temple of Skron. If necessary, I am ready to undergo any necessary inspections after this meeting."

"The Citadel believes that it should be present

at all meetings in which the Temple of Skron is involved," the cleric said. Once again, I felt like I was being pierced all over with needles by how the voice of the light one resonated through my body.

"You are breaking the agreement," I noted calmly.

"The agreement must be revised," he replied, refusing to back down. "The current iteration does not benefit the Citadel."

"I have a copy of the agreement signed by the pope in my hands. Do you have the authority to refuse his orders? If so, can you show me exactly where? If you want a new agreement, write one. For now, I ask you to leave my office."

"Are you prepared to defy the church?" The Light where his eyes should be flashed in displeasure.

"Do you doubt in the wisdom of the pope?" Two can play that game. "Do you believe that the document he signed goes against the interests of the church? Are you prepared to affirm these words before a conclave?"

How wonderful it was when you had strength behind your words. In this case, a piece of paper signed by the head of the church. The Citadel representative made a dissatisfied face, but had no reply. The agreement did give me the right to communicate with the dark ones in a confidential environment. Even if those dark ones represented the Temple of Skron.

The doors closed, and a familiar figurine appeared, shielding us from the watchful gaze of the *Phantom*s in the room.

"I am Four, and I have the authority to make decisions regarding our future cooperation. The Temple of Skrona has studied your requirements, your capabilities, your aspirations. Before we begin, I have a question: in what quantities can you mine essences?"

"Enough to make items from sets."

The dark one's head twitched. While before he looked at the table, now he was looking directly at me.

"Among the artifacts that I managed to obtain in the ruins of the Bartolomeo Clan was a recipe for creating gloves from the *Thunderer* set. It took fifteen krona essences to create them. It was a tedious task, of course, but quite doable. I was very disappointed that the Temple of Skron hid such information on essences from me. It really did seem to me that we had the opportunity to establish a long-term partnership, but in fact, it turned out that you decided to deceive me. Now I am not even sure that there really are aliens out there somewhere and you create creatures to fight them. My opinion is that you collect essences to start producing armor from the set, which will then take an active part in battles with light empires. Did I get anything wrong, Four?"

The dark one remained silent. Was he negotiating with his superiors? I thought he had just declared that he had the power to make decisions. Another blowhard.

"I asked the Citadel representative to leave so

as to not reprimand the Temple of Skron in his presence. But now I'm having second thoughts about ever working with you, Four. Because partners don't act like this. Con men do. And I don't want to have anything to do with con men. Now that I've voiced my position, I am ready to listen to the Temple of Skron."

"Did you create the *Thunderer* gloves?" asked Four. "We need them."

"I don't have them anymore. They were given as a gift. Does the Temple of Skron have recipes for the *Thunderer* set?"

"Six out of ten," Four answered after a beat. "New information requires new decisions. The Temple of Skron needs time to consider your words, Rift Conqueror."

"Tomorrow I'm leaving for Al-Khorezm and will stay there for who knows how long. Is the Temple of Skron prepared to wait?"

"Out of the question. We cannot wait. New information requires new decisions."

"That is your prerogative. I have stated my own terms and limitations. You can spend as much time making new decisions as you'd like, but now I know one thing — I need your six recipes for the *Thunderer* set. We won't reach an agreement without them. And I still have a restriction from Magister Meram. Has the Temple of Skron once again decided to forget its promises? How can anyone negotiate with you if you're constantly changing the terms? By the way, the question is — if I went with you to the Temple now, would they let me out? Or would they keep me until I agreed to your demands?"

I didn't receive an answer, and I didn't need one. Everything was perfectly clear. Dark, light — the only difference was what god you worshiped. In essence, they were all the same. Ugly people who had seized power. Or beastmen, in this case.

"Come," the dark one demanded. Grabbing me with his hands, the Temple servant pressed his head to my head, as Seven had, and my body began to burn. All the symbols that were on me, including the communication symbols, were destroyed. Burnt out of my skin. He let go of my head, and I immediately cast *Heal* on myself. It didn't help much — the pain didn't go away. I scratched the sore spots, turned away my shirt and stared in surprise at the terrible burns. Very similar to those on Adeline's face.

"Dark fire leaves scars, but completely removes other people's magic. From now on you are free from Magister Meram's influence. But that doesn't mean he won't be able to place a new symbol on you. This amulet disrupts the symbol guidance system. They will not fly after you if you move out of the trajectory, but they will land on your body if you remain in place. It is impossible to completely block symbol magic, but you can escape from it. The Temple of Skron gives you this as a gesture of goodwill and wishes to receive three rapse essences as a reciprocal gesture of goodwill."

"Have only my symbols been wiped clean? I have a few remote communication symbols. What will happen to them?"

"They were burned everywhere. Including on those with whom you were paired. In order to restore your remote communication, you'll have to contact Magister Meram."

"So you didn't think to warn me about that ahead of time?" I could barely contain my anger. Burning me was fine, but why my ladies? And how would I restore contact with the chancellor? True, I now strongly doubted that I needed it, but it still made things a little easier.

"You wanted to get rid of the restriction on visiting rifts. You didn't ask for anything else. The Temple of Skron needs time to formulate a new proposal."

"Okay, you have two days. No more. If you don't make an offer within this period, I'm leaving for Magister Meram."

The dark one took three rapse essences and left my office. Eleanore and Alia immediately flew inside. After casting *Heal* on both of them and realizing it was useless, I just sighed heavily, displaying my attitude to what was happening.

"What was it?" Alia involuntarily touched her shoulder, which was still burning.

"A gift from the Temple of Skron. They removed the rift restriction, but also all the other symbols I had on me at the time."

"Can you restore the connection?" Eleanore cut straight to the point. "It made things a lot more convenient. And proper."

In lieu of a reply, I made a few passes with my

hand in the air, forming the golden sigil. I'd managed to make a lot of ink, so I wouldn't have any problems drawing more. Everything I crafted remained in my inventory, and my runescribe skill could easily draw from it. But the symbols refused to stick to the burn marks. While this wasn't a huge problem for Eleanore or Alia — they could just place the symbol on their other shoulder — for me, it posed quite a dilemma. I had to use my thigh, as my shoulders and chest were now a terrible sight to see. Naira also had the same ugly burn...But it was easier for her, the dark ones knew how to remove the consequences of dark fire. Too bad that the portals were now closed for me, otherwise I'd fly off to Cedric and ask him how to remove these ghastly disfigurements.

"Eleanore, I need your advice. Alia, put up a canopy. To be honest, I'm not sure what to do next. Because I'm really upset by all that has transpired. My mind understands that there was no other choice, but my heart cannot accept it."

I told her everything that had happened at the Vyazemsky's event, including the challenges to duel and the elder count's subsequent decision to cancel them. Eleanore listened to my story all very calmly, as if I was telling her about the weather in another country, while Alia reacted with more emotion. At one point, she even covered her face with her hands and laughed. But not from glee, but from the realization that I had once again managed to get into such a convoluted mess.

"In an amicable way, we need to close all

projects with the Vyazemskys," Eleanore replied. The count was in the wrong. The fact that he openly threatened your fiancée, no matter what god she obeys, shows that you are not respected. He is the head of the clan, which means he should behave like a head, and not like a hot-headed young man. Perhaps you have already agreed to continue working with him and confirmed that what happened would not affect your agreements in any way, but my opinion is that you need to react harshly. If we were part of the empire, that would be a different question. But we are an autonomous city and have no right to allow people to talk to us like that."

"Can we go back on our word two days later? Our meeting was just yesterday."

"We can back out six months from now. We'll just pretend that yesterday you didn't want to ruin Count Vyazemsky's business reputation in the eyes of those present, so you answered the way you did. However, now, having returned home and having no restrictions in the form of an outside opinion, you have rendered your verdict. If Count Vyazemsky does not officially apologize to you and your fiancée within a week, you will shut down all ties and joint projects with his family. This will affect the construction time, but not its quality. Unless we can't do anything with the road, since the highways of the empire do not belong to us. In all other respects, the severance of relations with the Vyazemskys will not affect us as much as it will affect him. And yet, you did the right thing in not showing any temper and immediately returning to Hearth. Emotions are good where they are appropriate. The way the elder Vyazemsky acted, especially in front of such high society, is unacceptable. If you agree to continue working with him, you will lose much more. Restoring your reputation is more difficult than finding new partners. This is how I would do it. What we actually do is up to you."

"Thank you, that's exactly what I was asking for. Draft a letter and initiate the procedure for terminating the contracts," I said. "From now on we will do without the Vyazemskys. I don't think the Count will agree to official amendments. We're not such high flyers that others have started to care about our opinion. In two days I am leaving for Al-Khorezm. Is there anything that needs to be done before then?"

"We need to prepare you for your meeting," Eleanore nodded and handed me a piece of paper. "I could be wrong, but the problem with the Vyazemskys will seem like a minor misunderstanding compared to this. Do you still have the plate?"

I wish health and prosperity to Archduke Maximilian Valevsky. Peace onto you and your land. I have heard about your adventures and deeds, which are similar to the songs of my best bards. I know that you are going to Al-Khorezm to study with Magister Meram, so I invite you to visit. While you are studying, you can live in my palace, which is not far from the palace of the great master. I will be happy to listen to the true version of your adventures — one not distorted by storytellers. I won't accept no for an answer, you know that. I'll be offended.

Bayazid the Third, Padishah of the Shurgan Empire

Chapter 11

"ARE YOU SATISFIED, Sir Maximilian?"

"More than satisfied." I placed the large basket, loaded with all the essences I had agreed to transfer to the Temple of Skron, on the table.

"The Temple of Skron is interested in items from sets. We are ready to provide you with additional recipes and all the necessary ingredients."

"Not right now. First, I must undergo training with Magister Meram," I was still lying fully prostrate. The information transfer had been rough this time. Four held my head for about five minutes, no less. I think I even lost consciousness a couple of times.

"The Temple of Skron is willing to wait. Collaboration with us is profitable. And we are ready to prove it."

"Profitable," I agreed, evaluating my updated

status bar. Before, new pictograms would simply appear in the next slot over, but now it had been completely redesigned. Everything was more organic, sleeker and clearer. Everything in its place. There were new icons, a new quick access panel, new abilities and, what interested me most, a function for working with pupils. The beastman had accomplished the main goal — he had turned me into a mentor. Someone who could give others a status bar.

Then the dark beast left, allowing me to once again evaluate the results of our meeting. I didn't even know where to start. The Temple of Skron had approached its second proposal with special care, taking into account almost all of my desires, as well as adding some of its own.

First of all, as already mentioned, I was now a mentor who could bestow a status bar on one person a month. Moreover, if I didn't use the opportunity, it would roll over and accumulate for future use. Anyone I "converted" in this way will be registered with me as a student and will be displayed in a separate panel. Until they gave up their apprenticeship, I would be able to track all their progress.

An updated magic field. Now it looked entirely different, but it came with two incredible perks. First, I was able to adjust my magic stones. The tool that the Fortress was so adamantly against turned out to be a completely accessible tool that did not require any additional mechanisms. One nice element was that in order to get this function, all I had to do was drink three exclusive elixirs. The Temple of Skron stated that they wouldn't reveal the recipe for the elixirs, because it was a trade secret (and I wasn't giving away how I obtained the essences), but the ingredients were exorbitantly expensive and exceedingly rare. Consequently, very few dark ones could afford such a thing. Only the highest hierarchs of the clans of Skron, and even then not all of them. The second perk was that the size of my magic field had increased to six cells in each direction. Elixirs helped with this process as well, but the Temple servant immediately warned me that another increase wouldn't be accessible to me for the next ten years. The elixirs wouldn't work. This wasn't the best news, but it was acceptable. A six-by-six field was nothing to sniff at, especially now that it was possible to adjust my stones. An incredible field of maneuver had opened up to me, which I was going to take advantage of in the very near future. All that remained was to figure out how to correctly arrange all the stones in the field. I urgently needed facet elixirs, but in order to obtain them, I'd have to bow before Kimal Sarento. I needed to think about what we could offer him. Now, after the meeting with the Temple of Skron, such an opportunity existed.

The next gift followed from the previous — I had ten recipes for creating an elixir for increasing the level of a magic stone, twenty charges in each. One elixir gave one level, except that the ingredients for increasing levels varied depending on the strength of the stone. Every five levels an additional ingredient was required, ever rarer than the last. In total, if you believe the recipe, the stones could be leveled up to fifty, but there were names of ingredients listed that I didn't even have in my inventory yet. Checking my reserves, I realized that I wouldn't have any problems until I reached level fifteen, after which there was a huge drop off. I simply didn't have the right resources. I'd have to start closing twenty-level rifts and above, which I had never once done before. However, I believed my ladies and I would all be able to raise all our magic stones to level fifteen. Considering my current level at six, it would be a huge gain. This wouldn't make me equal to Kimal Sarento or Count Vyazemsky — they would still easily destroy me — but now I definitely wouldn't die from any old enemy popping up with level ten stones. It also became clear why all the heads of clans and leading light mages who are able to buy the necessary elixirs for themselves have stones of a maximum of level twenty-five. I have never seen anyone above that. Never! The answer was simple: because pumping to the twenty-sixth level requires resources that mined from the thirtieth level of rifts. While the Gourfans were known to delve below level twenty-five, they certainly didn't crawl all the way down to thirty. Which opened up a lot of possibilities that I was trying not to think about right now. In order to take advantage of these opportunities, I'd need to walk through a portal. Which I was cardinally against. The Temple of Skron might seem harmless now that I was in Hearth, but as soon as I entered the portal, there was one-hundred percent chance that I'd find myself in the dungeons of the dark pyramid. And they'd have me in there, making set after set of armor until I died of old age.

A word about the armor. The six new recipes for the *Thunderer* set pleasantly warmed my soul. With my gloves, this gave me seven out of ten. The only remaining issue was the ingredients, and then the bitterness of the realization came that I would have to make a choice. Either elixirs for powering up my stones, or armor. There was definitely not enough for all my reserves. Moreover, the problem was not that *Devour* was filled. No. The problem was that I'd gone through too few high-level rifts. I needed more. Much more. Preferably a dozen. In order to get ten Riftmaster essences, so that I could start crafting armor for Alia and Eleanore. I had to defend my ladies, even if my estate manager was leading her own life.

When the Temple servant pulled out his last gift, I almost rushed to hug him. It was astoundingly useful — an artifact to identify invisible people. Apparently, the Temple servants had realized that there were many *Phantom*s attending each of our meetings, so they solemnly handed me a thin bracelet that allows you to see all hidden creatures within a given radius. In my case, it was thirteen meters.

This was the full proposal of the Temple of Skron. They gave me exactly what I'd wanted, and also gave me independence from the clan artifacts. If Naira was to be believed, it was possible to adjust the magic field with the help of some kind of stationary piece, which even the highest hierarchs of the clan didn't have access to. This object expanded the magic field, but the girl did not know the details. I learned all this while traveling to Turb and now, after our return, Naira and I weren't talking. She continued to play the role of beauty terribly offended by the world, which, for whatever reason, refused to forgive her for her stupid joke. To Skron with her.

"Eleanore, come here, we have matters to deal with." While she was walking over, I tore the curtain from the window, laid it on the floor and began to embody a sundry array of items that I'd collected during my two campaigns in the fog. All these bones, teeth, crests, skin, scales and other alchemical rubbish. One of the storage facilities had already been rebuilt, so there was a place where all this could be stored. Why carry around resources that were useless to me? Alchemy as a skill set was forever closed to me. So I wasn't interested in wasting time fiddling with it.

It was quite an impressive heap. I couldn't even imagine that I'd picked up so many things out of the rifts. If the hoop-shaped artifact was to be believed, there were no invisibles in the office, so I did not worry that someone would see my process of extracting materials. Eleanore opened the door and froze on the threshold, staring at the huge mountain of materials.

"I'll need to store this somewhere," I said, and then grinned. A shadow entered the room along with Eleanore. The bracelet began to tingle, attracting my attention, but not so much as to cause discomfort. The *Phantom* remained outside my field of vision — I couldn't see the silhouette. But I saw a violet aura as it moved to the far wall and froze there.

"You have one minute to leave my office," I said, turning to the aura. "Then I'll be forced to kill you."

"Who are you talking to?" Eleanore said, looking around.

"The person standing right there." I pointed to the blank seeming space, where I saw the strange aura. "We have a *Phantom* backed into a corner. I wanted to give it the chance to get out of this alive. Open the door, please."

Eleanore complied, and the bracelet vibrated again as another two invisible people slipped into the room. How many could there be?! Alright, my patience for this nonsense was running out.

"My dear spies, I must ask you to leave my office. You have forty seconds, and then I'm going to get aggressive. Anything that happens after that is on your shoulders."

One of the violet auras twitched, hesitating for a moment, while another headed for the door. It didn't go out the door, however, as if not believing that I'd actually act on my threat in the presence of Eleanore, but also didn't occupy a strategically important place near the wall. The other two auras made absolutely no move to leave. They obviously felt safe. I decided to give a chance to the one that was frozen in indecision. Obviously, they had already witnessed my ability to identify strangers. I didn't even point my hand directly at the enemy. All I had to do was focus on the aura and everything else was done by the mithril glove. I didn't even see the flash of silver light — the bolt hit with such force that pierced straight through the *Phantom* and into the wall behind. My gaze immediately shifted to the next aura, and the second bolt broke into a flight. A moment later, two bodies collapsed on the floor. I pulled the masks off — both unfamiliar faces. The bracelet stopped vibrating. The third invisible person had heeded the voice of reason and fled. Now the office was secure.

I put my hand on the chest of the first one I'd killed and imagined his magic stones transferring to my inventory. I really didn't want to get on my hands and knees, tear into his chest and start digging around inside. *Devour* handled this perfectly. A moment later, my hands were full of eight-facet stones, as well as several fascinating little capsules filled with green poison. I did the same to the second body and poured the handful of stones on the table.

"I need more bolts forged," I said to Eleanore, who was hanging on my every movement. "Preferably today, so that I can take them with me. I don't have many left."

"Done," she nodded and looked around. "It it

safe to talk now?"

"As safe as it can be. One of the Temple of Skron's offerings allows me to identify wielders of the *Phantom* stone, but that doesn't mean that no one is standing on the other side of the wall, listening to our conversation. Come in here please, Alia."

I examined the first elite octagonal gem from all sides. The notebook immediately began to blink, and a translucent message appeared next to the stone:

Magic stone *Phantom*. Level 4.

I repeated the process with the rest of the stones, except that I had to cast *Analyze* on two of the ordinary stones. I'd never seen them before. When I opened the notebook, the complete information appeared in it on all the stones I'd just studied. Starting with the descriptions, ending with a complete set of numbers that no one ever paid attention to. The servants came in and dragged the bodies away. Flask appeared, and the wide-eyed stupor of my alchemist told me that the bits and pieces of rift beasts I'd managed to acquire were quite impressive.

"Can any of this stuff be used?"

"None of it," Flask said as he started to pick through the loot, handling things as if he was afraid they would crumble in his hands. These are from the rifts. A Fortress device is required to process them. They can't be used in their current state. Great Light! These are from exclusive beasts! Where did all of this come from?!"

"You won't be able to use them, even if you go through training?"

"What does training have to do with it? These objects have a dark aura. If they are used to produce anything without cleansing them first, they'll be poison. No exceptions. They can only be cleansed in the Fortress. And maybe at the magic academy, though no one's sure. But I know what this can be processed into, and so I hate to see such resources pass me by.

"Flask, write out a list of all the resources that can be made with these parts. Eleanore, negotiate the issue of cleansing the parts with the Fortress. Even if they take half as a payment, we'll still be coming out on top. Something is always more than nothing. In the meantime, hide the resources in the storage. Let's check how reliable it is," I said. If dark beast parts couldn't be used directly, there must be some recipes for them. I'd have to seek them out, but first I needed to understand how to use the resources at all. A whole crowd of people came in and out of the office, but somehow I managed to push them all back for now. Should I have used the curtain to carry all of these things? The fabric was starting to split, but it made the journey from the office to the hallway, and finally, Alia came to me. Seeing all of the resources, the girl closed the door and pointedly looked all around the office.

"There's no one here, but it's best to put a

canopy up anyway. The walls have ears."

The girl sat down opposite us, and a dome formed around us. I'd need to find an artifact that did the same thing. It was always useful to have, as practice had shown.

"Straight to the point. I want to give you a status bar."

"I knew you'd offer sooner or later. Max, I don't want to take a single step toward the darkness. I've had to make peace with the fact that I'm constantly surrounded by it. By people who should be burned at the stake. Yes, we try to bargain with them, and yes, we have permission from the Citadel, but this does not change my attitude to what is happening. I do not want it. Sorry."

"You have nothing to apologize for. You are who you are." I didn't like Alia's decision, but I didn't plan to try to persuade her. She was one of the few people whose opinions I actually respected and heeded. Taking out a notebook, I put it on the table.

"This is for you. It's already integrated with mine."

"What is that?" Alia looked warily at the artifact.

"Take it in your hands and you will understand. Don't you trust me?"

Alia resolutely grabbed the notebook, and the girl's eyes immediately widened in amazement. A few moments later, the artifact dissipated and was embodied in her pocket. It was now bound to her, and I was one hundred percent certain that Kimal Sarento's invisible men would not be able to do anything with this artifact while Alia was still alive. The intel was in good hands. The girl took out the book, opened it and couldn't help but gasp. Flipping through it, she stared, dumbfounded, back at me, demanding clarification. I pulled my notebook from my belt and placed it on the table.

"The two books synchronize their entries somehow. What I write appears in yours and vice versa. With the status bar, which you rejected, the process of entering entries into the book is greatly simplified. It becomes almost automatic. See how this works using *Amplify* as an example. This stone is not yet in the book."

I opened my inventory, where the fragments of various items were stored, and embodied one of the *Amplify*s. The notebook worked perfectly. As soon as the shimmering, red, octagonal stone appeared on the table, all the information I had about it appeared in the book. Including information about how to level up.

"Convenient," Alia said. Attached to the side of the notebook was something that looked like a pencil. The girl took it and jotted down a few sentences. No miracles happened — the book couldn't draw anything from her memory, but the text appeared in the notebook with the note, *Handwritten note by Mother Alia.* Another page appeared as she wrote notes about *Augment.* Another exclusive stone that I hadn't yet managed to create. She jotted down a lot of other information, some of which was already stored in the notebook. Without her automatic synchronization, the artifact refused to update normally.

I laid another notebook on the table.

"This is for Father Nor. I assume he'll also refuse a status bar, but at least he'll be able to see all the information we obtain. I don't see any point in keeping all the records in the form of a real archive that anyone could pocket. Now you and I have access to the artifact. They'll have to kill us to get access to it. There's no other way for anyone to get their hands on it.

Alia sat for a long time and looked at the book in her hands. She leafed through it, but it was clear that the girl's thoughts were far from whatever was written there. When she got to the different character sheets, and to Naira's in particular, a fire lit up in her eyes. After reading the rather dry text, Alia put the book back in her pocket and looked back at me.

"It's just a tool, isn't it? And only we can decide how to direct it? Toward the darkness or toward the Light?"

"Only we can decide. Remember Bishop Zwat? He walked under the Light, but at the same time was an ardent supporter of Skron and became his puppet. By the way, somewhere now in the dark lands there is a creature that was once Bishop Zwat. He opened a portal for Magister Meram without my aura, which means he was sent to the rebirth cycle. I wouldn't be surprised if we see this man again. Hearth was his patrimony. He probably has some hiding places here."

"I agree to the status bar!" Alia practically shouted. It was clear that the decision was not easy for the girl, but she was not going to back down. I understood perfectly well what this step meant for her. For eighteen years, she had been taught by the Fortress that everything dark is evil, and if you muddy your hands with the darkness even once, you'd never be able to wash the dirt off for the rest of your life. Alia adhered strictly to her own principles, but I had put a difficult choice before her. Either faith in the church and its ideals, or faith that we are doing the right thing. We are not the church. And the choice was made.

Instructions on how to initiate someone as your pupil were included with the function tab itself. I activated one katar blade. Taking off my mithril glove, I slashed first myself, then Alia, on the wrist. Uniting the wounds, mixing the blood, I said:

"Henceforth, I, Archduke Maximilian Valevsky, Hunter of Darkness, take you, Mother Alia, as my pupil. Let the Light be my witness!"

"Let the Light be my witness," Alia repeated, and her eyes widened once again, this time from the monstrous pain tearing apart every part of her body. I knew this would happen, so I picked up the unconscious girl and carefully laid her on the floor. Alia moaned, but using *Heal* or a recovery potion was prohibited. If the modification process was interfered with, my new pupil might die. A new entry "Mother Alia" appeared in my mentor field, by clicking on which I could see all the information about the girl. The binding was complete.

The moaning stopped. The adaptation was complete. The girl suddenly opened her eyes and sat up. Her eyes began to dart from side to side, like a madman's, while her face looked incredibly strange. Surprised, scared and bemused at the same time. Alia dealt with all the pop-up messages and pictures that were visible only to her. The girl took out the notebook again, and a moment later, all the information about the High Priest appeared in it. Appearance, description, a couple of pictures, strengths and weaknesses. Everything Alia knew about Father Urg. Opening the notebook, I supplemented it with his main stats obtained with *Analyze*. The result was an almost complete description of the man. Gulping, Alia looked up at me in amazement.

"No one aside from us has access?"

"Only you and I. I have two more books. One has been identified and is ready for installation, the other has not yet been identified. Look in the artifacts section, everything is there."

"Max, I don't think that giving Father Nor the other book is the right idea," she said unexpectedly. "What does the Evil Engineer know that you don't already know?"

"A whole lot. He spent time in the dark lands. And not in the clans, where there is peace and grace, but on the front line. Near the Wall. Among those who send Waves towards us. Among the orthodox and madmen, eager to sweep away even the very mention of Light from the face of the planet. He has seen and fought with various creatures that we don't even know about. He received a *Mentor* stone, which for me was a kind of pipe dream. I hadn't even found a single fragment. If anyone should be given this book, it should be one of these two. In fact, we could use both. Father Nor has a high level of access and will be able to add to the notebook what is stored in the Fortress. Something that even you don't have access to."

"True, but their information is limited. Sooner or later they will stop adding something to the book and will become only consumers. I expressed myself incorrectly — I am not against giving them the notebook, but only after you have at least one more copy."

"Do you have a good suggestion for another candidate?" I asked, surprised.

"Yes," nodded Alia. "I have already looked at the settings of the address book — it could only be synchronized in one direction. Giving information, but not receiving anything in return. Therefore, I suggest giving one book to Naira Jode. Since she is your fiancée, let her work it out. Everything she knows about the dark ones, their customs, abilities, etc., we will put in the book."

"I've been meaning to talk to you about this very topic for a long time. Alia, I could expound for hours about what an important person you are in my life and all that, but I won't. I know it's not necessary. So I'll go without all the unnecessary niceties: Alia, I don't want Naira. I want you. Marry me?"

Her pupils dilated impossibly wide, and the next moment I felt her two beloved hands squeezing me in an embrace. Her tender and sensual lips found mine, and the world stopped existing for a while. There was only me and Alia, and no dark magic perfumes.

Chapter 12

A VERY SATISFIED DARK HUNTER rode in a carriage, detachedly observing his surroundings. Alia agreed to become my wife, and within 24 hours this news spread throughout Hearth. Only the laziest among them didn't congratulate us. There was the feeling that the whole city, including the builders, breathed a sigh of relief when they found out that I wasn't going to marry a dark human, but rather a bishop of the Fortress. Naira handled the news well, without any hand-wringing or moaning. The only thing she clarified was whether our training would continue. Both her training in adapting to darkness, and mine in the dark language. The news that I was leaving Hearth did not affect her mood. I had to agree to the seemingly insane proposal, and now the dark one was sitting opposite me, immersed in the study of my textbooks. The same ones that her cousin brought. This year, Naira would no longer go to the Kerux Magic Academy, but this did not break her determination to become a strong mage. So she pored over textbooks on runes, trying to remember as much as possible. For me, this text still remained inaccessible — my dark tongue, although improved, was still not up to the task.

I decided to celebrate my wedding with Alia according to all the rules for the highest aristocracy of the Zarak Empire. Magnificent and stylish, and with invitations sent to all the prominent people of the empire, among others. Eleanore advised inviting several influential Shurgan merchants, as well as the heads of the dark clans with whom we were trying to establish trade relations. Valdez, Gourfan and Bartolomeo, at the very least. The autonomous city of Hearth must demonstrate to the whole world that it was focused not only on light empires, but also on dark ones. This choice influenced the date of the event. We couldn't, in good conscience, invite guests to the derelict ruins that the city of Hearth currently were. An additional restriction was imposed by Alia's pregnancy. As a result, we made a fateful decision: the wedding would take place exactly one year after I proposed. Eleanore assured me that by this time the city would be completely ready, and I no longer doubted anything she said. If Eleanore said it would be done, it would be done. The Countess didn't mince words.

Thus, I'd have two fiancées for the next year. The laws of the Zarak Empire prohibited having two wives, but you could have as many fiancées as you wanted. Naira did not end the engagement — who knew how the Temple would react to this. Although they promised not to touch the girl, as soon as she left the relationship with me, she would once again fall under the radar of the Temple servants. Neither Alia nor I objected. Let the dark one travel along with us, if she so wished.

"Halt!" a menacing order was heard. The carriage swayed and stopped. "Who are you? State your name!"

"Archduke Valevsky and his bride, on their way to Al-Khorezm!" Gustav replied. We had been on the road for two days already, and the map showed that the carriage had already left the Zarak Empire. There were uncharted lands ahead, and despite the fact that Alia had hand copied a map of the Shurgan Empire into her notebook, the scale was not sufficient to zoom in and see exactly where we had stopped. Somewhere near the border.

"The road is closed, take a detour!" I heard the strange reply, forcing me to get out of the carriage. A detachment of twenty horsemen surrounded us, preventing us from moving any further along the road, and another three dozen foot soldiers with long pikes were nearby. The points were not directed in our direction, but in the direction of the black clouds of smoke visible ahead.

"Who are you and what are you doing here?" I said. "Please give a full report on why we've been stopped!"

"That is out of our jurisdiction..." the commander of this strange little battalion growled, but immediately stopped short when he saw the padishah's plate. I knew why Bayazid the Third had invited me. So that I could personally explain how one of his three plates had come into my possession, when they were only issued to the most trusted persons. So there was no point in hiding it anymore, and I decided to take full advantage of this item as often as possible until we reached the padishah's palace.

"Do I have to repeat myself?"

The commander dismounted his horse and walked over to us. When he removed his helmet, I saw a seasoned warrior in front of me. Half of his face was disfigured by a terrible scar. One eye was missing. By the looks of him, the Shurganite was about forty years old and, if not for the slanted eyes and specific hairstyle, one could easily confuse him with Gustav. Military men were the same in all different countries.

Taking the plate, the commander checked it from both sides, returned it and knelt.

"I beg your pardon, sir, I was given no warning that you would be traveling along this road. But it is currently closed. There's a dev in the village ahead."

"A dev?" Naira poked her head out of the carriage. "Here? Where did it come from?"

"He lived beyond the Wall, my lady. For some reason, the monster escaped from its grounds and went south. The defenders of the Wall were not prepared to face a dev. The monster broke through and tore into the depths of the Shurgan Empire. A messenger has already been sent to the Citadel; soon a group of paladins will appear here and drive the monster away. But for now, it's impossible to pass through."

"What are devs, and why are they dangerous?" I asked.

"Devs are the second caste of Skron beasts. Dangerous, strong, practically invulnerable anthropomorphic monsters," the girl said as if from a textbook. "With an average height of three and a half meters, devs are monstrously fast. Their skin is so thick that even a crossbow bolt fired at point-blank range cannot penetrate it. Magic is a similar story — they simply ignore it. They eat meat, preferably live. They always travel in pairs with a horeb. They do not possess magic, but, thanks to their speed, they manage to grab the victim before it runs away. Even the best armor cannot withstand multiple blows.

"That is correct, my lady," nodded the commander without standing from his kneel. "The dev and horeb destroyed several villages along the way, continuing their march to the south. We are here to detain any of their companions."

"What about the people?" I nodded toward the village.

"They're already dead, sir. They were dead the moment the dev rolled into the village."

"So there could still be survivors?" I began to

take off my traveling robe. Gustav, who was driving the cart, understood me correctly and rushed to the suitcases to bring me a comfortable outfit for fighting evil spirits. Custom tailored from the best fabric this world has, brought from the Valdez Clan. They also sewed my suit. I didn't even want to think how much all this cost me. However, it had been worth it.

"Sir, what are you planning?" The commander became worried when I stripped almost naked and began to pull on a tight-fitting dark uniform.

"I want to go for a little walk. Tell me, if I kill the dev, will there be any negative consequences? Are they considered a rare and protected species that is bred in the Shurgan Empire?"

"Kill the dev?" Even Naira was astonished by my words. "By yourself? That's impossible! Neither steel nor vyrma does any damage. Devs die of natural causes in battles with each other or when an entire army of well-trained fighters goes against them! If it were not for the fact that there are few of them and they reproduce very poorly, they'd pose a real problem. And they each have their own territory, which they usually stick to. Devs are homebodies, so it's surprising that this one started getting antsy. Something must have happened to its habitat. And it must have been quite serious to make it start searching for a new home."

"They're sentient? Can they hold a conversation?"

"Their thinking is different from humans.

They could be called intelligent, they even communicate with each other, but not with people. I don't think this is a good idea, Maximilian."

"Listen, Madam, Sir, you shouldn't lay down your head for a handful of peasants," the detachment commander still refused to stand from his kneel. The hierarchy of subordination was powerful in the Shurgan Empire.

"Even if your son were among those who are now in that village?" I asked.

"Such is the will of the Light, Sir."

"You don't even have a weapon, what do you expect to do?" Naira was amazed when I did a few squats to warm up my muscles after the long journey.

"Weapons are for people who rely on such things. I rely only on myself," I replied. "How far is it to the village?"

"Three kilometers, Sir. The horses won't go any closer. They're scared."

"In that case, I'll go for a run. Gustav, full stop. Boil up some of your signature soup for my return. I'll try not to be too long."

Was I worried? Not at all. Even if the dev really was a strong and dangerous beast that vyrma could not touch, I always had two ultimate weapons. My level eighteen ousel and my mithril glove. With such a set, I could go head-to-head with almost any creature that used normal attacks. I'd felt much more confident since I upgraded all my stones to level fifteen. Even though this improvement cost me almost all my high-level resources and now I could not even think about creating items from the set, my greed never gave me peace. From now on, Alia, Eleanore and I were all protected and charged with magic to the maximum of my current capabilities. It was imperative to get to the twenty-seventh level of the rifts. I want to upgrade all my stones by another ten. What were level fifteen stones against someone like Kimal Sarento? But I even had a response for this: third-level *Amplify*s! I'd finally gotten around to piecing all the fragments of red stones into one whole, and then increasing this gem to the third level. I couldn't make it any higher, as I ran out of stones. I needed nine first-level stones to upgrade to level two, and then nine two-level stones to upgrade to three. So I limited myself to only the two *Amplify*s that were already in my magic field. But it was worth it! From now on, the parameters of all my paired stones had increased threefold! And with help from an exclusive stone, my level fifteen *Golden Dome of Protection* was upgraded to level forty-five! Now it would be impossible to pierce through to me, even if Kimal also had an *Amplify* on his lightning attack. I had no doubt that he did. But what pleased me most was *Praxis.* This stone was connected to two *Amplify*s at once and, as soon as they increased in level, it reduced the mana consumption for *Analyze* to ten percent! A mere trifle compared to the speed of mana recovery. As for other abilities, they became free to me! Even despite the significantly increased mana requirements due to their high levels. Now I could cast *Heal* with complete abandon.

It was a nice run. Sitting for two straight days, even in a comfortable carriage, still had a poor effect on the muscles. I tried to jog lightly, although my legs were eager to get me to the goal as quickly as possible. I was curious — what were these devs and why did they evoke such fear? Running out from behind the trees, I found myself in an open space. There were two hundred meters left of the cleared field before the fence, which looked like reliable protection, when I saw the first enemy in the form of red lightning, which was rapidly approaching me from the direction of the burning village. I always thought that a horeb was only a meter and a half tall wolf-like being with strange spikes and growths. Apparently, I had only encountered runts. The monster that rushed towards me was significantly taller than me. It bared a mouth full of gleaming teeth, prepared to bifurcate me in one massive chomp. Opening the latch on the ousel, I adjusted for the creature's speed and, as soon as the distance between us was just right, I used *Dash*. My new-and-improved stones didn't disappoint. *Insidious Blow* sent it into a nosedive a few meters away from me. Horebs proved extremely fast — in the time it took me to turn around, the creature was already on its feet, showing that no eighteenth level forces had any effect on it, and I could only scare small children with this weapon. Real horebs had no issue facing creatures from these depths. It didn't come in for a second attack right away. A flock of goosebumps ran across my body, but the horeb missed the target. As it jumped toward me to finish me off, I rolled to one side, sending a vyrma bolt into its side. Thanks to the key *Indestructibility* parameter, not a single creature in this world could stun me.

But another issue had arisen — the vyrma bolt that had previously been able to pierce through the hide of any horeb and easily penetrated metal was powerless against the enraged monster. Sparks flew and the bolt flew off somewhere to the side. It growled and again used some unpleasant ability. Its roar became so low that my stomach lurched and I suddenly wanted to go to the toilet. The exclusive monster growled and ducked to make its next leap, signaling my time to attack. The ousel was useless. Vyrma was useless. What was left? That's right — mithril. If it also turns out to be powerless against this bastard, then I'd be out of options. I'd have to turn tail and flee. But let us see who was tougher. Me or some monster.

Dash brought me right under the monster's belly. The difference in height worked in my favor. Thinking that the katars would also be powerless, I formed a blade with my fingers and struck, as I always did with other creatures. It worked perfectly — the mithril glove met no resistance, calmly entering the monster's body. True, my clothing had evaporated to the elbows as if it had never existed — the horeb was surrounded by some unknown field. I clenched and unclenched my fist, letting *Devour* do the work for me. Something hard and round immediately appeared in my hand. Jaws clanged overhead as the horeb tried to fight, even in this state. But by doing this, it only made things worse for itself. The creature twitched, and my fist withdrew from the body, holding a red gem. The essence of an exclusive horeb. Letting out an offended roar, the monster collapsed to the ground and lay there, motionless. Not even death convulsions. I put my hand on the monster, and *Devour* again worked wonders. A slew of materials flew into my inventory, including the valuable skin that Viscount Kurpatsky had spoken about. Now Flask would be pleased — there was little darkness in this monster. But the most interesting item came later, when only a huge pile of dark flesh remained on the ground.

6 of 12 *Mentor* fragments obtained. Total: 6.

Magic Stones obtained: *Block Vyrma, Shrill Cry, Booming Roar*

Despite the fact that I still did not understand the importance of the quality of magic stones, the fact that I managed to find some *Mentor* fragments made me happy. The Evil Engineer hadn't deceived me, they were indeed obtained from above-ground creatures with a red aura. But the quantity indicated that the strength in this monster was immeasurable. Six fragments at once! Here, a

Level 10 Riftmaster wouldn't drop that much! But even this wasn't the most valuable to me. *Block Vyrma*! An exclusive support stone, thanks to which, from now on, the arrows of the supreme dark converts would bounce right off of me! Give me two! I also needed one for Alia! No — four more, for Eleanore and my two future children as well. Maybe it would make sense to organize a hunt for devs and their minions? It was an extremely profitable venture. The other two stones were abilities, but I didn't see the point in them. They stunned opponents, which I could not do due to the key parameter *Indestructibility*. I'd have to change with Kimal Sarento — if he gave me ten facet elixirs, I'd give him two exclusive stones...Level eighteen? What kind of behemoth had I just killed?!

The temptation was so great that I couldn't resist and immediately inserted *Block Vyrma* into the free slot of *Golden Dome of Protection*. Thanks to the updates to my magic field, this could now be done without relying on crutches in the form of magic academy or Fortress devices. I'd definitely have to think carefully about how to rearrange and place my new stones. I might have to give something up, add something elsewhere — but I'd need to do it in a calm environment. Alia promised to think about what would be most effective for me, maybe even ask the High Priest about universal sets of stones, although it was unlikely that anyone prepared sets for six-by-six fields. This was too rare a phenomenon in the lands of the Light.

Opening the notebook, glad that I had used *Analyze* after *Dash* to enter the enemy's data into the journal, I could hardly resist a surprised gasp. A "horeb" section had appeared, which included two types of giant wolves. One was the kind I destroyed near the secret estate of the dark ones, the second was my current opponent. And the differences between them were vast! The notebook was amazing. It even indicated that the current creature was immune to ousels, therefore, the potential level of the rift at which it could be found was eighteen and higher. Perhaps it was a good idea to measure the strength of creatures by rift levels. It was a standard that would let me know instantly what I was up against.

A beast of level eighteen or higher could really wreak some havoc. Only specially trained squads of rift conquerors could do anything with such monsters, but there was no rift here. Here was just a clear area and an insanely fast, deadly creature that could destroy you with one bite. My defenses, of course, could cope with a bite, perhaps even two, but if I did lose consciousness, the horeb would destroy my shield within a minute and reach my body. What fine beasts they had roaming the Shurgan Empire!

There was no point in rushing anymore. Retrieving the bolt and returning it to my glove, I walked toward the village. The noise of splintering logs could be heard a kilometer away. The dev was tearing through houses as if they were made of straw. Half the village had already been reduced to ruins. Soon the clanging sounds of metal hitting stone were heard — one house was a little too tough. The stone domicile in the center of the village could only belong to the headman. The dev turned out to be an absolute giant. Naira had said they were about three meters, but she was deeply mistaken. This monster was no less than five meters tall. This freak used horeb skins as clothing, increasing its already daunting defense. Outwardly, it looked like a man: two legs, two arms, a torso, and a head, only there were horns on the top and its face looked like the muzzle of some kind of animal, although I wasn't sure which one. The details that distinguished the giant from humans began to emerge as it approached — disproportionately small, stubby legs, short powerful arms, each of which was thicker than my body, and only three thick fingers. The dev held a metal-bound club and slammed it into the stone house. The creature was amused that the house was not collapsing. There was no rage or indignation, but rather belly laughter and anticipation. One of the walls could not withstand the pressure and caved in. Screams of pain were heard: there were people in the house fleeing the monster. Those who tried to escape had apparently already been killed by the horeb. Dev put his hand into the hole, fumbled around and pulled out a man. Fortunately, he was already dead. The poor wretch's body caught on the hole as it was being pulled through and snapped in half. This did not stop the dev. Putting aside its club, it ripped open the belly of his prey, pulled out and threw the intestines to the side, after which he began to enthusiastically devour the prey. It was such a disgusting sight and sound that I almost vomited. This beast had no right to live! Even if it was sentient!

"Hey, gorgeous, I'm over here!" I shouted to attract its attention. By this point, it had already devoured the first person and was reaching for the second. I could not be called humanity's greatest defender, by any means, but it certainly was not pleasant to see people being devoured like that. Fortunately, not alive. The dev heard me and turned around. On its muzzle — it couldn't be called a face — there was an expression of unspeakable amazement. It even began to look around, searching for its little companion to help in the hunt.

"Looking for this?" I embodied the heavy skin of the horeb and almost collapsed. It weighed almost as much as I did. It produced the desired effect — the dev removed its hand from the hole, and there was no person in its fist. Its second hand reached for its club. The monster's eyes narrowed — it recognized its companion's hide. I returned the skin to my inventory and prepared for battle. There were barely ten meters between us, which allowed me to use *Analyze* to assess the dev's abilities. Another *Block Vyrma*! Just for Alia. The dev had the same stones as the horeb. So the master always had the same development level as its pet. It had no magical attack, only a few protective abilities. Although why would it need one? Judging by the stats *Analyze* spit back at me, I'd need a point-blank tower missile to even break through the skin!

The dev waved its fingers to demonstrate how quickly it could move, and in the blink of an eye covered the distance between us and brought down its club with a clang of metal on metal. It sparked so brightly that I was momentarily blinded! I'd never seen so many sparks in my life. Even when a whole horde of dark beasts fell upon me. I was pressed into the ground, but my defenses withstood! And it not only handled the next devastating blow, but also deflected it! The dev hadn't been expecting any recoil and didn't have time to react as the club flew straight to its forehead. No matter how strong and persistent this monster was, it was unable to handle its own strength. With a prolonged moan, the dev fell to the ground, raising little whirlpools of dust.

With a powerful leap to escape from the small crater the blow had driven me into, I found myself next to my vanquished foe. It was alive, but unconscious. The blossoming bruise on its forehead showed where the blow had hit, but incredibly, its bones weren't even cracked! They must be made from vyrma! The dev began to moan and its eyes twitched beneath the eyelids. It was gradually coming to. I could not allow this. Another jump, and I landed on its chest. The mithril glove ignored all the dev's defenses, and another gem appeared in my hands. This time, the essence of an exclusive eighteen-level dev.

Devour went completely crazy as it dug through the monster's insides. What didn't it take — bones, veins, even the skull! What in Skron's name was I going to do with this hulking thing?! What could be made from it? *Devour* didn't care — it tried to grab everything it could. The most unexpected, but pleasant surprise that sent goosebumps up my spine was not any of the individual pieces, but rather the dev's club. Thirty kilograms of pure vyrma! The metal was vyrma! Thirty kilograms! I'd pulled far less out of the eighteen-level rift. Where did an object of such luxury come from? The goosebumps were from the realization that if I had not set the stone in place as soon as I received it, the blow would have killed me. My dome had been useless against vyrma.

The dev's stones jumped into my palm, and the six new fragments of *Mentor* meant that I had a new exclusive stone. This was the most valuable drop. When *Devour* stopped ravaging the body, it was a terrible sight, but it remained whole, more than just pieces of flesh. Although it was missing a head. I looked around. Except for the burn up to the elbow on my jacket, I didn't have a single trace of the battle on me. I'd even managed to avoid the dark slurry that always drenched me after these fights. Approaching the stone house, I shouted to the huddled peasants:

"It's all over, you can come out! The dev and horeb have been destroyed! My name is Archduke

Valevsky of the Zarak Empire! Come out!"

I had to wait a while before they believed me. At first, someone's head appeared in the hole, but immediately hid, as if not believing what she saw. Another head popped out, but remained in place, examining the surroundings and reporting what he saw to those left inside. I sat casually on a log, demonstrating that it was safe. New heads popped out, until finally, there was a sonorous gong of metal on a stone. Something crashed, a muffled scream rang out, but it was clearly not urgent. The people freed the blocked doors and practically ran outside.

Soon, there was a crowd. My eyes narrowed — they did not look like peasants. Peasants didn't wear a full set of steel armor of the Shurgan cut and obviously did not drag long spears with them. A dozen warriors surrounded me in a half circle, but in their gratitude, did not point their spears in my direction. I got to my feet, looking with interest at a boy around my age that walked out after the warriors. For some reason, I liked him. He had open features, nothing rat-like about them, thin, fox-like eyes that pointed straight forward, a fleshy nose, athletic physique and long dark hair gathered into a ponytail. His expensive garments only complemented his image, showing that the boy in front of me was a high-born Shurganite, and not some peasant.

"Archduke Valevsky, you were right on time!" The stranger had a pleasant voice. "My soldiers were forced to hide in this house, although we knew perfectly well that this would not save us from the dev and his pet. If not for you, I would now be in the presence of the Light, listening with baited breath as my ancestors told tales of the past. I, Rustam Bakhtiyar, thank you for saving my life, and know that from now on, I am in your debt. As a sincere favor, I ask that you be my companion and accompany me to my house. There, we will arrange a feast in honor of your valor. Bayazid Padishah will want to personally embrace the man who saved his son's life!"

Chapter 13

"WHAT AN AMAZING COINCIDENCE. Do you always have this kind of luck?" Naira sat down nearby and watched the soldiers help the survivors from the village. There turned out to be quite a few — about sixty people had been hiding in the headman's stone house. The cunning old chief, who also survived, had dug himself a huge basement, which he used to store food reserves for the entire village. They had been able to keep the whole supply and fit everyone in there as well.

"What are you talking about now?" I also didn't really like the situation I was in, so I decided to pretend that I didn't understand anything and the explanatory brigade was required.

"We are stopping at the palace of Padishah Bayazid of the Third. And here, quite by accident, a dev appears on the path that the padishah's son was traveling along and drives him into this stone house. And it just so happens that of all the people on this planet, you are nearly the only one who can single-handedly destroy a dev, while losing nothing more than the sleeve of his jacket. Don't you find this all to be a little strange? As if someone set it all up ahead of time?"

"We chose our departure date ourselves. Judging by what the soldiers said, the dev must have broken past the Wall a week ago, and Rustav was just fulfilling his father's orders. You're right, of course, it does seem like a very strange coincidence, but sometimes it's just random chance. Do you know of any forces that could contain a dev not far from the village to await our arrival? Or did someone whisper in the padishah's ear that he urgently needed to send his son to some distant Fortress?"

"I sincerely beg your forgiveness for interrupting, but this heavenly beauty is right," Rustam Bakhtiyar finished giving instructions to his soldiers and approached us. "These events really do seem to have been guided by some ill will."

"Rustam, allow me to introduce my companion, Naira Jode of the Bartolomeo Clan. Naira, this is Rustam Bakhtiyar, second son of Padishah Bayazid the Third."

"Clan Bartolomeo? You're dark?" Rustam eloquently arched his brow and discreetly, as if by chance, placed his hand on his sword.

"Gray," Naira grinned, pretending not to notice Rustam's reaction. "Bearing official permission from the Citadel to travel in the lands of the Light."

The fact that for the next twelve months, she remained my fiancée, Naira kept quiet about.

"If we can return to your remark, what makes you think that someone's ill will has guided this?" I asked when Rustam lowered his hand from the hilt.

"Father wanted me to go to the Fortress for a check three months ago, but only four days ago he suddenly remembered this order and demanded that I leave immediately. My map showed the dev's movement — it remained in a dense forest for four days, as if it had started to build a new habitat, but yesterday, it suddenly broke into a rampage again and moved further south. Directly interceding with my detachment's path. The only thing that doesn't fit into the picture here is your sudden appearance. Clearly, it was preordained."

"Why would the padishah suddenly want to get rid of one of his sons?" Naira asked.

"Him? My father wouldn't dirty his hands in such matters. That's what younger brothers are for. One of them could very well be behind this. And Sayid had the opportunity. I've never liked that bookworm. Obviously, he read in one of his books about how to bait a dev and used this knowledge to try and destroy me. Well it didn't work, brother!"

"That story is so far-fetched that it crumbles at the slightest criticism. The dev has been roaming your lands for a week. You received the order from your father three days ago. We decided to leave two days ago. Three independent events requiring clear coordination. Say that Magister Meram himself was involved in this — it wouldn't work without a remote connection to him."

"Magister Meram doesn't meddle in such tiresome affairs," Rustam said. "And he would only be interested in a dev from a purely pragmatic point of view. But we agree that everything seems quite contrived, enough to be suspicious. Just as long as the chief of this village, who we'll still need to deal with, doesn't go on the run."

"What did the chief do wrong?" I asked.

"Shurgan law prohibits constructing your house out of granite. All the granite extracted must be processed and sent to the capital. This headman, however, has neglected to uphold the law. Not only did he build his house from this material, but also planted a tree to block the view, so that we would not suspect anything. And the whole village knew about it, but remained silent.

"Which ended up saving your life," I reminded him. I didn't really like where Rustam was going with this.

"Which ended up saving my life," he agreed. "Nonetheless, the law is the law, and he broke it. We need blood as repayment, otherwise father will be considered weak. Unable to conduct his own business. I believe the headman and every third person saved must die. The survivors will forever remember that the law in the Shurgan Empire is higher than human life! This is the only way we can resist the darkness."

Having uttered the last phrase, Rustam looked to Naira, but the girl did not react. She was rummaging through her purse, showing that she didn't give a damn about anything that was going on. The young man called the commander of his group, and within twenty minutes all the surviving villagers were lined up according to height. The chief stood alone, and his face was as white as his hair. The old man knew what was about to happen, but he could not prevent it. Every third person, including the children…I silently watched the sorting process, trying to calm the anger seething in my chest. What was happening was wrong. Inhumane. You cannot resist darkness by creating darkness. For what was happening clearly bore no resemblance to anything Light. If it did, then who needed the Light at all? The people were divided into two groups, and the one that was destined to remain alive was forced to watch what was about to happen. Rustam went to those unlucky few, taking out a knife. He intended to enforce the law himself.

"I'm wondering why the second son of Padishah Bayazid the Third decided to destroy my property," I said, having made a decision. Hearth would be neither light nor dark. Hearth would be gray! And anyone who broke the laws of my city would go through the courts, and not through the arbitrary decision of one influential figure. Yes, the headman broke the law, and he alone should be judged, not the whole village. And considering the circumstances!

"What are you on about?" Rustam said. Displeasure flashed in his eyes because I distracted him from such an exciting activity — the instruction and destruction of these obedient sheep. For some reason I no longer liked this man, despite how friendly he may look.

"The fact that I saved all the lives in the village makes me feel entitled to the right to punish or spare them."

"You are a guest in our lands, Archduke Valevsky." Rustam's voice was steely. "Because you saved my life, I will take your indiscretion without comment. These people are under my father's jurisdiction, and they broke the law!"

"Perhaps that was the case before I saved them. But after I destroyed the dev, the fate of this entire village passed into my hands. I started to develop a real concern for what's going on here. That's why I'm surprised at how easily you divide the people for whom I risked my life, how you were going to kill them. I'm interested to know what the laws of the Shurgan Empire have to say about this. Surely, there is some precedent, right?"

Rustam turned toward me.

"These people broke the law!"

"That's not what I asked you, second son of the padishah." My words could cut like metal as well, when I needed them to. Magister Tarra taught me so.

Rustam made a gesture, and his warriors immediately pointed their spears and crossbows in my direction.

"I am grateful to you for saving my life, but I won't tolerate this kind of treatment!"

"So you're telling me the dev and horeb were terrible monsters who frightened you, but the one who took them down so easily does not?" I arched my brow and took a step toward Rustam. "The people who survived in this village now belong to me, Archduke Valevsky. And if anyone decides that he has the right to punish my people, he must first have the power to punish me. Are you able to do this, Rustam Bakhtiyar? Are you ready to go against your father?"

With these words, I pulled the plate of the padishah from my pocket and demonstrated it to those around me. Rustam turned white. In relation to the Shurgans, it looked quite funny — they suddenly looked more like Zarganites.

"Where did you get this from?" the steel in his voice had vanished. It had been replaced by shock.

"It doesn't matter where I got it from. What matters is what it allows me to do." I returned the plate to my breast pocket. "So what are you going to do with my people, second son of the padishah?"

The soldiers put down their spears and looked to each other, not understanding what to do. They swore to serve the son of the padishah, but before that — the padishah himself. And I just demonstrated that the padishah's word was my own. And they were going to poke spears at me. Not good. You could end up on the chopping block for something like that. Legal issues were resolved quite quickly in the Shurgan Empire, as I understood it.

"They are yours, Archduke Valevsky. When we reach my father, I'll question him myself."

"Nobody will stop you," I answered and approached the headman. "Did you know that you were breaking the law by building a house out of granite?"

"I knew, sir."

"Why did you do this?"

"People in the neighboring villages get kind of rowdy, there are so many robbers these days that it makes your head spin. We already contacted the padishah's governor, but no one did anything. They sent several soldiers, who stayed in the village for a week, ate our food, and left. And then the robbers came, halved our supplies, killed half the people, and also burned half the houses. To teach us a lesson. It was then that I decided to build a house in which I could hide. Granite was found in those mountains, and we found a small quarry there. In five years, we collected the required amount and built a house. The robbers came twice more, but left with nothing. We could be happy in there for at least a week. We keep everything important there, and building new houses is not a problem. And they've learned to hit back; every house has crossbows. So the robbers started to avoid us. This is my decision, and I must stand by my decision. There is no reason to let people die."

"It's your decision, you should bear the

punishment," I agreed, after which, with a lightning-quick movement, I separated the old man's head from his body. I'd already found out everything I needed to know. The residents were still divided into two groups. I approached them:

"Choose a new headman, bury this one with honors. He deserved it. The house will be dismantled and the granite sent to the capital, as required by law. After you deal with this, collect all your things and go to the city of Hearth. They'll find work for you all there. Burn the village. Only the ashes should remind us that people once lived here. Go!"

The peasants silently turned around and went to the headman's house. Everyone got to work, even the kids who started pulling the boards away. I returned to the gloomy Rustam:

"These people need protection so that they can reach my lands without hindrance. If the deputy of the padishah fails to handle his duties, I will handle them myself. And you are right, second son of the padishah. When we arrive at your father's, I have a few things to ask him myself. Gustav, what's the deal with the soup? Has it cooled off yet?"

"All good, your Radiance!" My old mentor got his bearings quickly. "It's ready!"

"Please allow me to invite you to share a meal with us, Rustam Bakhtiyar," I said as if nothing had happened when I was done with the mandatory scolding. I knew that this would come back to haunt me later, but I couldn't have done otherwise.

"Thank you for the invitation, I'm not hungry," he replied curtly, setting the tone for further communication. Or rather, lack thereof. Well, to Skron with him. I didn't force my friendship on anyone. In my opinion, relationships between members of different empires should be purely businesslike.

"You sure know how to make friends," Gustav said, handing me a plate. "If a Shurganite refuses to share a meal with you, he is openly declaring you his enemy."

"What, should I run over there now, fall on my hands and knees and beg him to slaughter two dozen people? Just so he'll forgive me?" I couldn't resist being sarcastic.

"What do you need peasants for, anyway?" Gustav was almost the only one who was allowed to ask me a direct question. Even slap me on the head if I acted out of place.

"Eleanore will find a place for them. We always need more working hands, especially in Hearth."

"So, if we come across twenty more villages like this ahead of us, you'll take them all?"

"If there's a dev in each one, why not? It's a profitable business. Do you know anything about horeb skins?"

"How would I?" Gustav asked, surprised. "We only killed two or three when I was on the Wall. The commanders immediately took such valuables into their own hands. Do you have something to brag about?"

"I do, but I'm not going to show you here. Too many prying eyes around. Including our dark guest. Great Light, Gustav, what did you put in here? This is delicious!"

"May I have a taste?" Naira asked, intrigued by my exclamation.

"Please don't blame me, madam, it's really just a very simple stew." Gustav poured a bowl and handed it to the girl. While I had a simple wooden camping bowl, she had a dark steel one with some engravings. Even something as small as her eating vessel was a chance to express a sense of aesthetic. And it didn't matter that metal utensils heated up faster and burned your hands. The main thing was aesthetics. I wouldn't be a true aristocrat for a long time yet.

Rustam left several soldiers with the peasants, and soon we slowly moved on. There was no longer talk of any visit to the distant Fortress. Rustam hurried back to his father to ask a burning question. At some point, the impatient young man even left my carriage in order to ride further with his group, but returned, as if fearing that we would veer off the right road. But we had no intention of turning anywhere, nor were we in a hurry. There were still ten days left before Magister Meram's training began, so I was still fine on time. But I didn't much like the look of Naira right now. She pretended to be reading a book, but looked up every now and then, as if assessing me. This was pretty annoying, but I decided to develop patience. When you learn to handle your frustration, you become stronger.

"How did you kill him?" Naira couldn't resist asking an hour later.

"With a knife."

"I'm not talking about the chief. I mean the dev. I saw the corpse — it was five meters tall! How did you manage?"

"Why should I reveal my secrets to you?" I asked. "I was actually lucky. The horeb attacked me outside of the settlement. If the two beasts had coordinated, I would have been toast."

"So you're not invulnerable? Just lucky?"

"Precisely! Well, you were lucky to be at this point in space and earn yourself an enemy."

"I still don't understand why you did this. Rustam was perfectly within his rights. These are his people, and it is up to him to decide how to punish them."

"His father's people," I corrected her. "Not Rustam's. Even the group that accompanies him belongs to Bayazid the Third, not his son."

"Okay, these are his father's people who broke the law."

"Are you certain about that?"

The dark one scoffed at my question.

"That's what Rustam said."

"That is, you will believe the first person you meet who calls himself the son of a padishah if he, for example, says that in the Shurgan Empire there is a law obliging all dark women he finds attractive to strip naked and perform a dance for the amusement of the whole group?"

"Maximilian!" Naira said, outraged.

"What's the difference? Why do you believe him on that point, but you're indignant on another? After all, the law is the law. He would be in his right. Rustam was going to execute twenty people just because they survived. This is not normal behavior. The chief was to blame, he knew what he was getting into. The reasons that prompted the old man to do this should not be discussed here, maybe at another time. But for his decision, the old man received a well-deserved punishment. He is dead. For what are the others to blame?"

"Alright, Max, let's say you're right. Then why did you decide to burn the village? Why send the people to Hearth?"

"Because if they had stayed in the village, they would all have been killed. Not by the robbers, but by the padishah's men. Rustam would return here in a week and slaughter everyone. Just because he can."

"What do you care about these people? Aren't you meeting them for the first time in your life?"

"You're right, these people won't make my life any easier. They're peasants; I don't have free land in Hearth where they can grow crops. They will have to be trained, new jobs will have to be found for them, and effort and money will have to be spent on them. But there is a huge difference between the people for whom you risked your life and those who simply live under one or another control of the governors. The commander of the detachment that stopped us clearly defined the fate of those wretches — they had been given over to the dev. As had Rustam himself, by the way. When I intervened, I became responsible for their fate."

"If it weren't for the dev, you wouldn't have lifted a finger?"

"Naturally. These are local standoffs between peasants and their rulers. Interfering with them is the last thing I want to do."

"Got it," Naira nodded. "Tell me, where did the skin from the horeb go? I saw the scraps — not a single hair left, as if you had collected every one. I flipped it over just to check."

"The cost of destroying dark beasts," I did not go into details. "Unfortunately, after I finish them off, there's not much left of the bodies. And even more so from the skin, which is as strong as steel."

"Maximilian…"

"I have nothing else to add, Naira. There was no loot. Period."

"I understand, I rescind my question. Then answer me this: why did you refuse to marry me? Is this beneficial for your city? We would have a complete monopoly on duties on imported goods. From both your side and mine. As Adeline says, 'I'm for any business that involves me. Even a little bit.' And there is nothing better than to enter into a political marriage like the one between Kimal Sarento and my cousin."

"Would such a marriage suit you?" I couldn't

help but ask.

"Previously, no. I agreed to become your fiancée, and then your wife, only to save my father. You were right — I had no idea who or what you were. But now I'm standing next to you. I'm communicating with you, trying to understand the logic of your actions and, I want to say, at the moment I'm not against such a union. It would really be beneficial to both parties at once. Moreover, by taking me as your wife, you would receive the support of the third-highest clan of Kerux. Yes, our position has recently been shaken, but we will regain our former glory. And much more. The last time the Bartolomeo Clan presided over a clan meeting was before I was born. We have significant resources that can help Hearth become the second capital of the Zarak Empire in a couple of years. We have vast territories with many high-level rifts and Pharapho ruins. This means artifacts, resources. Everything that can make Hearth a strong and attractive city for trade. But you chose Alia. Why, what does she have? A title equal to or higher than yours? Apparently not. She belongs to the church and, as soon as the Citadel gives an order, she will immediately rush to carry it out? Because she's a bishop? The fact that she was given the incomprehensible status of 'independent' does not say anything. She left the control of the High Priest of the Zarak Empire, but not the pope. And as soon as the head of the Church of Light becomes interested in you, he will simply order Alia to give out all the information available to her about you, and she will not dare to disobey! Because she has no freedom!"

"So that's what you have in the Bartolomeo Clan? Freedom?" I barely restrained myself from yelling at the dark one. "Please explain how? Because you are free to resist the will of the Temple of Skron? That misty Temple servant decided that from now on, you will be a rift conqueror, and the third-most powerful clan in Kerux did what to challenge this? To interfere? Did you stand your ground and firmly declare that you weren't going anywhere? I don't remember anything like that. Alia has freedom. She can leave the church and become independent. Yes, she will lose her rank, lose her influence, but she has the opportunity. Can someone from your clan leave the Temple of Skron? Sure, maybe. Until they use a portal again. Then they'll vanish forever into the depths of the dark pyramid, and no one will ever recall them again. I found out the hard way what freedom is as interpreted by the Temple of Skron. I don't want to repeat this mistake. Your proposal is interesting, but it involves the fact that I will have to use portals. Which automatically makes this very proposal unrealistic. All your resources, rifts, ruins..."

"Stop!" A cry interrupted this titillating conversation. Gustav stopped the carriage so abruptly that we almost got hit. Surprised by this behavior, I jumped out to investigate.

I didn't like what I saw. A motley looking crew was moving towards us from the direction of Al-

Khorezm. Two High Converts and a Commander of the Citadel. Two dark and one light. Together. This would only be possible in one case, and I felt a sinking sensation when I understood the reason why the commander had not yet beheaded the supreme converts. Rustam and his group dismounted and knelt before the highest hierarch of the Citadel.

"Dark Hunter Maximilian Valevsky, you are the one I am looking for!" the commander said loudly, neglecting all my titles. The Church of the Light generally did not care about such conventions.

The trio reached us, after which one of the supreme converts ran a hundred meters away and began to chant the dark portal summoning song.

"You must go with this supreme convert!" the commander ordered, pointing to the second dark one. "An infected rift appeared a hundred kilometers from here. Now it's level eight, but every hour its level increases by one. There are too many small rifts around. You must destroy it as quickly as possible!"

"Master Meram handles infected rifts," I replied. "That's what he gets paid for."

"The gray master headed to another infected rift, located three hundred kilometers from us. That rift is already twenty levels deep and has begun to attract the rift that you must destroy. If these two merge, the entire northern part of the Shurgan Empire will become uninhabitable. Including Al-Khorezm! I'm going to the rift where the dark ones and Magister Meram are located. Everyone is being called there now. As soon as you manage, the second convert will send you to us. The Temple of Skron has guaranteed your immunity. You will be taken to the portal and returned to Al-Khorezm as soon as the rift is destroyed. You!"

The commander pointed to Rustam.

"Everyone who is here, except Valevsky and this dark one, must undergo a darkness test in the Citadel tomorrow! If even one person has been lost, the Bakhtiyar family will be punished! Such is the will of the Light!"

The commander considered his mission accomplished. He was not interested in the opinion of some insects. The convert opened the portal, and the light one disappeared. The remaining convert brought me a horse, indicating that I should hurry. A gentle hand touched my shoulder. Turning around, I saw Naira.

"You say the light ones have freedom? While you are running along rifts, think about how far it extends, this freedom, for the head of an autonomous city."

Chapter 14

"ALIA, I NEED ADVICE..."

I recounted everything that had happened. I wasn't too pleased with the commander's actions. He just showed up, set my task and left, without even worrying about whether or not I would carry out his order.

"I don't know, Max," my future wife said thoughtfully. "Formally, you didn't sign a contract to close rifts. The Citadel is a unique organization, of course, but even they don't have the right to order you around in this way. Clearly, they're facing something relatively serious, otherwise they wouldn't be acting like this. Two infected rifts, you say? They've been popping up a lot more frequently, don't you think? None at all for several decades, and then four in the past month. Something's fishy here."

"Can infected rifts be man-made?"

"I haven't heard anything of the like. I'll have to ask the High Priest. What did they say about the distribution of extracted goods?"

"Absolutely nothing. The commander didn't say a word about that."

"Yes, something really out of the ordinary happened there. The Citadel usually pays close attention to such details. Where is the rift located?"

"About fifty kilometers from the border."

"So three hundred kilometers from Hearth. If this rift isn't closed on time, what will happen to our city?"

"Nothing good," I sighed.

"That's the answer to the question of what we must do. We will talk to the Citadel separately — their behavior is unacceptable. However, this rift now threatens Hearth and needs to be dealt with."

"But only this rift. The rift behind the Wall is Magister Meram's problem."

"I support you in that. Let those who receive privileges for their work handle this problem. You're not authorized to handle such things now."

I had this simple conversation while the supreme convert and I were rushing forward, driving the horses. Every once in a while we had to stop to extend the life of our transportation. I understood perfectly well that the poor animals would die — a race of a hundred kilometers, especially over rough terrain, had never brought anyone any good. We didn't spare the animals at all, and in just three hours, as everything inside me was twisting and turning, we reached our goal. There were still two hours left before sunset, so I decided to take a little walk after the hurried journey.

"Stay here, I'll walk through the ruins," I pointed to the Fog of Pharapho visible nearby. With the rift no longer blocking the Scourge of Black Mountain, he happily burst forth into the world, sending his fingerlings of fog out into the world in search of prey. The fog had just appeared in the local ruins, so there wasn't much to profit from here. In two hours I only managed to find four soldiers, increasing the number of cutting stones. There were no artifacts to be found.

The rift had grown significantly by our arrival. The commander had said it was a level eight, and the Riftmaster would appear at twelve. Only three hours before the metamorph! *Devour* took all the most valuable things from the rift and again I received several strange stones called lyog. Strange colorless crystals appeared only at the last level and were in such minute quantities that they immediately caught my eye. Even vyrma I'd already accumulated enough of to create a good set of armor, if I decided to craft it, but I only had nine pieces of lyog. Three crystals per each infected rift. This made me think — the presence of this stone did not depend on the level of the rift. My previous rifts were level eighteen and fourteen. This one one twelve. Which was peculiar. I needed to consult someone more knowledgeable, and my conversation with Naira immediately came to mind. The Bartolomeo Clan would be ideal for this purpose. They probably knew what lyog was used for and how to process it. What if I could use this resource to build a superweapon that would destroy any enemy? That'd be pretty cool.

I didn't want to go back. I'd practically cleaned the whole rift out and only low-level resources remained, which were useless to me due to my lack of recipes. The magic stones were outright garbage — nothing of interest there. Apparently, the time had come to start collecting stones for my second- and third-level friends and family. I'd need to denote a special person to structure the stones and form sets with them for subsequent integration. I didn't think the Fortress would refuse such an amount. I no longer wanted to go through Kimal Sarento.

A surprise awaited me on the surface, and I can't say that it was pleasant. The supreme convert performed his ritual self-sacrifice, opening a portal, and three people appeared to me through a shimmering veil. The commander, a misty Temple servant and another high convert. Evidently, in case anything went wrong with the portal.

"You were in no hurry," the commander said, dissatisfied. There were no more than three hours left before sunrise.

"No such need was expressed to me," I answered. "The infected rift has been destroyed, I'm not going to give away the magic stones."

"We don't care about your stones," the

commander clearly did not know how to communicate in any way except from a position of strength. "Go to the portal, there is another rift ahead. The Temple of Skron guarantees to get you there and back."

"Why should I? The dark clans, the Citadel and Master Meram are dealing with the infected rifts," I answered, deciding to cut to the chase. If I obeyed now and agreed with the commander, I'd be running errands til the end of my days like a powerless sheep, not even daring to raise my voice. "When I was in the Bartolomeo Clan, it was still possible to somehow get me involved in this work. But I was lucky enough to leave the clan, and the fact that Naira Jode is my bride does not in any way oblige me to jump through portals at the first request. It's not my job, Commander."

"Are you refusing to submit to the will of the Citadel?" the light one appeared to grow in size.

"I refuse to do something that I didn't sign up for and that I'm not paid for. If this goes against the will of the Citadel...Well, I'm ready to accept the punishment I deserve. I've lowered my defenses, Commander. Try to kill me quickly. I don't want to suffer."

"You will be punished!"

"For what? For the fact that I don't want to die in a rift and would rather you just kill me right here and now? What does a corpse care how it's punished? I'm ready to accept the wrath of the Citadel. I repeat — my defenses are down. You can kill me without any fear of retaliation."

"The Temple of Skron would like to know what you want in exchange for your help?" asked the Temple servant.

"He must submit to the will of the Light!" The commander clearly had some kind of grudge against me. Why was he suddenly so heated?

"What reason should the Hunter of Darkness have to fulfill the will of the Light?" The Temple servant turned to the commander. "An agreement to destroy the infected rifts was signed between the Temple of Skron, the clan council, the pope and Magister Meram. If the latter fails to seal the rift, the combined forces of the signatories are sent into the rift in order to fulfill their mission. There is no Archduke of the autonomous city mentioned in this treaty. You'll have to go into the rift yourself, commander."

So that was the reason! I thought that the light one must hate me for some reason, but he just didn't want to die himself!

"What level is the infected rift?" I asked, wondering what beneficial terms I could negotiate for myself.

"Twenty-eight. In two hours it will be thirty-one — another rift will soon be swallowed up. Then it will stagnate for a while. There are no new rifts in the area, and the old ones are slow to move toward this behemoth. We estimate that in twenty-eight hours the infected rift will attract a level twenty rift. The Temple of Skron does not want to turn these vast inhabited tracts of lands into a desert."

"Rot starts appearing at level twenty five. I don't know what it is or how to destroy it."

"The Temple of Skron remembers your demands. You will be given rings, amulets, and additional armor that reduces the influence of darkness. A thirty-one level rift has not been closed for eight hundred years. Especially an infected one."

"I'll need steel boxes."

"You will receive containers for new ousels. They have already been made."

"Why?"

"The idea to create a dark mirror didn't just occur to the Church of the Light."

"You say that as if I already agreed. This infected rift is quite far from Hearth. Even if it hits the northeastern part of the Zarak Empire, my city will not be harmed."

"It won't be harmed," agreed the Temple Servant. "That's why we're here. In order to come to an agreement, Rift Conqueror."

"Why couldn't Magister Meram handle it?"

"Rot. It showed up before he applied the seal. His runes have no effect on rot. He started developing a new word, but Skron knows how long that will take. Maybe he's already done it. Or it might take an eternity. Maybe the rot can't be sealed at all. We do not know."

"A thirty-one level rift, despite the fact that my current maximum is eighteen. And you want me to risk my life and go into the rift out of sheer altruism?"

"It is your duty!" The commander intervened. "You are a servant of the Church!"

"When did that happen?" I was genuinely astonished.

"When you were recognized! When they gave you a personal attendant! The existence of dark ones in light empires is regulated by laws that define you. The fact that your life was returned, turning you from a doomed soldier into a human being, does not change anything. For the Church of Light, you will remain a doomed soldier until the end of your days! Those who are sacrificed first of all to save ordinary people. We're wasting time! If you don't go to the rift voluntarily, you will be sent there by force!"

"Commander, I will repeat: my shield is down. You can finish me off with any ability of your choosing. I humbly bow my head to you and your might. Send me by force into the rift, I'll settle there on the first level and won't go anywhere. I don't care about the droves of dark ones who will die due to the infected rift. I don't care about the territories of the Shurgan Empire, which the enlarged rift may touch. I am responsible only for my city and my people. And neither one nor the other are located in the territory of the rift. As for my duty...the High Priest of the Zarak Empire removed me from the Church of Light. Did the pope reverse this decision? Or does the commander of the Citadel have the right to ignore the decision of the High Priest of a sovereign empire?"

"You refuse to fulfill your duty. The Citadel remembers those who went against it," the commander said with undisguised anger, but he didn't go anywhere, nor did he try to overpower me and throw me into the portal.

"The Temple of Skron repeats its question: what would you like?"

"What does Magister Meram receive for each sealed rift?"

"The agreement prohibits the disclosure of this information." The Temple servant didn't want to reveal Magister Meram's salary.

"In that case, pique my interest. Offer something that will make me forget about the sense of self-preservation and descend to the thirty-first level of the rifts. And no talk of debts — I don't owe anyone anything. If you want to kill me, kill. You have Magister Meram, who can easily cope with all adversities."

"All the resources extracted from this rift are yours," he said.

"Very funny. Infected rifts are empty by default. I've already gone through three of them and haven't found anything except nux and chrone."

"The Temple of Skron needs time to make an offer, but we don't have it. In twenty-eight hours this conversation will be meaningless anyway."

I turned my gaze to the gloomy commander.

"The Church of Light will not offer you anything, Dark One," answered the servant of the Light, but immediately added: "We are ready to fulfill your reasonable demands, but not come up with them ourselves."

"My demands? No problem! I want Hearth and I to be recognized as free from the influence of the Church of the Light. I am not happy that every time they try to charge me with some kind of non-existent debt. I need complete and as detailed maps as possible of the key locations in all empires. I need a hundred artifact recipes. I need official settings for producing elixirs for mana, stone levels and facets. I need access to the Citadel archives. I need resources and manpower to rebuild Hearth. At least one hundred work teams for a period of one calendar year. I need gold. You wanted my demands, there they are."

"Your demands are unrealistic," the commander once again loomed over me. I even closed my eyes, expecting a blow, but it didn't come. When I returned to reality again, he had regained his former appearance.

"I have similar demands for the Temple of Skron. I need complete location maps. I need access to your archives. My lack of information is really starting to piss me off. The metamorph appears at the fifteenth level of the rift. Rot is on the twenty-fifth. What appears on the thirty-fifth? You know, but remain silent. Then I too will be silent."

"The Temple of Skron has heeded your words and will provide a worthy offer after the rift is destroyed. We are ready to take on the obligations of the Citadel — we are more interested in ensuring that our lands remain inhabitable."

"I need independence from the Church of the Light," I repeated stubbornly. "Even if it's only partial — if there's one person who can order me around, it's the pope. Personally. No commanders, paladins or even Inquisitors will have this right. I am not going to rush off in an unknown direction at the first call of any representative of the Citadel who comes to me. And Hearth needs devices. We are a trading city and want to produce what we will trade ourselves."

"The Citadel is ready to discuss your demands," the commander said forcefully. "Only the pope can make the final decision. Even the conclave does not have this right."

"I want to meet with the pope and discuss my participation in closing the rifts."

"The pope doesn't meet with dark humans!" The commander barked. "Your participation is insignificant! You must close this Skron-damned rift, period! Magister Meram will deal with the rest!"

"I told you my demands, decide for yourself. By the way, it only now dawned on me that you said a rift of this level has already been closed? By whom?" I turned towards the Temple servant, but the commander replied.

"The First Emperor! He freed our lands from the rifts that appeared here during Skron's entrance into our world; He laid the foundation of the Church of the Light!"

"An additional demand is that I need

complete archives on the first emperor. What he did, what he could do, what he had."

"Access to this information can only be obtained with special permission from the pope!"

"In that case, I repeat: I need to meet with the head of the Church of the Light. Temple Servant, why are you silent? Do you also have anything similar? An archive to prevent the dark ones from collecting information on the first light emperor? I will never believe this."

"I have no authority to discuss access to this information with you," came the answer. "Only One does."

"I need a meeting with One. I will be happy to meet him at Hearth."

"One does not leave the pyramid. One is the pyramid," the dark one said mysteriously. "The Temple of Skron will discuss your demands. Every minute we stand here, a normal level twenty rift is getting closer to becoming infected. We can discuss your demands endlessly, but this conversation will not lead to results. In two hours, the sun will rise and the rift will close. When it reopens, you'll have fourteen fewer hours. Don't forget: you still need to be prepared for the descent. This will also take some time. Rot is an extremely unpleasant substance."

Unlike the Citadel, the Temple of Skron knew how to urge on with facts: they even reminded me that rifts open only at night. I met the commander's gaze. Even though there was pure Light shining in his eye sockets, it did not bode well for me.

"I need lifelong guarantees that the Temple of Skron will not take advantage of its position and will not transport me to the pyramid against my wishes. Otherwise, I will never enter another portal. Ever."

"You have them," he assured me. "If the Temple of Skron wishes to speak with you, it will send a messenger."

It was a kind of feeble promise, but they couldn't give me anything better right now. What would stop the Temple from breaking its word? Did I have a contract? They didn't care about such things. Control by the Citadel? Not an option at all. The only guarantee they could give was their word. Which they would keep as long as it was profitable for them.

"Okay, I await the reasonable proposals from the Temple of Skron and the Citadel. You know my minimum requirements. Have you already finished off the metamorph?"

"The Gourfan Clan is on location," the dark one answered, which sounded more like, "Naturally, what a stupid question." However, just in case, I clarified:

"Does the portal lead to the infected rift?"

Waiting for a nod, I entered the shimmering veil. The gloomy, dissatisfied and clearly embittered face of the commander was a repulsive sight to see. I definitely had beef with the Citadel. I'd deal with it when I got out of the rift.

If I got out of the rift. Not when…

The last remark I almost said out loud. As soon as I exited the portal, the air, saturated with some kind of unpleasant rot, began to weigh on me. My lungs immediately began to burn, as if I had inhaled a good portion of caustic construction dust all at once. *Heal* helped — the burning in my lungs stopped. Holding my breath, I looked around. As far as the light from my crystal could reach, there was a barely noticeable haze hanging everywhere, giving off a green hue. Unlike the fog of Pharapho, the haze rose high above the ground, expanding into all the available space. People around were wearing special masks, fleeing from the caustic abomination. Neither the commander nor the Temple servant had bothered to warn me about what was awaiting me. Was it revenge? I'd told them that I had no idea what rot was.

"Follow me. We don't have much time," the servant's voice said. The haze clearly did not cause him any discomfort. Still trying not to breathe, I entered the huge tent after him, and only then exhaled noisily. There was no haze inside — the magic field blocked it. Again the same round table that I had already seen before, and around it stood the heads of clans and leading rift conquerors. Cedric Jode was also here, ready to carry out any order the onyx pyramid gave him.

"Rift Conqueror Valevsky," the dark one introduced me to the crowd. Although it seemed to me, everyone already knew perfectly well who I was. Including Magister Meram. The old man did not look very good, as if he had descended down as far as possible and sat there for several days. Dried up like a mummy, he was nevertheless cheerful and active.

"Valevsky, then," He said, looking at me appraisingly, as if for the first time. "In nine days you should be in Al-Khorezm. If you're late, I won't accept you! Just bear that in mind!"

"The rift conqueror needs protection from the dark influence," said the Temple servant, preventing me from answering Magister Meram's remark. "The thirty-first level of the infected rift requires the maximum attention of all those present. Gourfan Clan?"

"Unidentified metamorph ring," the new Gourfan clan head did not remove his helmet, so it was hard to say what he looked like.. However, his armor really caught my attention. It didn't look like steel. *Analyze* was once again completely useless, as was expected. It was now only suitable for identifying dark humans. I no longer saw the point in all these enhancements. I sure hoped Alia could master my new magic field as quickly as possible. It was time to step up.

"In addition, two of our best rings for blocking the influence of darkness," two more appeared next to the first red object.

"A darkness-blocking amulet," Cedric placed a heavy stone on the table. "Also exclusive — Heirloom of the Bartolomeo Clan."

"Three rings from the Temple of Skron," the misty servant put three more exclusive rings on the table.

"This will help him with the darkness, but what will he do about the rot?" Cedric Jode asked. Judging by how everyone remained silent, no one could help me with this. Because only a few had ever encountered it.

"What is rot and how can it be defeated? Masks?"

"Masks only work for ten minutes, then they become infected," answered a man I didn't know. The clan symbol was unfamiliar to me, but I didn't want to demand that everyone introduce themselves. Who cared?

"Rot is a special state of matter that can be found from the twenty-fifth level of the rifts and deeper," the Temple servant began, but fell silent. A few moments later he was next to me.

"It's easier to transfer the knowledge to you immediately and in its entirety. You'll figure it out."

My head almost exploded with the new knowledge. I even fell back on the ground when the Temple servant let me go. No new functionality — just information. The notebook began to blink like crazy, so I had to open it and immerse myself in reading. Rot. Mold. A special fungus that covered rift beasts, giving them new powers, skills, and abilities and making them immune to one or two types of damage. The fungus ate away everything, even standard resources, turning them into something new. But the rot had the worst effect on the guards: they were altered beyond recognition. They became smaller, more dangerous, more furious. The air on levels infected with rot was poisoned. Staying there for more than five minutes was tantamount to suicide, and only complete healing magic could guarantee at least some kind of salvation. Another unpleasant thing was that there was no light at the rot-infected levels. The blue crystals did not work, as they quickly became coated in green fungus. And, as a final kicker, the beasts reacted extremely negatively toward any sort of illumination, be it light crystal, torch or lantern.

And you think that sounds bad? If only that was it! Even ordinary clothing became infected with a fungus and began to infect its wearer. If the clothes were not removed, the person died. Once again, the only defense was complete healing. You couldn't go into the rift without *Heal*. The current descent record, level twenty-eight, belonged to the Gourfan Clan. Of the fifty rift conquerors trained to the highest level, only ten people had gotten out of the rift. They couldn't get past the guards.

But this group was working with a standard rift. No one knew what an infected rift with a rot infestation would bring. For example, normal rifts of level twenty-five and above didn't produce a haze from rot. And yet there it was, and not just on the surface, also on the first three levels. The Gourfans wouldn't go any lower. That's why they had me. About ten minutes later the blacksmiths appeared and began to fit a full steel suit of armor to my body. And I had to wear the steel on my naked body. Magister Meram actively strengthened the armor with various symbols, even a few whole words. Everything took more than an hour, and when I was considered ready, the rift had begun to close. The runescribe finally hit me with a communication symbol, and I couldn't dodge it. I simply hadn't expected such a nasty trick from Magister Meram. He placed the symbol when my back was to him, and in a place that I couldn't touch in polite society. Magister Meram connected me with Cedric Jode, my potential relative. They weren't yet aware of the fact that I didn't plan to take Naira as my wife.

The armor certainly didn't make it any easier to breathe. The rot still easily penetrated wherever it wanted. However, using the *Heal* stone once every half a minute completely cleared the inside of the armor of rot, and it had to refill the available space. So *Heal* destroyed rot...Hmm...What if...

A level fifteen *Healing Aura* filled the surrounding space, completely burning out the very mention of rot. A simple, unreliable, useless ability in most cases worked great. I removed my helmet and took a deep breath. No rot. Jumping into the hole, I turned around and sighed heavily. The rift had closed. I had just over twenty-five hours left to reach the thirty-first level of this madness. And, what unnerved me most was that I wouldn't be able to use *Healing Aura* inside the rift. Because the rift beasts will immediately see me as an enemy. I had the sneaking suspicion that I was in deep trouble by agreeing to this recklessness. Although, to be honest, I didn't have much of a choice. I'd wanted to get into a level twenty-five rift or below to gather resources to level up my stones? Dream accomplished. Next time I'd only dream of busty lasses. It would be safer that way.

Chapter 15

TROUBLE FOUND ME in the first cave. I don't know what the Gourfans were doing here, but the kronas hadn't gone anywhere. Six creatures sat in the center of the cave and, as soon as they were touched by *Healing Aura,* they rushed at me in a blind lust for blood. The monsters were not interested in the fact that they saw me as the same beast as them. They only wanted to take out the one who was doing them wrong. *Golden Dome of Protection* threw the kronas back, and they spread over the stones as a repulsive dark liquid. I had four steel cubes hanging from my belt. Two of them contained levels five and eighteen, and it was the last one that I unleashed now, smearing the beasts into the ground. The other two cubes were empty. I was going to put creatures from levels twenty-five and thirty in them. As long as they were there, these ousels. It would be an unpleasant surprise to find no floating yellow spheres in this rift. *Devour* automatically dragged some pieces into the inventory; I was even too lazy to figure out which ones specifically. What was important was the fact that without a healing aura, I would not be able to burn out rot in the air, and with it, all the creatures of this rift would rush at me. For I would be their greatest adversary.

I reached level five in about thirty minutes. I didn't want to travel floor to floor, searching out beasts in every cave. But this level had a range, so I had to devote some extra time — this is where the first exclusive beasts would be found. I even flipped off *Healing Aura,* since the rift inhabitants died before I even approached them. The effect was instant — the rot in the air attacked me with redoubled force. I had to take extreme measures. Holding my breath, I cleared the room of red creatures, tearing out their essence, then turned on the aura, destroying all the remaining monsters and rot, after which I inhaled, held my breath again, turned off the healing aura and ran into the next cave to get the rest of the exclusives. Not the most convenient, but quite effective. The rot didn't affect me and I got the spoils. True, it was infuriating that I had to leave all the magic stones behind — I didn't have a backpack. And one more thing: the essences of creatures subject to rot were different from standard essences. My inventory delegated a special spot for them, and the recipes for creating a set from the *Thunderer* set adjusted. For example, while the simplest gloves cost fifteen normal krona essences, there was now an additional line saying that I could spend only ten rot-infested krona essences on those same gloves. The difference was quite noticeable. Moreover, the essences themselves began to be ranked by level, transforming my inventory into an incredibly complex organizational system. If I had not seen the original, parsing the current one would have become much more difficult.

There was no point in clearing all of Level Five. As soon as I saw the descent to Level Six, I took it, leaving the loot behind. The only resource vital to me now was time. Unfortunately, even *Devour* couldn't give me another twenty-four hours.

The journey to Level Nine was marked by a new event: resources finally began to appear in the inventory. In particular, vyrma, as the remaining slots of low-level crystals were filled to capacity. There was not much valuable metal, but it was enough to understand the main point: at low levels, rot did not affect resources. They do not lose their properties.

Level Nine gave me pause — this is where the exclusive rapses began to spawn. *Phantom* and *Silent Tread* were too valuable stones to just throw away. I had to take a risk and pull off my helmet, where these stones fell. While moving between caves, I had to hold my breath as the haze from the rot began to affect me more strongly, it tickled my nose and sore throat, but I simply could not leave these stones behind. I needed my own army of invisible people!

My brain switched on again at Level Seventeen, when I started choking after each cave. The rot here was so dense that I couldn't see more than five meters in front of my face. When I turned on *Healing Aura* to disperse all this smog, it reminded me of the good old days, when I had to actively fight with dark beasts. One thing was good: the monsters could not do anything with my protective dome and my mithril glove worked real miracles. Having cleared the room in this way so that I could once again breathe, I cast *Heal* on myself in order to drive out even the tiniest particles of rot, and opened my inventory. It would be impossible to move further without a helmet, but I couldn't even raise my hand for a whole armful of exclusive stones. So I decided to create a helmet myself! I had seven recipes from the *Thunderer* set, so all that was left was to figure out which one would be most effective as a backpack. I settled on the helmet: the depth and the seal created by the visor gave me hope that I wouldn't be using these resources in vain. Except that there was a problem with essences — I didn't want to spend high-level stones on something that would be given away. In the end, I settled on a dozen rot-prone krone essences. An object shimmering with green gold appeared in my hands, and this time I could not resist trying it out. It was interesting how much the choice of parameters depended on the place where the parameters were selected. I put the helmet on my head, for a few moments the world plunged into complete darkness, but then everything returned to its original form. Except, perhaps, for the notification I received:

Helmet from the *Thunderer* set. *2 parameters available. Increase lightning damage by 50%, lightning damage penetrates 10% lightning resistance. Recruitment bonus: none. Additional parameters may be revealed by a rarer essence.*

I grinned. Kimal Sarento would probably give an arm and a leg for a full *Thunderer* set. I'd need to send him a description. As I understood it, the stats did not actually depend on the location in which they were crafted. It turned out that it didn't even matter which essence you used initially, be it a krona or a master. From the postscript, it seemed like the item could be improved at any time, as long as you had the resources.

The only sad thing was that this item was practically useless to me. Switching to a lightning attack would mean a definite loss for me. My fighting style was strange as is — I was sort of a mage, but was still constantly trying to get into close combat so that I could destroy the enemy with the help of vyrma or mithril. In extreme cases, there is always the reliable *Dark Spike* that would scatter opponents in all directions.

The helmet was extremely capacious — almost twice as much space on the inside as my previous one. With the helmet on, I immediately felt the difference. Breathing came much easier.

Level Seventeen, which was the third range, I had to clear almost completely, as the descent to the next floor was located in the farthest cave. Rotten essences and *Amplify* shards flowed towards me like a deep river, so I had no right to be indignant. I flew through the eighteenth and nineteenth levels almost instantly, as the passages were near each other. The pressure of the dark influence slowly started to creep up, but it was still tolerable. The rings did their job. I had immediately donned everything the dark ones gave me, except for the one uninitiated ring. The later I waited to do this, the stronger the ring would be. Sure, I'd have to give three back to the Gourfans, but who said I had to return all of them? Compared to the other two, this ring was significantly weaker. For me, +1 to my *Mana* parameter would not make much of a difference.

On Level Twenty-Four, I made a pitstop. I needed rest and a thorough healing — I was frankly tired of coughing up blood. The effects of *Heal* only lasted ten seconds, then the rot again crept into all my pores, transforming me into a revolting corpse of a man. Ulcers and scabs appeared all over the body; it was scary to even think about what must be happening inside. Holding my breath did little to help. Considering the amount of healing magic that I was pouring into myself, I should have been downing a whole cart of mana elixirs. *Golden Dome of Protection* remained permanently on, and I began to wonder if it was even doing anything. From what I could tell, it wasn't! Rot easily passed through my defensive line, ignored the dark mirror, and only *Heal* allowed me to still feel relatively alive.

The cave had already been cleared, so I turned on *Healing Aura* and grimaced. The density of the rot decreased significantly, but I was not able to completely drive it away. My stone was still too low level! Opening my inventory, I pulled out the recipe for increasing stone levels and tossed in all the necessary ingredients. The Fortress had sold me a whole box of empty elixir bottles, and what pleased me most was that they fit perfectly into my inventory. Crafting five elixirs was easy enough, and soon my *Healing Aura* was level twenty. It helped — the cave was completely cleared of rot. I had to do a similar thing with *Heal* and, just in case, *Golden Dome of Protection*. Now I'd be ready to have another sparring session with Kimal Sarento. However, I didn't stop there and for the first time since receiving the functionality, I removed one magic stone from the field. *Healing Aura* had only one facet, so I had to take a risk and put *Cost Reduction* in the free field. Instead, I inserted the level-three *Amplify* that I had just created. I had a huge amount of fragments.

I didn't have to wait long for the result. Not only did this significantly strengthen the power of my healing magic, but also the range. Dark beasts immediately rushed towards me from a nearby cave, forcing me to jump up and prepare for battle. However, no battle occurred — *Healing Aura* slowed the creatures down until they were moving at a snail's pace. Moreover, these were elite monsters, not some common runts. All that remained for me was to finish off the monsters and regretfully throw their stones on the floor. Only two facets.

The new improvements gave me strength, and without turning off the aura, I descended to level twenty five. The level at which, in normal rifts, rot began to spawn. The very first cave on this floor showed me that everything I had experienced thus far had been a cakewalk compared to what was coming. There was absolutely no light, so I had to use a light crystal. The green fungus was everywhere, covering the space in a soft, dense carpet. My steel-toed boots were covered with soot, so the rot tried to eat away at them, but couldn't break through. The density of the haze here was lower than at the level above, which seemed quite surprising to me. I could even see the opposite wall. *Healing Aura* began to actively drive the rot away, starting from the air, ending with the slime covering the stones. A terrible stench arose as the rot reluctantly burned away, making one final attempt to poison me. If there were six more levels of this ahead, I was in for it.

Level Twenty-Five was a range, so the beasts here let me know how unwelcome I was right away. Six krona-like creatures rushed at me from all sides. While *Healing Aura* slowed them down, it did so very subtly. The monsters moved with monstrous speed and, if I had not bothered to increase my defense, they could have devoured me in a few moments. The dome held, although it began to drain mana like crazy.

Attempts to reach them with my gloves didn't bring any success. They were exponentially faster than me and managed to jump away before I could touch them. The vyrma bolt also didn't do much — the beasts managed to dodge. Not the nicest situation to find myself in. I was starting to consider making a tactical retreat and asking the Gourfans through Cedric how they managed to pass through two levels with such fast creatures, when my gaze fell on the *Heal* icon. My most used ability in this rift. My thoughts began racing even faster than the twenty-fifth level kronas. Fixing my gaze on my opponent, I cast *Heal.* Since the aura alone could slow down opponents, targeted healing should stop them in their tracks!

It worked perfectly. The creature froze, allowing me to use *Dash* and rip out the essence in one swift motion. *Devour* once again ran wild, throwing a strange selection of pieces from the dead beast into my inventory. Moreover, this time it acted with utmost efficiency. All that was left of the krona-like creature was a magic stone. Everything else, including flesh, skin and bones, and even amulet blanks, went to my intangible storage.

Dash! Why didn't I think of it before? I turned toward the other monsters and in a flash was next to my next target. I couldn't stun them, but I did manage to knock the beast off its feet and, while it was trying to buck and jump away, I spared it from this condition called life. Once again everything fell into my inventory bins except for the magic stone. I had developed a strategy for destroying the creatures, and soon there was not a trace left of the six dangerous opponents. I looked into my notebook to see what I had encountered. I shouldn't have used *Analyze,* which, by the way, already had three third-level *Amplify*s attached! If it failed to break through the blocking amulets after this, then I didn't even know why I had it in the first place. I'd remove it and put something useful in its place.

The thing in the picture was clearly once a krona. An oblong pillow on four thin legs with three joints and a growth that acted as a head. But life in the rot took its toll on the krona — its body had been changed beyond recognition. Tentacles had sprouted, the body was significantly deformed, the head had disappeared, the once dense skin was covered with ugly dark veins, scabs and ulcers. But I was especially horrified by the teeth: they had become even bigger, even more dangerous. The notebook made sure to make a special point of this. The current iteration of this creature did not have a name, but the notebook had assigned it the name "Rotten Krona."

"Max, what are *Add* shards?" I heard Alia ask. My personal attendant was worried about how things were going and was keeping a close eye on the changes to the notebook. I didn't immediately understand what she was talking about until I came across a note on the rotten krona — it produced fragments not of *Amplify*, but of a certain *Add*. Six dangerous creatures gave me six fragments, but I did not receive the same notifications as before. *Devour* now took everything into the inventory without informing me.

Opening the list of available shards, I stared at the strange image. Yes, there was a new line for *Add*, but it didn't list a maximum quantity. As if these fragments could be accumulated indefinitely. But the strangest thing was that next to the lines *Amplify, Augment* and *Mentor,* a small green plus appeared. I mentally clicked on the plus sign next to *Augment*, since I didn't have this stone yet, and chuckled at the effect. The number of *Add* shards went down, and the number of *Augment* shards increased by one. Oh, wow! That was Skron-damned convenient!

As if it had been waiting for me to do this, the pages of the notebook began to fill again — information about all types of fragments, including ones dropped in the Fog of Pharapho, as well as methods for obtaining and using them. Alia piped up:

"Max, I have a proposal. I want to test a theory."

"Alia, I'm cleaning out an infected rift here! What kind of test?"

"It's important. About *Devour*."

"If so, then go ahead," I was surprised.

"Look, in the archives that I managed to find about the first emperor, it said he had a fifth-level

Devour."

"Can you imagine what a huge inventory Kimal Sarento must have?" I couldn't resist making a remark.

"Don't interrupt. Look, in order to get *Amplify* to the next level, you need to take nine stones from the previous one. The situation is most likely similar with the other two stones. But we know that it is impossible to obtain a second *Devour.* This means that this method does not work with this stone. Just as cement through elixirs does not work. I thought about this for a long time and came to an interesting conclusion: what if you increase *Devour* by using nine exclusive stones?"

"It would be too simple," I answered, but still thought about it. I had enough stones; pulling out a rare one and returning it back takes just a minute. I wanted to take a break anyway, right? I'd wait until Level Twenty-Five and then I'd do it. It will still take me some time to adapt — despite the rings, the aura of the rift was already beginning to affect me. It was impossible to take food with me, so I began to gradually turn into Magister Meram — a shriveled up poisonous mushroom.

"But should you check?" Alia said, refusing to let up. "Will it take a long time to do?"

"Gimme a couple of seconds," I reassured her and removed *Devour* from the magical field. I instantly felt a pang in my soul, as if I had torn out a part of myself. A vital part. The status bar faded a bit, and many different icons appeared that had previously been collected in one place. It was so disturbing that it even overpowered the dark influence for a while. I looked at the stone, memorizing its pictogram. I had never held *Devour* in my hands before. Placing the stone on the floor, I placed nine *Phantom*s around it. An expensive pleasure, of course, but something needed to be sacrificed. Unfortunately, nothing happened — the stones remained still, making no move to unite and integrate into a cohesive whole.

"Nothing." I took the stones back, but hesitating, decided to leave *Devour* in place. Alia correctly noted that this stone cannot be upgraded using the standard method. Nor using nine regular red stones. But what if the exclusive stones were not quite ordinary? Not the ones dropped by monsters, but ones that need to be collected from fragments?

A moment later, three magical octahedrons shining with red light appeared in my hands. *Amplify, Augment* and *Mentor.* The first increased the parameters of support stones, the second increased their quality, and the third increased the amount of mana consumed. An important stone, by the way, for any person who does not have *Praxis. Devour* was already on the floor, and I began to lay stones around it, drawing lines from each edge. It wasn't perfect, but it didn't seem like it needed to be. Either it would work or it wouldn't. It wasn't a matter of accurate placement.

Devour level increased.

The flash almost blinded me. It was even brighter than my light stone! Rubbing my eyes, I stared at the floor. The three octahedrons had disappeared, leaving behind only burnt stones. *Devour* had not changed in appearance. I grabbed the stone and, burning with impatience, returned it to my magical field. Level Two. My inventory had reached Level Two! A strange sensation arose, as if the air around me had begun to be drawn into my body. It lasted only a moment and immediately subsided, but the results were clear: all the resources that were previously at the maximum level increased to 450 conventional units. Plus one hundred and fifty units! It was not just a lot, it was a monstrously large amount.

"We need to start hunting for converts," Alia said thoughtfully, and I completely agreed with her. Logic dictated that in order to upgrade *Devour* to the next level, I'd need to feed it three valuable stones of the second level. And so on, ad infinitum.

"Or just hunting in rot-infected rifts," I corrected. "*Add* is a substitute for any stone."

"How much time do you have left?"

"A little over sixteen hours. Currently at Level Twenty-Five. The beasts here aren't giving me an easy time. The kronas almost tore me apart. And there are six more levels ahead."

"Then let's not be heroic. To destroy faults with rot, you need time to study it. Understand its nature and how to fight back. You can't get by with just a mirror…"

My mood improved significantly after talking

with Alia. It was telling that we managed to increase the level of the *Devour*, albeit almost by accident. What a bastard Kimal was! If he surrounded his stone with eight *Amplify*s, then his inventory could hold all the loot from all the rifts of this world! I wonder if he had a status bar?

My speed dropped to a minimum. I had to completely destroy the caves through which I moved. At some point I even turned off *Healing Aura* and hid the light crystal to try to slip past the creatures unnoticed, but the dense fog of rot that immediately rushed to fill the cave almost finished me off. I had to double back, heal myself, and continue progressing according to the previous strategy.

I found the ousels in the second-to-last cave. Like all creatures of the twenty-fifth level, it turned out to be significantly altered. The creature no longer looked like a blooming yellow ball floating freely in the air. Now it was something filthy, unpleasant, devoid of any growths. The monster rushed towards me, and I was able to stop it only by continuously casting *Heal*. Placing the monster in a steel box, I watched with repulsion as rot began to creep over the surface. In just a few moments, the creature had dissolved the steel and rushed at me again. I had to tear out its vile essence and accept the fact that the maximum level of my ultimate weapon was twenty-four. And even then, I'd have to go find it in an ordinary rift.

At level twenty-six problems began. I realized that I was gradually suffocating. I hadn't given my body enough of a break and the darkness had begun to take its toll. The unpleasant pressure on my solar plexus wouldn't let up, even after three doses of *Heal*. *Devour* absorbed resources from the twenty-fifth level, but nothing I could use to raise the levels of stones by another five units. The creatures attacked in batches and died in droves. I trudged forward on sheer willpower, and after a few caves I was lucky — I found the next descent. As I stepped through, I nearly lost consciousness. The rings I had now were not sufficient to help me feel comfortable. My body fought back and tried to adapt, but I was descending too quickly. I should never have agreed to this with no food rations.

With a trembling hand, I pulled out the uninitiated ring from the helmet with magic stones, put it on over my mithril gloves and fell to my knees. The strength had drained from my body and I needed another break.

Exclusive ring of the stubborn rift conqueror. *Significantly reduces the influence of darkness, significantly reduces the influence of rot, allows you to block rot infection, grants the passive ability Rot Breath, grants the passive ability Rot Vision.*

My mind became clearer, as if someone had suddenly removed a bag I'd had tied around my head! Two new icons appeared on the quick access panel, which explained the essence of what was happening. *Rot Breath* allowed one to breathe air saturated with rot without any consequences for the body, *Rot Vision* allowed one to somehow use rot as lighting. I hid the light crystal in my helmet, covered the crystal with magic stones, and gulped. The space that had previously been hidden from me by impenetrable darkness was now in full view. It was lit in an eerie green light, but visibility was high! Switching off *Healing Aura,* I braced myself for pain, but none came. Recognizing the ring at level twenty-six played a role. The Gourfans definitely weren't getting this back. Something told me that the cunning dark ones had more than a dozen such rings, but they didn't want to share them with me. They'd be asked to "surrender" them to the Temple of Skron. We'd see how the Gourfans would get out of that one.

"Maximilian, we have a problem," Cedric Jode's voice appeared in my head. "Four ordered you to tell me that the Temple of Skron made a mistake in its calculations. The next rift will be absorbed in ten hours, not fifteen. You need to hurry!"

Was he joking?! I'd need to bust my ass and burst all my blood vessels for them again?!

Chapter 16

LEVEL TWENTY-SIX, SURPRISINGLY, was a walk in the park. Thanks to my new ring, I did not need to use *Healing Aura*, which allowed me to return to my usual method of conquering rifts. I simply walked past the monsters, stopping only next to especially valuable creatures, took their essence and ingredients, sighed heavily, looking at the next red stone, and threw it away, contemplating how unpleasant this monstrous muck was and how no one should face it without preparation. Why was I thinking this now? Because I had to walk through the last levels naked! Just before I reached Level Twenty-Six, my steel armor became covered with a thick layer of rot and, as soon as I walked through several caves in the dense dark fog, looking for a passage to the twenty-seventh level, it began to fall off. The steel was actually rotting, no matter how unusual it may seem. A similar situation happened with my ousel cubes — they had been completely eaten through. My ultimate weapon had simply crumbled to pieces. The two yellow balls inside were shredded into tiny bits before they even reached the floor, decaying midair. A similar situation happened to the helmet I'd crafted. First, all of its precious contents melted into one solid mass, then dissipated, including the light crystal headpiece, after which the rot began directly on the helmet. It devoured the thing almost entirely, with one exception. When all the contents disappeared from the helmet, and the inventory refused to accept the rotted armor, I tossed the remains aside as useless, and *Devour* finally kicked in. It had taken two kilograms of vyrma to create the helmet and exactly the same amount was returned. The rot had no effect! The notebook immediately recorded this with the note "requires more research." Because now I needed new cubes that could hold beasts above Level Twenty-Five. The only thing that the rot did not affect was the mithril gloves and what they hid underneath. I should definitely look into making mithril armor. I needed mages, and now I knew exactly where to get them: I'd make them myself! I had the stones, elixirs, and, most importantly, the human resources! All I had to do now was get out of the rift alive and preferably in one piece.

I had to crawl down to Level Twenty-Nine, which was the final range. Not because the darkness was pressing so hard on me, or because the rot was ingrained in my skin and threatening to dissolve my bones. It was even more banal — I was starving to death. The darkness couldn't break through the rings, but my body still couldn't cope. It was devouring itself, trying to find the smallest grain of additional energy. I was already smeared from head to toe with rot. The beasts didn't even acknowledge me, and not because of the dark mirror, but because to them, I had turned into a moving piece of furniture. Nevertheless, I cleared the level entirely, making sure to pass through each cave. The essences I mined here ended up at the very end of the recipe list. They were even superior to the Riftmaster essences that I was able to obtain from low rifts, and, if I understood correctly, set items crafted from them would have at least five different properties. Five! I'd craft a whole suit of armor, stick Alia inside, and there won't be a bastard in the world able to defeat her...

"Maximilian, we're starting to get concerned! There's only an hour left! How are you faring?"

"How am I faring? I'm practically a corpse. I've got the guards ahead of me," I replied with a wheezing cough. My four main stones were already level twenty five, but this was no longer enough. *Heal* couldn't cope, *Healing Aura* was powerless against the dense clouds of rot, the darkness pressed me into the floor, and for the last two hours I crawled on my hands and knees, unable to rise to my feet. One hour... I only needed a minute to gather my strength and enter the last cave, but where could I find the strength to gather?

I tried everything possible, forcing myself to get up. It was all futile. A huge cave with thirty-one guards was nearby, behind the last corridor. Essentially, all I had to do was crawl through them, get to the Riftmaster and finish it off, but it simply wasn't working. Just now I noticed that all my amulets, including the gift from the Bartolomeo Clan, had been destroyed — darkness blocking, fatal damage blocking, interference in the rube scribe guidance system — even the stone hiding me from *Analyze* had vanished without a trace! The rot had stripped me completely! It had even chewed through my hair and easily devoured everything that appeared in my hands. To test this, I had manifested a krona essence, and it dissipated in an instant! Rot was deadly. If it weren't for the ring, I would have died four levels ago. But now in front of me lay only one cave, thirty-one guards and the Master. And the full realization that I would not make it to the end.

"Max, we have guests," Alia's voice said suddenly. "Kimal Sarento is in Hearth."

"What does he need?" I croaked.

"He and his wife have remote communication. Adeline is near your rift, acting as the deputy head of the clan. She told her husband where you were sent and why. Kimal came to help."

"I'm on Level Thirty One. No strength. No potions. Nothing left. How can he help?"

"That's why he came. Via portal, if you're interested. I had to tell him why your own remote communication sigil with him had burned off. But the chancellor knows about rot and its effect on humans. He said that you must now look like a skeleton, lying naked on the floor, exhausted. *Heal* doesn't help. Kimal says you are in front of a cave with guards."

"Correct. I can't go further."

"Max, I can give you some of my power," Alia said. "You and I are connected. We're having a child together. A part of you is in me. Kimal Sarento brought an artifact that allows for the transfer of powers between parents. It is usually used to ensure that a man can give part of his power to a pregnant woman, but it can also travel in the opposite direction. I know where you are and what is happening to you. You need help. We're almost out of time. If I don't give you strength, you will die."

"If you could transfer powers without consequence, you would have already done it." Somehow, I found the strength to string together such a long sentence.

"That's right. There are consequences. By giving you my power, I will kill our child and, most likely, myself."

"No!" I barked and started coughing, nearly hacking up my own lungs.

"Max, I'm not asking. I'm letting you know. I wanted you to be aware before I did it. Right now, it's not about me or our child. There is a task that needs to be completed to save hundreds of thousands of people. Light, dark — it doesn't matter. The important thing is that they stay alive. One life — okay, even two lives, is not worth thousands. You must close this rift, and I am ready to give you everything I have."

"Alia, no!" I cried again. My rage gave me strength, and I managed to get onto all fours. "I'll do it! Myself! Don't you touch that artifact! I'll do it! Promise! Promise me!"

A bloody veil appeared before my eyes, blocking my view. But I no longer paid attention to such trifles. Kimal was a monster! He knew perfectly well what would happen to Alia if she used the artifact, but he brought it anyway! The beast! What low-life scum he was! Not even human. This was a man who deserved only one thing: death! If Alia didn't listen to me, if she used the artifact...I would wipe the magic academy off the face of the planet! The whole world would forget that Kimal Sarento ever existed!

I didn't remember how I crawled through the huge cave with the guards. There was only one thought in my head: if I collapse, Alia will commit a monstrous and irreparable act. Once again, they wanted to take my family away from me, but now I had the power to prevent this. As long as I didn't collapse and completed the task. Alia must not use the artifact, and I would kill Kimal Sarento the first chance I got!

The Master of this infected rift had been changed beyond recognition. Once upon a time it had been a cube, in the center of which a huge heart beat. The heart was now so large that it bulged between the ribs on all sides, trying to escape its cage and continue expanding. As with human hearts, this one had huge veins, from which clouds of rot flew out every second, which immediately dissolved into the surrounding air. Next to the Riftmaster was a projection of a new beast being spawned, and, if my vision served me right, it was the metamorph. The creature was almost entirely formed. All that was left to complete was the lower part. Three or four hours and the metamorph would be fully manifested. If the Temple of Skron's calculations were correct, I would take a risk and wait for the incarnation. I couldn't say no to another level thirty-one ring. But I didn't have that kind of time.

"Max, I..."

"Alia, no! I'm already at the Master!" there was no time to evaluate the creature. Just in case, I used *Analyze* to put this monster in my notebook, I crawled to the place and stuck my glove inside the creature, tearing out its essence. That was it, it was over! The Skron-damned rift had been destroyed, and my future wife would live! As would our child!

I had no idea how long I lay next to the motionless Master. As the rot vanished, so did my vision, so I found myself in complete darkness, periodically falling into unconsciousness. There was a constant buzz of voices in my head. Alia, Cedric, even Eleanore. But I couldn't make out what exactly they were saying. I lay there just glad that Alia was still talking to me. She hadn't taken advantage of Kimal Sarento's monstrous gift. She was alive!

When I opened my eyes again, I saw light. It got closer and expanded to fill my field of vision and I saw a room of people — clan heads, the commander, a Temple servant, several supreme converts and rift conquerors, and some others. One of the dark ones leaned over me and poured several recovery elixirs into my mouth, which spread warmth throughout my body. Even if they didn't do much, the sensation alone was wonderful.

"What, you burned my seal off?" Magister Meram said, surprised. The old man also reached depths that no modern man had ever been before. Unable to move, I opened my inventory and without much emotion, looked at the three more units of lyog obtained by *Devour*. My stone took everything most valuable from this level, even when I was unconscious. Including these three suspicious stones. I had a bad feeling about how these pebbles could be used. I needed a rift to test it.

"What a mess!" The rune scribe made a pass with his hand, and several symbols appeared in front of me, forming a word that was so familiar to me. "How many rifts does that leave him?"

"There is no need to impose restrictions on him," the commander said in a deep voice, to which the old runescribe only snorted:

"It's not for you to decide, Light One! I want you to have one and I'm sealing it on you! Five rifts a year, I think, should suffice. If you need help with rifts like this, I will increase the number by one. No, stop! You removed it with dark fire, right? Of course, what else? I don't see any burns. So. This means we need to make sure that this doesn't happen again. But how? We'll have to think on it a while. Making the same mistake twice is unbefitting of me. Hmm...What an interesting dilemma."

The old man became immersed in his thoughts, losing all interest in me.

"You have completed your task, Rift Conqueror. The Temple of Skron will prepare your reward and see that it is sent to Hearth," said the Temple servant. He approached the creature that was once the Riftmaster — only a skeleton remained. Everything else was in my inventory.

"I would like to receive information about the appearance and parameters of this monster. The Temple of Skron is willing to pay you well for this information."

"Where are our rings?" Naina of the Gourfan Clan stood above me, staring down at my hands. There was nothing there, and the mithril gloves had adjusted to fit my considerably bonier fingers.

"From what I see, they have dissolved," remarked the servant of the Temple of Skron. "Just like the armor, steel cubes and amulets. The rot took everything with it. All that remains is an exclusive amulet from the Riftmaster. I believe that the rift conqueror has every right to it. Commander?"

"The Citadel doesn't need dark trinkets," he replied, but Naina clearly did not let up. The nasty woman even flipped me over, thinking that I was lying on something valuable. She didn't care that I was naked.

"If there are no rings or amulets left, how did he survive? Why wasn't he eaten away by rot?"

"He used *Heal* and *Healing Aura,*" someone suggested.

"Where did he get so much mana?"

"It's easy to check," said the Temple servant. "The rift conqueror does not have an amulet that blocks *Analyze.* I think Cedric Jode has already seen everything."

"Well? Where does he get his mana from?" Naina turned sharply to Adeline's brother, but he remained unperturbed:

"Information on the stones and development parameters of Maximilian Valevsky is a secret of the Bartolomeo Clan. We do not intend to reveal the abilities of one of our members."

"The light one does not belong to your clan!" she barked back.

"He is Naira Jode's fiancée," Cedric answered. "That makes him an important part of our clan. The clan council decided that the Hunter of Darkness would be considered the highest hierarch of the clan, temporarily residing outside the clan."

"Four rings!" The Gourfans weren't going to let it go that easily. "He destroyed four of our rings!"

"And our heirloom as well," Cedric nodded. "This is the sacrifice we made in order to be able to stand here having this discussion now. If it weren't for the rings and the amulet, the rift conqueror would not have been able to reach the Master. And we would have to do it ourselves. Or lose most of our lands. Your lands as well, Naina Moises. The entire Gourfan Clan. Maximilian Valevsky is associated with the Bartolomeo Clan, and we believe that you owe us a great debt."

"The Temple of Skron believes that all debate on this issue is now moot. As well as questions about why the Gourfan Clan did not provide rings that block the influence of rot. We will discuss this issue separately, in another place and in another format. Now the rift conqueror is in a monstrous state. He needs recovery. We will open a portal to Hearth and return him home. As promised."

"He will not be returning to Hearth!" the commander unexpectedly declared. "The dark doomed soldier named Max will appear before the court of the Citadel conclave! He refused to carry out the order of the commander of the Citadel, refused to fulfill his duty. The Conclave will make its just decision and determine his punishment."

"Max, Adeline is reporting everything that's happening to Kimal," Alia's voice rang out. "The chancellor demands that you remain silent and agree to everything. Even if you are sent to the Citadel and called a doomed soldier. The High Priest will get you out. Just don't interfere."

Gathering my will into a fist, I did the incredible: I put my hand on my thigh, where there was a symbol of connection with my future wife.

Fortunately, this required minimal movement.

"Kick him out!" I growled. My words barely resembled speech, but Alia got the gist.

"Max, there's no reason to kick him out. There was no artifact. Kimal Sarento asked me to tell you that I would sacrifice my child and myself to motivate you. If you don't believe me, look for yourself: there are no artifacts in the notebook. Forgive me, Max, but we couldn't help you any other way. This was the only way you could get through this rift. We'll discuss it when you return. For now, just stay quiet. The commander is violating every rule the Citadel has. Apparently, he was only recently given this position and does not yet understand the basic principles of the relationship between light and dark.

"The Temple of Skron promised to deliver Maximilian Valevsky to Hearth," the Temple servant said, unexpectedly taking my side. "Does the Citadel Commander want us to break our word?"

"I care nothing for your words and promises!" He wasn't backing down. "The doomed soldier will go to the Citadel, where he will stand trial. And only they will decide his future fate. Or does the Temple of Skron wish to challenge my decision?"

"Magister Meram?" The misty servant turned to the runescribe who was sitting nearby and scribbling something in his books. Raising his head, the old man looked at everyone with an indifferent gaze, after which he returned to his notes, ignoring the question.

"Magister Meram!" The Temple servant raised his voice.

"What do you want from me?" the old man answered irritably, looking up from his notes. "Valevsky will not go anywhere until I finish developing a new block. One you cannot burn out with dark fire. Then do whatever you want with him, it doesn't matter to me. If you don't show up for training this year, I won't accept you for another five years. That's all I have to say. That's it, shut up everyone. I'm sick of you all."

"I need a portal to the Citadel," the commander said. Surprisingly, no one dared to resist. Except for the runescribe. Magister Meram looked up from his notebook and said:

"Do my ears deceive me? Has the Citadel decided to ignore my words? Is this the official position of the Church of the Light or the will of a specific commander?"

"The dark doomer will go to the Citadel after the seals are applied to him," the light one retorted. "We need a portal so that the dark ones don't throw some kind of surprise. This doomed soldier will appear before the Conclave!"

"That's better," Magister Meram snorted, continuing to fiddle with the notebook. The servant of the Temple of Skron silently looked at the commander, and it was as if a battle was being waged between them on levels inaccessible to mere mortals.

"The Temple of Skron agrees with the Citadel's decision. The Riftmaster will be sent to the Citadel. Open the portal!"

"Finally!" Magister Meram exclaimed joyfully. "Got it! Now let's see how you cope with these runes! So they decided to burn everything off with dark fire. Won't work here! Magister Meram can handle it. So, Valevsky, lie still and don't move. It might hurt a little. In fact, it will most definitely hurt. You'll have to be patient. Or not. I don't care. Cover his mouth. I don't like it when someone screams while I'm working. These symbols will have to be applied to the body manually."

One of the converts rushed to carry out the order of the evil old man, and everything inside me sank. The journey to the Citadel did not frighten me as much as the rift-restricting runes. Although the trial that the commander threatened here did not make me too happy either. I didn't expect anything good from the Church of the Light. Nor from the Temple of Skron. They had just clearly demonstrated that even on their own territory, they are ready to bend to the will of just one commander, forgetting all about their own promise. Who said that they would not renounce their words later of their own volition? The precedent had already been set.

Magister Meram leaned over me, and there was unbridled madness in his gaze. He didn't care at all about my pain, my attitude to what was happening, or the opinions of others. He only did what he wanted. And didn't do what he didn't want to do. Why was he given this free reign? Was it really just because of the rifts? Was everyone really ready to put up with this bastard's incursions, just so as not to trudge into the rifts themselves? Now this old man would get rid of his potential competitor and would once again breathe freely.

How tired I was of being treated like an obedient little pawn to be used for anyone's purposes! Enough! There were forty-two sealed rifts down to Level Twenty-Five in the world, and who knew what would happen to them if Magister Meram was gone? As far as I remembered, all symbols disappeared if their scribe died. I didn't remember who said it, but the information had slipped through to my brain. Did the same principle work with rifts? Maybe. Maybe not. For these were seals, and not just some symbols on the body. Well then, whatever happened would happen! Since both the light and the dark were dependent on Magister Meram, I had to do everything to make them dependent on me instead!

Gathering all the strength that I'd gained after downing the recovery potions, I prepared to deliver a single blow. I wouldn't have another chance. Magister Meram even stuck out his tongue in his zeal as he drew symbols on my stomach. They burned, but not so much that I started screaming. Or was this just the beginning, and soon it would completely engulf me? The runescribe moved closer to get a more comfortable angle, and at that moment I struck.

The mithril glove easily pierced the rotten old man's chest as if it were paper. It flashed brightly several times — the fatal-damage-blocking amulets were trying to save their wielder, but it was difficult to do this when his heart was already outside his body. The old man's thigh caught fire — the *Az* symbol burned there. But even this absolute protection was powerless against the mithril glove. The supreme convert holding me reacted too late. He threw me aside only after Magister Meram had collapsed on the floor, staring at the ceiling with glassy eyes. I hit the wall and lost consciousness. The last thing I saw before clocking out was the notification in front of my eyes:

Runescribe skill has been updated.

That was it. Apparently, my studies in Al-Khorezm would be delayed indefinitely.

Chapter 17

I RETURNED TO CONSCIOUSNESS extremely reluctantly. Reality constantly eluded me, like a fidgety mistress. It seemed that I was about to catch her, but then the darkness was sweeter and closer. It didn't want to let me go, plunging me into the black over and over again. It was nice, cozy. Only one thought haunted me: where was I, exactly? Surely I had been snuffed out for good, and this was when I would meet either Skron or the Light. If so, then this was a rather strange place, because the malicious and extremely unwanted voice of Kimal Sarento was ringing throughout it:

"How long are you going to lie around? Get up, you self-taught hero, and face the consequences of what you've done."

This was enough to bring me back to reality and I opened my eyes. My soul sank deep into the bowels of the earth: I was in a prison cell, the walls, floor and ceiling of which were made of pure steel. One wall consisted of two rows of bars spaced close enough to one another that mages couldn't stick their hands through to attack. There were steel hoops on my neck, arms and legs, and my hands were chained to my belt so that I couldn't take a swing at anyone. My gift of the Temple of Skron that allowed me to track invisible people had also fallen victim to the rot. However, I was still wearing the mithril gloves. Either no one knew they were there or had no idea how to remove them. Although, if they knew about their existence and could not remove them, they would simply just cut off both hands. What also surprised me was the state of my body. I was still thin, but it no longer looked like a skeleton. It was as if I was being actively fattened for several days before being brought back to consciousness. I really had to strain to stand — it wasn't easy, in my constrained state.

Kimal Sarento stood on the other side of the bars, grinning across the full width of his satisfied face. I opened my map and smiled as well — I'd ended up in Al-Khorezm after all. My attention was drawn to the skills icon that was actively blinking. Opening it, I grinned even wider — more than thirty new characters were available to me! All those that I saw performed by Magister Meram, as well as a whole bunch of others that currently had neither a name nor a description. However, I could already use them, and this inspired certain hope for the future.

"I always considered you a rational person who knows how to adapt to circumstances. But to tear out a person's heart like that in cold blood...Really, Maximilian, this is an egregious act. They say Magister Meram was so upset by your actions that he even canceled several of his meetings."

"What do you mean, upset?" The news almost cost me my balance. "He is dead! I tore his heart out!"

"Young man, in order to destroy a runescribe, especially one like him, you need to show more ingenuity than just tearing out his heart. Just think, our old man lay there for a couple of minutes, regenerated and jumped up as if nothing had happened. By the way, if it weren't for Magister Meram, you wouldn't have survived. Exhaustion of the body plus hitting the wall had a detrimental effect on your well-being. You were dying, and the runescribe had to save your naive little soul. You know, let me fill you in on what's going on so that you don't pester me with a hundred stupid questions. So! Magister Meram survived and returned home. The rift was closed, and all resources went to the Citadel. You were brought here a week ago, but you refused to regain consciousness. All this time, the Citadel was deciding how best to burn you — with dry wood, so that it would be nice and quick, or with wet wood, so that you would suffer before death. The soul only returns to the Light only after suffering, you know. That's what the churchmen say."

"Maybe you can get straight to the point? Why are you here?"

"Maximilian, where are your manners?" The chancellor was poignantly indignant and then became serious: "No, until we discuss the weather, no one will get down to business. And the weather is changeable these days. In some places it is sunny and pleasant, in some places there is precipitation and even deadly lightning."

"And how can you be on the sunny side and not get hit by heavy lightning?"

"What a good question," the smile returned to Kimal Sarento's face. "Now the Citadel is deciding how to put pressure on you most effectively to ensure that they don't pay a cent and have you closing infected rifts for the rest of your life. Magister Meram has already stated that from now on this responsibility passes to you."

"Now I'm really in the dark. Why is he refusing to perform the service that made him unique? He is devaluing himself."

"Thus becoming even more valuable. Infected rifts were a side gig, but this is not the only reason the Citadel is forced to endure his chronic overstepping. Magister Meram's main occupation lies in a different field. He's a runescribe, not a rift conqueror. He is valued and his actions are tolerated in exchange for his seals. Blockers of fatal damage, life extension and, of course, elimination of the consequences and influence of psychotropic drugs. There are more and more people greedy for oblivion crystals every year. The Citadel is already tired of burning them. In addition, some particularly cunning dealers have slipped crushed crystals to the servants of the Light, getting them hooked on the drug as well. If it were not for Magister Meram and his symbols, we'd all be in trouble."

I opened my jacket and looked at my stomach. It was clean. The symbols that the runescribe had begun to draw on me were not there. My garments, by the way, were painfully familiar — a doomed soldier jumpsuit. There was even a special symbol on the front to show others who I was.

"Magister Meram still hasn't determined your punishment. He is still deciding how to poke and prod you most painfully to break you while still keeping you alive, but he has already told everyone that from now on you are his pupil. In two days you start school. No matter what the Citadel comes up with, even it cannot keep Magister Meram's pupil in prison. Therefore, they will bargain with you. I respect and appreciate your determination to solve global issues on your own, but at this particular moment you need a representative. You are not yet ready for negotiations of this level. They will lure you with beautiful candy that costs nothing, and they will force you to work. But I am ready to defend your position almost on a voluntary basis."

"Kimal Sarento, altruism?" I couldn't resist sarcasm. "What do these two opposite words do in one sentence?"

"What altruism? There is no need to scare me with such terrible words, young man. Only mutually beneficial cooperation. Moreover, it is mutually beneficial for everyone, not just me. I became aware of certain notebooks integrated with each other. I want to synchronize with the recordings. In only one direction. Mine."

"Forget about it." I even found the strength to grin. "When they burn me, dig around in the ashes. There might be something left. Or kill Alia — she will also drop an artifact. But if you do, our next visit will be your last. I will do everything in my power to kill you. I'll make a deal with Skron himself, if necessary."

"Nevertheless, we will have to share, Maximilian."

"Synchronization in one direction is not going to happen. Either complete, in both directions, or forget that we have notebooks. There is too much unique information that should not be available to outsiders. For example, I managed to figure out how to increase the level of a particular stone without using *Amplify*. Does this interest you?"

"Our meeting is private, you don't have to speak in code. No one will overhear here."

"Alright. I was able not only to determine the method behind, but also to successfully increase the level of *Devour*. My stone is now Level Two. Although...I agree, this is not my most valuable information. What difference does it make to you how to level up? Eight second- or third-level

*Amplify*s around a fifth-level *Devour* and any capacity issues you may have with your intangible inventory will be solved for life."

"That particular stone, as you put it, cannot have facets added in the standard way. The stone that I got has only one facet. Why are you always getting off topic?"

"The runescribe functionality," I answered, finally realizing what had seemed wrong to me all this time. I clicked on the skill icon again, but this time I paid attention not to the set of symbols, but to the panel below. Previously it was empty, but now dates appeared on it. Moreover, the dates were not in the past, but in the future. And the nearest one was a month and a half away. I focused my gaze on this entry, and a map with a rift mark unfurled before my eyes. An infected rift. It was located not far from Al-Khorezm and had reached Level Eight. I closed the map and counted the number of entries. Forty-two. The Temple of Skrona hadn't lied — the seals on the infected rifts would soon degrade. The process had already begun and could not be stopped. The seals must either be updated or the rifts must be destroyed. The latter was preferable. Especially for me.

"Judging by your face, you just had a realization."

"Infected rifts. The first of them will open in a month and a half near Al-Khorezm. The last one is twelve years from now. This is the maximum period. When I tore out Meram's heart, albeit to no avail, I took some of his information from him."

"Only a month and a half before everything starts collapsing? Not bad leverage for negotiations. We will definitely use it. But let's get back to the notebooks."

"Double-sided synchronization, Sir Chancellor. Only then will I give you access to our notes. I'd rather agree to be deceived and forced to destroy infected rifts for next to nothing than give you such useful information. Or do you not want to know how infected rifts appear?"

"Are you saying that this is a man-made creation?" A note of interest slipped into Kimal's voice. Aha! He definitely didn't know.

"Two-way access, Sir Chancellor, and you will find out everything. Only this way and no other way. Where is Alia?"

I could not contact my personal attendant, as the steel cage blocked our magical connection.

"In Hearth. I'm afraid she won't be able to leave the autonomous city now. Otherwise, the Citadel will call for her to account for her misdeeds. She neglected her duties as a personal attendant and agreed to become your wife. This, to put it mildly, is prohibited. The rules clearly state the main restrictions between the dark ones and their personal attendants, and one of them states in quite plain words the impossibility of such a relationship. For now, you are protected by the status of your city. As soon as she leaves it, she will fall under the jurisdiction of the church."

"Alia didn't mention anything of the sort," I answered, looking at Kimal with suspicion.

Trusting the chancellor was the last thing I wanted to do. "Wait, what do you mean by the status of my city? How does it protect us?"

"Weren't you the one making a big fuss about how Hearth must be free from the influence of the Church of the Light? Well, you got it. Detachments of darkness monitors will be on duty near the city and check everyone who leaves. There are no more church representatives inside the walls. The Pope signed a decree giving the autonomous city of Hearth special status. From now on, it is a gray city under special control of the church. Actually, this is what we are talking about. The status of Hearth is already a done deal. But they may present it to you as a great gift to make you agree to close all of the infected rifts. There are still a lot of small nuances that you simply don't know about and because of which you can lose. But with my help, you can get out of this cage on top."

"Okay, let's discuss your participation. What are you willing to offer me to represent my interests in the upcoming negotiations?"

"Maximilian, don't tell me that blow to the head was much more serious than it initially seemed? I'm starting to worry."

"You came here for very clear purposes that you aren't discussing. You need something and you plan to get it by using me as a bargaining chip. If this brings me good benefits, I'm ready to agree to this, but obviously not for free. All this talk about how I'm not yet ready for such negotiations, that they'll eat me alive and won't leave a crumb behind — this is all poor man's talk. I'm not interested. And incidentally, I am a pupil of Magister Meram. In two days they will let me go, even if I don't say a word to anyone, so that they don't offer me anything. It is the Citadel and the dark ones who need to negotiate with me, not the other way around. It's their rifts that will begin to open in a month and a half, not mine. And on top of that, I recall the commander raging on about how I'm a doomed soldier and must follow his orders. I've never heard greater nonsense from the church!"

"I wouldn't be so certain about the doomed soldier thing," said Kimal. "That's another point for negotiation. Don't you see, Maximilian, that according to church rules, the emperor only has the right to return a doomed soldier to the land of the living if that doomed soldier is light. Which doesn't apply to you, as you understand. Formally, you belonged to the Church of the Light, so you belong to them to this day. They even gave you a personal attendant and, mind you, did not take her away. Father Urg knew this very well, so all he could do was get you out of the control of the petty churchmen. But not the church itself. You are a doomed soldier, whether you like it or not. As is the Evil Engineer. There is no other way for you to officially exist in the lands of Light. If you turn gray, do as you please, all paths are open to you."

"Going gray isn't a problem. Just twenty minutes of fiddling with the development crystal. Will this be enough to revoke my status as a doomed soldier?"

"We will determine that after you become gray, but we were discussing my participation in the negotiations."

"I refused you in Hearth, and I will refuse you now. There will be no synchronization of notebooks, and you will not participate in anything. I need information. As for threats and all that...In a month and a half, Al-Khorezm may come to an abrupt end. I reiterate: it is they who need to negotiate with me, not the other way around."

"The rift near the capital isn't very deep yet. The Gourfan Clan can handle it themselves. Regarding your refusal, I apparently need to clarify: you will appear before the Citadel Conclave. A full hearing, headed by the pope himself. According to the laws of the Church of the Light, a dark one, even if he is already gray, has no right to communicate with the pope. Either he must appoint his own negotiator, or he will be given a representative of the church. In your case, it will be the commander with whom you are already familiar. Moreover, the commander's word is the words of the Conclave. You will sit behind an impenetrable dome. You will be seen, you will not see anyone. The negotiator will move in and out of the dome, communicating the position to the other side. You can, of course, use this option, but are you sure that the commander will speak on behalf of the Citadel, and not on his own? For some reason he clearly doesn't like you. He was far too emotional when speaking about your place in this world."

"Are you trying to tell me that you would report everything verbatim? You won't try to slip something in?"

"Of course I will, how else? But in my case, we are both interested in Hearth continuing to flourish. So that he becomes stronger, and you have the opportunity to move freely across our lands. Besides, I don't like the 'doomed soldier' status; I would like to remove it. Would the commander want the same? A controversial issue. That's why I'm here. This may seem strange to you, but I'm on your side, Maximilian. No matter how much you might believe the contrary."

"So it's either you or the commander? Is there no third option?"

"Why not? Of course there is. You can refuse representation. In this case, the pope will announce his decision, which will be recorded and handed over for you to execute. With no right to make any amendments. And who knows what he'll put in there. Hearth exists now purely due to his goodwill. If the pope decides that it is too early for an autonomous city to appear in our world, it will be swept away. You've been gone for a week. When they told me where you were and what was wrong with you, I came to Al-Khorezm and managed to catch General Khabensky's army moving towards your city. Order from the Citadel, carried out by the Fortress: if you do not agree, the city will be swept from the face of this world. Along with its residents. Including two pregnant women. The Citadel can be very cruel at times."

"They wouldn't dare." I almost threw myself onto the steel bars at the news.

"Believe it. Do you think that your ability to pass through rifts makes you unique? Now you're just getting on everyone's nerves. You flew too high too soon, you don't share with anyone, you insist on your opinion, you wave your rights in everyone's faces. Instead of focusing only on the Zarak Empire and gaining strength and connections there, making people dependent on you and Hearth, you climbed higher. Started arguing with the Citadel. I asked you to agree to everything! No, he needed an audience with the Pope. You wanted it, you got it. You want a serious conversation? Let's talk seriously. The Citadel really has its doubts about letting you live. You're too unpredictable. Too dangerous. If it weren't for the decision of Magister Meram, who announced that he wanted to see you among his pupils, there would be no conversations about what to offer you now, but rather about how much to punish you! Yes, you have some obvious useful qualities, but what do the decision makers get for it? Nothing! They don't see you as the source of their strength. This is not the Fortress with its clerics mired in corruption, craving only gold. This is the Citadel! Here they have one goal: to destroy darkness in all its incarnations. And what do they see? A dark human accumulating special privileges left and right who has decided that the ability to close rifts and destroy the Fog of Pharapho makes him one of a kind. No, Maximilian, it doesn't. Magister Meram is one of a kind because he helps people. Saves them. Frees them from drugs. Extends people's lives. He works for others, without forgetting, of course, about himself. Haven't you ever been surprised by the fact that Magister Meram travels through empires and puts seals on ordinary people, despite all his supposedly great power? Because this is his contribution to the work of the church. He's keeping his end of the deal. You only work for yourself. Rifts, fog…'Fifty percent is mine, or I won't budge!' Aren't you the one who screams like that all the time? What are your reasons for making such a ruckus? A show of force? You don't have it. Connections? You don't have them either. What do you have, young man, besides ambition and luck? The ability to collapse the usual market for magic stones, resources and elixirs? No one needs it. These items were considered valuable because they were difficult to obtain. During all the time that you have been conquering rifts, you have obtained more magic stones than we have seen in twenty years! And this is not an exaggeration, it's just a fact. They allocated a city to you, called you autonomous, allocated resources, but it seemed like that wasn't enough for you. You demanded a meeting with the pope. For what purpose did you decide to leave the Church of the Light? Do you want to become independent? I repeat — what will this get you? An army on your doorstep will show you what true independence and strength are. If you and the Citadel don't come to an agreement, Hearth will simply cease to exist. Do you think that if you run away to the dark ones, it will somehow solve your problems? Are you ready to meet the Inquisitor again? The Citadel may not care about the cost and will send this ghastly creature after you. The dark ones themselves will finish you off, just to keep the Inquisitor out of their lands. I hate to upset you, Maximilian, but you stuck your nose where it wasn't wanted too quickly. And you will have to pay for it."

Kimal Sarento fell silent, allowing me to digest this information. After a couple of minutes, he continued, in a calmer voice:

"Maximilian, I'm on your side. I have certain plans related to Hearth and its greatness that require it to be managed by a person who's loyal to me. Yes, I have plans for you too — it wouldn't hurt to have my own runescribe. Who knows what Magister Meram might teach you? But all this will not happen if the Citadel decides to rescind your autonomy. I ask you, as an older and more experienced person, don't get carried away. Don't show ambition. Give me a chance to figure out what's going on. Become stronger, acquire support, your own army, and then you will have the opportunity to somehow oppose the Church of the Light. Not now. Now you cannot oppose even me, and I am much weaker than our ardent commander."

"I will not integrate your notebook in only one

direction. Do you want me to trust you? Believe you? So prove that you are really on my side. Now you are anything but a kind uncle who wants to protect a little boy. Now you are the insidious and cunning chancellor of the magic academy, who takes advantage of my lack of information about what is really happening in the world and puts pressure on me with eloquent, heart-felt speeches. Even trying to frighten me with the fact that General Khabensky's army is moving towards Hearth, although it should have arrived two weeks ago. However, unplanned exercises delayed them. Eleanore consistently informs me about what is happening with Hearth, and I have become accustomed to listening to her, not missing a single detail. But you do not take any counter measures, demanding submission from me. You won't get it. Either we work as partners on mutually beneficial terms, or we don't work. It will be exactly the same with the Citadel. Either we will work as partners, or we will not work together. I am not a doomed soldier who will prostrate myself before the pope and his Conclave and beg for forgiveness. Yes, I have no power behind me, no connections, no army. But I have something else — the ability to destroy level thirty rifts. The ability to destroy the metamorphs that occupy vast spaces of the Kaliman Empire. I have something to offer the church and something to interest them. But there is no Kimal Sarento in this process. You'll only be a part of it if we can synchronize our notebooks in both directions. Only this way and no other way.”

There was the piercing shriek of a sliding door whose hinges had not been lubricated for several thousand years. Kimal Sarento grimaced with displeasure and turned to the side. A clergyman approached us, his face was hidden by a hood.

“Time is up. Kimal Sarento, have you agreed on your participation in the Conclave?”

The chancellor looked in my direction and grinned.

“We have. I will be the voice of the dark rift conqueror at the meeting with the pope.”

Chapter 18

"SIT DOWN!"

The clergy were not known for their friendly demeanor.. I was taken to a large round room, somewhat reminiscent of an arena. In the center, on a flat area about four meters in diameter, there was a simple stool and several steel rings to which my shackles were chained. Next there was a solid wall of about my height, above which stood stands with comfortable chairs for the highest hierarchs of the Citadel. Cardinals, as I'd learned. However, there was another tier: directly in front of my face, above the chairs of the cardinals, there was a snow-white throne. The distance was great, so it was impossible to appreciate the elegant design of the pope's chosen repose. But it looked impressive.

My nose itched and I had to concentrate to try to stop the sensation from driving me mad. The stool was extremely uncomfortable and I constantly fidgeted, trying to find a better position. Minutes dragged on, but the cardinals were in no hurry to take their places. Finally, leisurely steps were heard and Kimal Sarento stood next to me. The chancellor looked fresh and content with life. Not at all like the man who visited me in the Citadel prison yesterday.

A seemingly solid dome immediately appeared around us, shielding us from the stands. Kimal Sarento walked out from under it, but immediately went back in.

"Interesting solution. An opposite canopy of silence. You can be seen and heard, but everything that happens outside is hidden. Are you ready to face the inevitable?"

"My notebook still hasn't been synchronized."

"Maximilian, sometimes I feel like I'm talking to some uneducated hillbilly from some remote village. Are you suggesting that I integrate two artifacts that are recognized as dark, right in the center of the Citadel? The place where the power of Light reaches its apogee? I have no desire to find myself chained to a chair next to you. Once again, this is the Citadel. A place where the veneration of Light is at its highest. Everything related to the dark is prohibited here. Have you turned gray?"

"No. I created the *Dark Indifference* parameter, but it had no effect on me. Skron has been indifferent to me from the beginning."

"Not great." A shadow of displeasure ran across Kimal Sarento's face. "Okay, it's not critical. Alright, sit here and wait."

The chancellor left the protective dome again, and I found myself in my least favorite state: waiting for others to make decisions when nothing depends on you. I sat for a long time. Sometimes it even began to seem to me that there was no one left in this world except me. The dome perfectly hid all sound and vision. However, it soon began to flicker — Kimal had returned. His face looked slightly discouraged.

"I won't beat around the bush — the pope thinks that you are too uncontrollable and unruly a force, and that you bring too much chaos to the established order. He doubts that you will be useful to this world, even considering your upcoming training from Magister Meram. There are more worthy candidates. Loyal and agreed upon by the church. It's easier for him now not to fulfill the runescribe's demand and pay him some kind of compensation than to give birth to a new monster. All the arguments presented in your favor proved unconvincing. They were heard, but were not heeded. And now something will happen that has never happened. The pope wants to hear from you in person. Never before has the dark one had the right to talk to the head of the Church of the Light, so I have no idea what will happen next. You will have a few minutes to prove your usefulness to the pope and the Conclave of Cardinals. Maximilian, I don't know what you're going to say, but I ask one thing: don't do anything rash. Your task is to leave the Citadel and return to Hearth. Focus on that."

Did Kimal Sarento actually care about me? Why such tenderness all of the sudden? Was he trying to pull one over on me? All I could do was nod, indicating that I understood my task.

"He's ready!" said Kimal Sarento, and at that moment the dome disappeared. I found myself in the arena again, but this time the stands were full. Around the perimeter sat cardinals dressed in golden-purple robes. The highest hierarchs of the Church of the Light were few in number — only thirteen. Simpler clergymen were bustling around next to each big-wig, but I didn't see any food or wine. Papers, papers and more papers. One got the feeling that those gathered were really working. Despite the fact that I was shackled with steel hoops, I could not resist going over the cardinals with *Analyze*. I wanted to know what kind of people they were.

The snow-white throne was also occupied. The pope was a fairly young man for his position. At first glance, he could be about fifty years old, no more. Definitely not a venerable old man, like most cardinals. What showed his age was his gray hair, styled in a long braid, typical of the inhabitants of the Shurgan empire. Thick eyebrows, as gray as the hair on his head, hung over his shining eyes. The pope was one of those followers of the Light who had given themselves to it, body and soul. The cardinals, on the other hand, had quite ordinary eyes. Which wasn't surprising, considering what I'd just found out. The pope's cassock was vibrantly colorful. It consisted of patches of all kinds of colors that can only be found in the Church of the Light. Black, white, red, purple...Colors of all shades and hues were united in the pope's clothing, showing the unity of the church.

Next to the head of the Church of the Light was a creature already familiar to me. The Inquisitor. The commander, who disliked me with all his bright soul, was in the company of his comrades. Finally, the time had come for me to use my *Analyze* with three *Amplify*s attached. If there was no result now, then I would throw this useless stone away and make room for something truly useful. For a while nothing happened, but then my heart started beating faster — it had worked! *Analyze* managed to break through the blocking amulet and gave me all the ins and outs of this being.

Commander of the Church of the Light. Modernized man.

I'd already come across the words "modernized man" before. At the time, I had not asked the man what they meant, deciding it would look bad on my part. But now I regret it. It was much easier to strategize when you knew what you were working with. The commander did not have stones — he used some kind of his own, Light magic. For example, the sword that tortures by fire was an ability that appeared contrary to all logic known to me. Tailored just for this being. As for the parameters...Now I understood why Kimal Sarento responsibly declared that he was an insignificant slug compared to these men. The commander was powerful. Incredibly powerful! He was also immune to Skron's magic, as if he had been forged from pure steel. I turned my gaze to the nearby commander, used *Analyze* again and frowned. Something wasn't working, and I didn't like it. However, I wasn't given the time to get to the bottom of it. The pope decided that the silence had gone on too long, and his voice filled the arena. Strong, penetrating every cell and chaining you to the floor. Nevertheless, I managed to resist. My previous experience with the Inquisitor had given me practice. The pope's influence pressed down on me, but not with as much strength as his had.

"Maximilian Valevsky, the Church of the Light has made its decision and wants to voice it to you personally. We consider you guilty of breaking the law. As a doomed soldier, you refused to comply with the demands of the Citadel commander. This is a critical violation for which the doomed soldier is obliged to bear a well-deserved punishment. And the punishment for this is one thing: the fire. The decision has been made, but it has not yet been approved. We know that Magister Meram wants to see you among his pupils. We know what benefit you bring to this world by destroying the rifts and the Fog of Pharapho. However, this cannot justify disobeying a direct order from the Citadel commander. Your voice, Kimal Sarento, was convincing in defending you, but his arguments were also assessed as insufficient grounds for saving your life. Before we make a final verdict on your fate, we grant you the right to the last word. Speak, Dark Rift Conqueror."

"I am grateful, Your Holiness," I said. The anger that began to boil inside my chest was extinguished amazingly quickly. Now wasn't the time. "Yes, I have something to say to the Conclave and the pope. There is something to motivate my actions. But before I begin, I want to correct the venerable head of the Church of the Light. Rift Conqueror is my side job. What I do better than anyone in the world, but what I do in my free time from my main job. First and foremost, I am a Hunter of Darkness. And my task is to find the dark ones everywhere, in whatever guise and in whatever place they hide. This is my mission and I plan to fulfill it for the rest of my life."

An uproar rose among the cardinals. If they had expected me to fall to my knees and start begging for my life, they had come to the wrong show. Kimal Sarento coughed eloquently, telling me to shut up and not do anything rash, but I was unstoppable. I'd come up with a strategy for my defense and was going to stick to it to the last.

"During my travels, I happened to obtain information that there are traitors among the highest hierarchs of the Citadel. Those who pretend to serve the Light, but in fact revere Skron. And not just revere him — they are dark themselves! I couldn't believe it. I was always taught that the Citadel is a stronghold of Light, that the people here are ideal role models for the rest of the light world. But the one who delivered such incredible news was convincing. He made me doubt. And then I realized that I needed to check, even despite the risks of being destroyed. But the question immediately arose: how can I check the highest hierarchs? How can I know if one of them is a traitor? I didn't know who they were, I didn't know what they looked like, and if I had come to the Citadel with such a proposal, they would have simply sent me to the stake without any questions asked. When the commander came to me, demanding the immediate destruction of the infected rift, I realized how I could do this. Only through the Conclave! I needed to gather all the highest hierarchs of the Light in one place to be convinced of the madness of my informant. But how could I do that? The answer was simple: refuse to comply with the commander's demand. Yes, I knew what price I would have to pay for learning about the integrity of the cardinals. Hearth. But I was ready to do it because I couldn't risk it. I couldn't sleep well at night knowing that a dark one was sitting in the Conclave. And here I am, among the full assembly of the highest hierarchs of the Citadel. I was warned that the dark one has no right to see or talk with the pope, but in extreme cases, when the church decides to destroy a creature it does not like, the rules may change. This is what happened today. This allowed me to look at all the senior leaders of the Church of the Light and understand who they really are. True servants of the Light or those who have sold themselves to darkness!"

I fell silent, catching my breath, and the thirteen cardinals began to buzz. These were unprecedented words for the Conclave, and they required action. All I could do was wait. The pope thoughtfully propped up his head and did not take his eyes, filled with true Light, off of me. It felt like I was being pierced right through, but there was nowhere to retreat. If what I'd said was of no interest to anyone, I would have to escape from the Citadel. I didn't think they'd burn me on the spot. They'd try to arrange a nice ceremony. Since they left me the mithril gloves, it wouldn't be difficult to escape. But I really didn't want to turn into an outcast. Someone who would be hunted for the rest of his life. Of course, I could go to the Bartolomeo Clan, but when I imagined having to live under the same roof as a Riftmaster, it made my soul go dark. Such creatures must be destroyed, even if they serve people with whom you're on good terms.

"And what is your verdict, Hunter of Darkness?" The pope's voice sounded, and the hall plunged into complete silence. The head of the Church of the Light showed interest in my words.

"I understood the main thing, Your Holiness. That my informant was wrong. He stated that among the highest hierarchs of the Light there is a dark one. This is wrong. There are two dark ones here! I, Maximilian Valevsky, Hunter of Darkness, appeal to the Inquisitor. Please verify two people in this room. I'm ready to pay any price the Inquisitor deems reasonable. To the point that I will voluntarily climb onto the fire and light it myself. I cannot point with my hand, since I am tied, but I can turn towards the one who is hiding behind the Light, being darkness. It's him!"

I turned towards one of the cardinals. Outwardly, he was no different from his brothers, with the exception of one small detail. According to *Analyze*, there was an eighty percent chance that this person was dark.

"Request received, price accepted!" a voice sounded, making me fall to my knees. I could not stand when the Light itself was speaking. In the blink of an eye, the Inquisitor found himself in front of the cardinal I was staring at. One got the feeling that he used some kind of teleportation, how quickly everything happened. The Inquisitor looked at the white-faced cardinal and a moment later the owner of the golden-purple robe collapsed to the floor.

"Dark!" the Inquisitor proclaimed, and such an aura fell upon me that I lay flat on the floor, unable to even breathe. I had to fight not to die, so I couldn't appreciate what was happening around me. When the aura disappeared and my lungs, flaming with fire, convulsively drew in air, I felt myself being jerked to my feet. Little black circles of gnats danced before my eyes, but soon it was all over. It took me great effort not to recoil — the Inquisitor stood next to me, casting me a withering look. Leaning to the side, I saw that the place with the cardinal, to whom I had pointed, was empty.

"Who is your informant, Maximilian Valevsky?" the pope asked in a heavy voice. The voice of a person who has made a difficult decision and understands that he has no other choice. "The Church would like to speak with them."

"You won't be able to. He's dead," I replied.

"You haven't given a name."

"I didn't know his name. The one who told me was a commander who descended with me into the Pharapho dungeon. The one who forced me to go lower and lower, before he and the former head of the Valdez Clan delivered an insidious stab in the back."

This time there was no whispering among the cardinals. Twelve people suddenly realized that the crazy words of the dark one were not so crazy.

"Commanders of the Citadel cannot be dark," the Pope said after a pause. "Their eyes shine with Light."

"There is no darkness in my eyes, and yet they call me dark," I replied.

"We don't want to get into a useless dispute now. You said that your informant was mistaken. That there are two dark ones in the Conclave. Who's the second?"

I looked around, peering at the cardinals, and as my gaze settled on each of them, the influential people froze. Some turned white, some turned red. Not one remained indifferent. Turning around, making a full circle, I fixed my gaze on the strange commander. The same one that had the postscript "modernized man." The other commanders who stood next to him did not have such a postscript.

"Him," I replied, staring at my enemy. "However, it won't be possible to check him just like that. Even the Inquisitor. Before testing this creature for service to Skron, all amulets must be removed from him. And then the Church of the Light will understand that even eyes filled with Light can hide darkness behind them."

The commander extended his hand in my direction, a fiery sword even began to form in it, but that was where his freedom ended. The Inquisitor again showed inhuman speed and was suddenly next to him. The hideous aura appeared again, which made me collapse on the floor and fight for a breath of air, but even in this state I heard the sentence:

"Modernized!"

When I could breathe again and came to my senses enough to assess the area around me, I was back on my feet. Except that the Inquisitor was no longer next to me — he was standing next to the pope. Kimal Sarento was holding me upright. Judging by the fact that everyone was silent, the word was still mine.

"Before the Church of the Light decides what to do with me next, I want to pose a question: for what am I at fault? The fact that I refused to carry out the order of a Citadel commander who gave himself up to darkness?"

"Don't overdo it," Kimal Sarento's warning

whisper was heard. "You've already said and done everything that needs to be done. Now just wait."

The chancellor's advice seemed sound, especially since after a double dose of the Inquisitor's aura, I was noticeably unsteady and dizzy. I wanted to lie down and never get up again.

"Are these all the dark ones that you managed to discover among the highest hierarchs of the Citadel, Dark Hunter?" The pope asked.

"Among those who are in this room, there are no dark ones, or those who are close to them," I answered, but immediately corrected myself: "Except for me."

"Why do you need independence from the Church of the Light?"

"Not from the Church of the Light — from the highest hierarchs who may sell themselves to darkness. I recognize the primacy of the pope and the Church of the Light over myself and my city and sincerely wish that representatives of the church will reside in Hearth. If darkness is allowed to take root in one city, it will spread further. I recognize that I am part of the world of the Light, and that my mission is to destroy the darkness. I don't really understand where the idea that I need independence came from. This question should be addressed to the person who informed the Conclave about this, but obviously not to me. I..."

They didn't let me finish my sentence — the impenetrable dome reappeared. Kimal Sarento looked at me for a moment and then walked out from under the dome, leaving me completely alone.

All I could do was sit back on the uncomfortable stool and await my fate. I wondered if the canopy was a good sign. Or should I start preparing my escape?

When the dome disappeared, I found myself in an empty arena. No pope, no commanders, no cardinals. The Inquisitor had also fled off on some important business. Even Kimal was gone! Some churchman came up to me and, without further ado, began to remove the steel hoops from me. Soon another person appeared and brought clothes. My traveling suit, which I had worn on the journey to Al-Khorezm. The situation seemed so unrealistic that I changed clothes without any questions asked. Maybe I just fell asleep and had a pleasant dream about being released from the Citadel? Just in case, I pinched myself. It hurt, but reality remained in place. They were not going to put me in a steel cage anymore.

I was taken to an office. Kimal Sarento sat at the table and enthusiastically wrote something in a flickering notebook. His was much larger than mine and looked like an ancient tome. Looking up from his notes, the chancellor pointed me to a chair and returned to filling out his artifact. I didn't argue. Apparently, this was my fate today — to wait. Nevertheless, I did see one important detail: the chancellor was using writing instruments to fill out his notebook. Which meant that he didn't have a status bar. Or he just liked his own handwriting.

Finally, making one final scribble in the book,

the chancellor closed it and held it out in my direction.

"Debts can be repaid," said Kimal Sarento. "As agreed, there will be double synchronization. Set it up."

"What about this being the Citadel and all that?" I couldn't resist sarcasm, but I pulled the book closer to me.

"Now everyone is busy with much more interesting things than keeping an eye on you and me. The two highest hierarchs of the Citadel turned out to be supporters of Skron. This has never happened in a thousand years of history. No, of course, it is quite likely that it happened, but it has definitely never been revealed. I would like to take part in the interrogation, but ordinary chancellors of magic academies are not allowed. Is everything set up?

Number of synchronizations: 2

The notebook pictogram began to blink actively. When I opened it, my eyes immediately became wide — I didn't even know what to investigate first. Kimal Sarento hadn't lied, and had provided access to his one notebook. One where he had been accumulating his knowledge for many decades. There was so much information that I couldn't even come up with a study plan. There was everything here, from magic stones to — and this came as an unexpected and pleasant surprise — data on the first emperor.

"I hope there is no need to say that if this knowledge ends up in the Fortress, a certain Maximilian Valevsky and his personal attendant, Mother Alia, will meet a sudden and unpleasant end? I would not like to share with strangers what I have spent my entire life collecting."

"Strangers?"

"That's right, Maximilian, with strangers. It took me a long time to make this decision. At my age, trusting someone is tantamount to a crime. However, I took a risk. Maybe for the last time in my life. Sometimes, you know, you want to believe in humanity. The Temple of Skron owes you. I owe you a lot. You see, I am a very inquisitive person and I cannot allow you to demand from the dark ones what you can easily get from me. The same goes for the Citadel. Today you showed that you can protect yourself. You have become useful to the church. Not just one who can pass through the rifts and Fog of Pharapho, but those who can detect darkness in all its forms. The Citadel paused to formulate a proposal to involve you in closing the infected rifts, but one thing I can say for sure is that from now on you have a responsibility. Once every six months, a certain dark hunter must appear at the Conclave of the Citadel to check all its representatives for aiding the darkness. Moreover, you must carry out similar activities with both the Fortress and the Stronghold. Letters to the supreme bishops will be sent out shortly. Your status as a member of the doomed legion has not been removed, but it will not affect anything. From now on, only the pope has the right to order you to do anything. All other representatives of the Church of the Light are deprived of this right. Your belongings, as well as all the loot you got from the rift, are waiting in the carriage at the entrance to the Citadel. Padishah Bayazid the Third has already been notified that you are delayed and that from now on you travel with the pope's protection. Are you going to stay with him? But that's where the good news ends. The Inquisitor has named his price, and I doubt you will be very pleased."

Kimal Sarento handed me a piece of paper signed personally by the pope. There were only a few sentences, but my head became heavy when I understood their meaning.

"The Citadel remained true to itself," sighed Kimal Sarento. "Despite your help, it will not turn a blind eye to the violation of its laws. I managed to defend Mother Alia's life, but no more. She will remain your personal attendant, but... You see the Inquisitor's demand. And you have no right not to pay this price. You yourself voiced this before the Conclave."

"The Inquisitor has set his price for his services: he forbids the marriage between Mother Alia and Archduke Maximilian Valevsky. If his will is violated, Mother Alia and her child will be executed by flame. Everyone is equal under the law!"

Chapter 19

"WHERE AM I SUPPOSED to put all this?" I asked dumbfounded when I walked out of the main gate of the Citadel and saw an entire convoy of caravans brimming with loot. The clergy stayed true to their word and gave me everything that was obtained from the infected thirty-one level rift. But there was so much loot that it took twenty huge carts, filled to bursting. A churchman in a blue robe stood next to my carriage and wrote something in a book. Noticing me, he waved his hand welcomingly, as if I was not a terrifying dark human, but a brother in the Light.

"Archduke Valevsky, please sign here and here." He handed me several reports in which I understood absolutely nothing. Numbers, lines, a lot of information which definitely required action, but exactly what action was unclear. Therefore, I simply put my signature on the bills detailing the transferred resources, correctly assuming that there was no point in the Citadel deceiving me.

"Very good," the churchman put away the documents and immediately pulled out new pieces of paper. "I understand that such issues cannot be resolved on the street, however, another opportunity may not present itself. The Citadel wants to buy back everything in these carts. Here's our proposal."

This time the report was clear even to me: it was just a single figure. For all the resources that the miners managed to pull out of the infected rift, I was offered an amount of nine hundred thousand gold. Why so little? Because there was nothing high-level in the rift, except perhaps the yem from the guards. All resources that were of any value were in my inventory and I had no intention of sharing them with the church. Nine hundred thousand would go far for Hearth. It would allow us to hire additional work crews, purchase high-quality materials and bring my city even closer to...to what? Now, when it became clear that in a year there would be no wedding, I did not see the point in the forced transformation of Hearth into a glorious garden city. Nevertheless, I easily parted with the carts. In order to use all this good loot, I'd need processing devices. They were not provided to me there and, as I understand it, they would never be provided.

"Thank you," the clergyman put the document in a folder. "Information about the transfer will be sent to banks today. In two days your funds will reach the Zarak Empire."

The servant of the Light made a gesture and the huge procession, as if awaiting his signal, trudged off. Only my personal carriage remained in place.

"You part with your hard-won loot so easily?" Naira came out of the carriage, looking with undisguised sadness at the departing carts.

"These crystals and gems are useless to me. We won't be able to turn them into elixirs. Stick them in a warehouse for safekeeping? I don't see the point. What did you do while I was visiting the Citadel? Have you been living life to the fullest?"

"If you consider the Citadel's fierce and invasive checks as entertainment, then of course! I had as much fun as I could. Do you know that more than half of Rustam Bakhtiyar's detachment was recognized as having given over to darkness and was solemnly burned four days ago? People died only because the commander ordered the supreme convert to open the portal. Since when did the Citadel's highest hierarchs travel with supreme converts?"

"I believe that Rustam or the padishah himself can demand compensation, because..."

"Because the affairs of the Citadel must remain the affairs of the Citadel," a voice said. Turning around, I saw a clergyman in a red cassock. He was a textbook Shurganite — the almond eyes, dark long hair tied into a tight ponytail, athletic build, and the gloomy, in some ways even menacing face. A representative of the security service had honored us with his presence, and judging by the Light shining through his eyes, this man was no novice cleric.

"No one should know about what happened at the Conclave, Hunter of Darkness," the cleric continued. "It's not promising that I have to tell you such small details. Moreover, you must never discuss what happened at the Conclave in the presence of a representative of the dark empire. Even though Naira Jode has been recognized as gray and given the right to travel through our lands, she remains a member of the Bartolomeo Clan, the leading clan in Kerux."

"Leading?" Naira's eyes even lit up.

"This is not a topic that I would like to discuss with a gray human," answered the clergyman. "I've already said everything I wanted to."

"What topic did you come to discuss?" I clarified.

"Your ability to keep your mouth shut. For some reason, your personal attendant, Mother Alia, has temporarily left her ward, so in her absence, this responsibility was entrusted to me. I'm Brother Lin. I will be your personal attendant for a while. We don't need to sign an agreement. When Mother Alia returns, I will step down."

"Just 'Brother?'" I asked incredulously. Usually common brothers of the Citadel did not walk with Light beaming out of their eyeballs.

"For you and those we meet, just Brother Lin," confirmed my new monitor.

The news was not very pleasant. I was already

out of the habit of considering myself a doomed soldier and rejoiced in freedom, but from now on my freedom was significantly limited. Moreover, I couldn't even claim that the Citadel was giving me any sort of special attention. Since Alia was not with me, I was given a temporary escort. Few people cared about the actual rank of this escort.

My personal items had been placed into a small backpack. Upon opening it, the first thing I did was take out the plate of the padishah — it would need to be returned. I'd played around enough. I threw the unidentified exclusive amulet into my breast pocket. As if I didn't have enough going on without some sly thief stealing my valuables.

"Gustav, we are going to see Padishah Bayazid the Third," I ordered, after which I sat down more comfortably and opened my notebook. First of all, I was interested in information about the padishah. Exactly who was he and what was he capable of? Unlike my notes, the chancellor's lacked pictures. Only bare text, but it was enough to understand that a difficult meeting was ahead. Bayazid the Third was considered the strongest of the padishahs of the Shurgan Empire and, in accordance with his position, was accustomed to having everything done for him. The padishah did not recognize the word "no." No weaknesses were identified and no illegal actions had been observed. Or those who could speak about such things were already dead. Not the easiest person to talk to, and I was even grateful to the Citadel for providing me with an escort. The padishah would not go against the Church of the Light. In the Shurgan Empire, power entirely belongs to the Citadel. The padishahs, and even the emperor, played second fiddle.

The palace of the padishah was located on the outskirts of the capital in the middle of a huge park. I'd seen this approach to construction before. The magical academy was built in a similar manner, with one main difference. In the Zarak Empire, people could freely walk around the park and even get close to the academy buildings, but here, a huge fence and squads of guards blocked any attempt to enter the closed area. The carriage was stopped several times, but each check was limited to the inspectors peeking inside, meeting the eyes of my escort, and immediately letting us pass on. Soon we arrived at the main building, and I once again had a feeling of déjà vu. I'd come across similar houses before. And I wasn't the only one. Naira also appreciated the palace of Padishah Bayazid the Third, which looked exactly like the palace of the Bartolomeo Clan.

"Something on your mind?" The cleric was quite attentive to detail. My reaction told him enough.

"This is not information that I would like to discuss in the presence of the dark one," I tried to avoid a direct answer, but then suddenly a dense dome appeared around us.

"Speak," demanded the clergyman. A simple attendant? Ha-ha-ha! The Citadel sent me a high-ranking figure--if not a commander, then someone close!

"The palace of the padishah is exactly like the palace of the Bartolomeo Clan and the estate that I managed to destroy in the Zarak Empire. In both cases, there was a Riftmaster on the top floor of the building. It produced broxies that served as guards, but here, as I see, there are no broxies. However, the buildings are too similar to avoid an unpleasant feeling of recognition. What if there is also a Riftmaster here managing security on the estate? Maybe even without broxies. The mental defense alone will be more than enough."

"Why did you refuse to talk about this in the presence of the gray one?"

"Because only a few top hierarchs of her clan know about the presence of the Riftmaster on the top floor. The rest remain in the dark. I promised the head of the Bartolomeo Clan that I would not reveal such details to Naira. Not everyone is ready to accept the fact that the clan has to kill hundreds of ordinary people a year to ensure protection."

"I hear you," the clergyman removed the dome, and at that moment the butler approached us:

"Padishah Bayazid the Third welcomes dear guests to his home and invites them to share dinner with him. Your rooms are ready, you can clean up, wash, change clothes and relax before dinner. Follow me."

Inside, the palace of the padishah was also not much different from the house of the

Bartolomeo Clan, except that there were a lot of people gathered. The dark ones, unlike Bayazid III, preferred living minimalistically. We were given three rooms. Despite the fact that Naira was still listed as my fiancée, she was given separate accommodations. What was this? A demonstration of the fact that the padishah is aware of our true relationship? Or just a meaningless courtesy? A fiancée is still not yet a wife. What if we had some special agreements regarding living together? Still, I was glad that I wouldn't have to share a dark room. Now was not the time for romantic relationships. However, all thoughts on this matter disappeared when I entered the room and fell into the tenacious clutches of two beautiful maids. They helped me undress, bring myself into human form, and without any unnecessary inclinations toward sex. The padishah's servants knew their job well, even when they gave me a massage, which, logically, should have turned into something more. But it didn't. Nevertheless, when the attendant came to pick me up, I felt rested and fully satisfied with life. Which, given my current physique, was pretty hard. My week in the Citadel had done nothing to fatten me up. I still looked like a flesh-covered skeleton.

In the dining room where I was taken, there was a huge table. Judging by the fact that almost all the seats were already taken, they had been awaiting my arrival. The padishah himself sat at the head of the table. Bayazid the Third was very different from his picture on the plate. The real owner of the estate turned out to be a very well-fed man of fifty with sparse hair that had nothing in common with the thick-haired image on the plate. His glowing red rings instantly caught my eye. Bayazid the Third was demonstrating his greatness, wealth and connections with dark clans to everyone around him. There were simply no other places where he could have gotten those rings. A colorful robe, similar to the pope's, hid a heavy body sitting on a mountain of pillows. Only now I noticed that there were no chairs here at all. Only pillows. But what I didn't like most was the look of the padishah. It felt like an animal was leering at me. Predatory, bloodthirsty, deciding the best angle of attack to seize me and swallow me whole.

In addition to the padishah, his four sons were at the table, including Rustam Bakhtiyar. The second son was sitting not far from his father and pointedly did not look in my direction. Naira and Brother Lin were already here, enthusiastically talking about something with their table neighbors. Outwardly, everything looked dignified and decent, if not for the gaze of the padishah. It didn't bode well.

"Archduke Valevsky, I am glad to welcome you to my home," the fat man spread his arms to the sides, feigning friendliness, and pointed to the place next to him. 'Take a seat, dear guest! Taste the dishes and dishes of the Shurgan Empire! I'm sure you've never tried anything like this in your life! Music!"

The padishah clapped his hands and several musicians struck up a jaunty melody. I was taken to the padishah and seated on pillows in close proximity to him. *Analyze* supplemented the chancellor's notes with pictures and images of both the padishah himself and all his children. Surprisingly, his wives were not at dinner. Naira was the only female given a seat at the table.

The less-than-desirable company did nothing to lessen my appetite. I hadn't had a decent meal in over a week. The contents of my plate disappeared with amazing speed and the servants barely had time to bring me new dishes. It got to the point where everyone present looked with undisguised surprise at how quickly I devoured the food. But even this could not affect my appetite. I wasn't just hungry, I was starving! My body, finally having reached its long-awaited meal, tried its best to replenish its energy supply, so that when I again had an indelible desire to go into the rift, it would have enough resources to do so.

"A good appetite is a compliment to the host!" the padishah remarked when I finally looked up from the plate. Judging by how warm I felt and the sweet bliss that spread throughout my body, I'd managed to put down half the table myself!

"What else can I do, when everything is so delicious," I answered, not at all disingenuously.

"Finally! My friend, you made me worry! I was already starting to think that something had happened to you!"

"What could have happened to me?" an old

man's voice rang out, making me turn towards the door. The mood and state of complete relaxation evaporated in a matter of moments. Standing in the doorway were the two people I least wanted to see in my life right now. Magister Meram and Karina Fardi. The old man's gaze settled on me, and he let out a malicious laugh:

"Indeed, what could have happened to me, when the only person in the last forty years who managed to kill me is here?"

"Kill?" the padishah repeated, and the glances of those gathered were again drawn to me. I was getting a little uncomfortable. Magister Meram settled down not far from me, and, as if on purpose, Karina Fardi sat on the pillow next to him. The girl sat with a straight back and looked strictly in front of her, not allowing herself any distractions.

"Kill is putting it mildly. The young man tore my heart out. Insidiously, without warning, one might even say that it was very unkind. For a moment, I was even upset. But only for a moment."

"And this young man is still alive?" the padishah was surprised.

"Let him run free, I don't mind," Master Meram waved him off. "My friend, let me introduce you to my pupil, Karina Fardi. I have to teach her, along with this idiot, the sacrament of imposing runes."

"My friend, I'm completely confused," the padishah made a gesture, and the musicians fell silent. "Archduke Valevsky killed you, but you are both sitting at my table, next to each other, alive, and it also turns out that you are taking this man as your pupil? Moreover, you find yourself with two pupils at once, which hasn't happened for decades? This sounds more like one of the bard's tall tales than reality."

"And yet, it is true. Valevsky will indeed be my pupil. Oh, what a beauty! My friend, I always knew that you have a penchant for beautiful women, but I never thought that you would share a table with them. Brother Lin, I can't say that I'm glad to see you, but I understand that it's impossible to refuse your presence. Are you here in lieu of his personal attendant?"

The cleric nodded, showing that the master's thoughts were correct.

"Naira Jode is at the table as a guest," the padishah explained. "This is the bride of Archduke Valevsky."

Karina Fardi showed emotion for the first time since joining the table. She turned her gaze to the girl. However, she quickly turned back and continued to study the opposite wall.

"Is that so?" Magister Meram turned his gaze to me. "Not only is he strong, but he's also nimble? Snatching such a beauty shows rare talent! What did you do to the Bartolomeo Clan that they gave you their treasure?"

"I believe Maximilian Valevsky will tell us this now," the padishah once again turned his predatory stare toward me. "I've heard so much about his adventures lately that I don't know what's true and what's fiction. Besides, one of my sons owes this man his life. Can you imagine, my friend, that there was a dev hunting in the Shurgan Empire!"

"Yes, I heard something like that," nodded the runescribe. "It's a pity that I didn't manage to get to him first. This would be the cherry on top of my collection of rare creatures. But on the whole, you are right, my friend, I would like to hear the story of this young rift conqueror. Maximilian, can you tell the old people how a common doomed soldier managed to become one of the most fascinating citizens of the Zarak Empire?"

"Why not tell me?" I smiled, but immediately the voice of the man with the Light-filled eyes rang out:

"Everything related to Maximilian Valevsky belongs to the category of classified information of the Church of the Light. He is not permitted to speak of what has happened to him during his adventures and how he reached the position he currently occupies. This is the will of the Citadel."

All I could do was shrug.

"I'm sorry, gentlemen, but apparently we'll have to go without this exciting tale. Brother Lin is against it. Although there is still one matter of business I must attend to. Dear Padishah Bayazid the Third, this belongs to you. I return it to you, safe and sound."

With these words, I took out a plate bearing the graven image of our host, placed it on the table and slid it towards the padishah, as if it were an ordinary card. His gaze gained even more malice. There was nothing human about him at all anymore!

"How did you get this card?" the padishah was in no hurry to take the item.

"I took it off the corpse of a man who dared attack me. He called himself Faceless. This beast kidnapped Karina Fardi and, using her image, for some time accompanied me and my companion on a trip to Hearth. In one of the villages, I don't remember which one specifically, he decided that it was time to act and attacked me. When I was sorting out the things that were left behind, I found this plate. An amazing item that has saved my life several times."

"So you used it without my knowledge? "The padishah's voice could have made my blood freeze, but after such a hearty dinner I could no longer be frightened.

"Before his death, Faceless reported that he acted on the orders of Padishah Bayazid III, who wanted to kidnap Baron Valevsky at the time and take him to his palace. I suppose it was slander. The revered padishah would never give such an ugly order. However, I was not able to give the plate back right away: I did not know a single trusted representative of the respected padishah. So I had to keep it for myself and, to be quite honest, even use an item of such value a handful of times."

"What happened to Faceless?" Brother Lin

asked.

"He exploded. When he realized what fate awaited him, he detonated his magic stones. The plate was the only thing left."

"The explosion in Verse," Brother Lin nodded, showing that he was well acquainted with the situation. "Yes, that explains a lot."

"And at the same time, you used my plate without my permission," Bayazid the Third once again gave the conversation an unpleasant turn. Twisting around, staring straight into the animal eyes of the host, I nodded:

"I did. If the respected padishah had not invited me to his house, I would have used it as many more times as I considered necessary. I have no information regarding how the plate fell into the hands of the person who wanted to kill me. I used the plate as a battle trophy."

"Father, how can you tolerate this behavior?!" Rustam exclaimed, jumping to his feet.

"Sit," the padishah said calmly, and everyone in the room held their breath, even the servants. "Archduke Valevsky, you understand that I did not give this order to Faceless?"

"Now that I have come to your house, shared dinner with you, and am sitting next to you, of course I understand how deeply I was mistaken. Such a wise ruler couldn't do anything so illegal. I sincerely apologize for using the plate without the will of its true owner and am ready to spend my time, effort and resources in order to pay off the debt that has accumulated during this time. I believe I will be able to find something that will interest even such a demanding person as Bayazid the Third."

"Are you speaking of the amulet that is in your pocket?" The padishah demonstrated that the maids did not just appear in my room, but were performing a very specific task. They had searched me and reported to the owner about all the little things that I had.

"Who would I be if I offered the respected padishah something that he already has so much of at his disposal?" I gestured to a whole heap of amulets that hung around his neck.

"Then I assume we are talking about these gloves?" Bayazid the Third made a gesture and the servants brought in armor that was familiar to me. Gold, shining with green light. So that was what I got for giving the Vyazemskys something valuable! *Analyze* showed that this is not just a coincidence--it was my creation. This connoisseur of rarities had gotten his hands on my gift!

"Not the gloves, exactly. Rather, all of the accompanying items. The *Thunderer* set consists of ten pieces. As a sign of my repentance, I can make four more items for the respected padishah."

"Let me have a look!" Magister Meram's interest was finally piqued. The padishah nodded, and the servants brought the gloves to the rune writer. "Wow! What fascinating work! And you have the recipe for five of the ten items in the set?"

All that I could do was nod.

"Where did you get them?"

I looked at Brother Lin and he shook his head, indicating that I should not speak. Although everyone already understood perfectly well where it came from. From the Temple of Skron.

"When will I receive my items?" the padishah asked.

"As soon as I get to the forge," I answered. "Just because I have a recipe doesn't mean I can create this item. Tomorrow I will be ready to provide our respected host with my sincere apology in the form of four items from the *Thunderer* set."

"I think the issue with my plate can be considered closed," Bayazid the Third grabbed the plate that had been lying in front of him all this time and hid it in one of the many pockets of his robe. "However, we are greatly saddened. You cannot tell about your adventures, because the Citadel does not grant you such a right. I cannot scold you for unauthorized use of the plate, because you repented and even apologized. I may, of course, recall that you stole an entire village from me, but I believe that the life of my son is worth several dozen peasants. Moreover, you personally punished the criminal. The evening is starting to get boring. At least give us one interesting tidbit, my friend. Did I invite you here this evening in vain?"

"If only!" Magister Meram rubbed his hands contentedly. "As I already said, Archduke Valevsky will become my pupil. At the same time, he tried to harm me. Even tore out my heart. Something

I've grown accustomed to, incidentally. It proved that I still have a heart. And they all said I was heartless...It was starting to get insulting. But that's not the point. My friend, will you mind if I punish my pupil a little before announcing the purpose of my visit?"

"I fully support this," answered Bayazid the Third. "Since I myself, by a strange coincidence, do not have such an opportunity, I will have to enjoy watching you punish him, my friend. I hope it will be something special that will give everyone a good spectacle."

"And more! I haven't taken on more than one pupil per cycle for a long time. I am unaccustomed to the need to manage several people at once. Therefore, Maximilian, until the end of your studies, you and Karina Fardi will be one. Eat together, sleep together, wash together and pore over my knowledge. There is no and there will not be Maximilian Valevsky or Karina Fardi. There will be one being called the disciple. And if at least one of you begins to spoil my mood by not preparing well for classes, and cannot come to terms with the presence of the other, I will punish both."

"Magister!" Karina Fardi couldn't hold back. All her feigned apathy had disappeared in an instant.

"My friend, what kind of punishment is this?" The padishah was surprised. "Being with such a beauty is more a pleasure than a punishment."

"It's all about the nuances," the old man grinned contentedly. "I have a little story about this. I think you'll like it, my friend."

Magister Meram gave the audience some backstory on why Karina and I weren't fond of each other. The runescribe mentioned not only the fact that her father destroyed my entire family, but also that I sent a steel bolt straight through her forehead. This news became a real revelation for many. Even Naira started looking at me with condemnation! Like, 'How can this be true? She's a girl!' How dare I raise my hand against someone who had higher status than me?

"The only thing that excuses him is that everything happened within the framework of a duel," Magister Meram still added a little objectivity. "Karina, in her stupidity, called an innocent young man to slaughter and he needed a defender. She is the only one to blame."

"Yes, my friend, you know a lot about punishment," the padishah rubbed his chin contentedly. Bayazid the Third looked extremely pleased, as if he had heard some fantastically good news.

"So, it's decided. If you both want to learn, you will put your individual emotions, desires and ambitions aside. You will become one. I will order you both to love each other with all your hearts. But enough of that for now. It was not for the sake of punishing my careless pupils that I came to you, my friend. What brings me here is much more exciting. I need a map. That one."

"My friend, it seems to me that we have already come to an agreement," steel flashed in the voice of Bayazid the Third, and his gaze again became bestial.

"We did," Magister Meram agreed easily. "New circumstances have just appeared, my friend, that don't allow me to just give up on this idea. And this very circumstance sits next to you. The infected rift of the thirty-first level was closed. Not sealed as before, just closed!"

"This is not information that should be disclosed," Brother Lin chimed in.

"Why not?" Magister Meram was surprised. "When did data on closed rifts become a Citadel secret? No, Brother Lin, I will say as I wish. And you have no right to forbid me to speak. Learning to listen can do you good. Especially you."

"Level Thirty-One?" The padishah turned in my direction, and I had to make an effort to keep a straight face and not meet his gaze. I hadn't decided what to do with Fardi yet. I didn't want to agree to the old runescribe's crazy demands, but I also needed training badly. I needed to find a compromise, but in order to do that, I needed to understand where this was all going.

"That's right, Level Thirty-One. I'm planning on taking a stroll down there myself. If I have a map, we will reach the desired point in just a couple of months. Right, Brother Lin? Will the Citadel go to the extent of delving through its vaults and pulling out nine mysterious and captivating crystals?"

"You..." Brother Lin choked on his rage.

"Of course, me!" Magister Meram's eyes

sparkled with madness. "We have a chance to stop the offworlders and throw them away from our world. Put a stop to the havoc they were wreaking. Return to humanity the lands that were captured by these creatures. I have Valevsky. I will train him and he will become the embodiment of power. I need a map to get to the point where the forces of these creatures are concentrated. I need crystals to open the passage. And when I do have them, and I do intend to get them, this world will shake beneath our feet."

"The Citadel cannot allow you to take such a risk by sending you on such a dangerous journey."

"I will have converts and disciples with me. This is more than enough to brush aside any adversity. Twenty years ago they didn't listen to me, so listen now. Or is the Citadel not interested in destroying the offworlders?"

"We are," Brother Lin answered after a pause. "But I can't leave the capital."

"Why do I need clerics on a campaign?" Magister Meram was surprised. "We will do things there that will cause us all to be sent to the stake. So no, thanks, we don't need any extra spies. Two pupils, three supreme converts from my personal reserves. This will be more than enough to implement any crazy plan we may contrive. Find the point of power of the offworlders and strike at it with an insidious blow. I love those kinds of plans."

"Let's say this idea appeals to me. What do I stand to gain? The map will lose its uniqueness."

"The Citadel will find a way to pay you," Brother Lin made a decision and, what was surprising to me, showed that he has the right to make such decisions. I hadn't seen him at the Conclave.

"Fantastic!" Magister Meram rubbed his hands together like a child being offered a piece of candy. "We'll move out tomorrow! I'll hang a beacon on myself. If you need my help, send a convert. But try to make sure that we are delayed as little as possible. Who knows how the physics of portals work in the lands of offworlders! Maybe they won't work at all? No, we can't take that risk. The less connection, the better. I already finished with Valevsky while he was lying around in the Citadel, Fardi was left. She also needs to be run through the symbols. My pupils must be as one!"

"Sorry, Magister, but I cannot abide by this. I swore on my life that I would kill this bastard, and you are forcing me to work with him! It will not happen. The only place where this doomed soldier belongs is the grave. And I'm going to send him there!"

"Maximilian!" Naira shouted a warning. I turned towards Fardi and saw Karina's distraught eyes. There was no intelligence left in them. Just a dull determination to see her decision through to the end. And now this decision was staring me in the face in the form of a hand crossbow attached to the girl's wrist. Even more disturbing was that Fardi's hand was inside my protective dome. The dome wasn't working. My gaze began to move to the quick access bar where *Dash* was located, but I missed it by just a moment.

"Die, beast!"

Fardi activated her weapon and when the padishah's children rushed at her, it was all over. I didn't even feel any pain — the bolt easily pierced my forehead and entered my brain. The darkness came instantly, and there was no returning from it.

End of Book Six

Want to be the first to know about our latest LitRPG,
sci fi and fantasy titles from your favorite authors?

Subscribe to our **New Releases** newsletter:
http://eepurl.com/b7niIL

Thank you for reading *Condemned!*
If you like what you've read, check out other sci-fi, fantasy
and A LitRPG series published by Magic Dome Books:

NEW RELEASES!

Crossroads of Oblivion
a portal progression fantasy adventure series
by Dem Mikhailov

Gakko Academy
a portal progression fantasy adventure series
by Evgeny Alexeev

War Eternal
a military space adventure LitRPG series
by Yuri Vinokuroff

The Hunter's Code
a LitRPG series by Yuri Vinokuroff & Oleg Sapphire

The Order of Architects
a portal progression series
by Yuri Vinokuroff & Oleg Sapphire

I Will Be Emperor
a space adventure progression fantasy series
by Yuri Vinokuroff & Oleg Sapphire

An Ideal World for a Sociopath
a LitRPG series by Oleg Sapphire

The Healer's Way
a LitRPG series by Oleg Sapphire & Alexey Kovtunov

A Shelter in Spacetime
a LitRPG series by Dmitry Dornichev

The Village
a LitRPG progression fantasy series
by Dmitry Dornichev & Alexey Kovtunov

Ghost in the System
An apocalypse LitRPG series by Alexey Kovtunov

The Last Portal Jumper
a LitRPG series by Konstantin Zubov

Lord of the System
a LitRPG progression fantasy series by
Alex Toxic and Furious Miki

Kill to Live
a LitRPG progression fantasy adventure series
by George Bor and Yuri Vinokuroff

Kill or Die
a LitRPG series by Alex Toxic

The Strongest Student
a portal progression action fantasy series
by Andrei Tkachev

Living Ice
a portal progression alternative history series
by Dmitry Sheleg

Law of the Jungle
a Wuxia Progression Fantasy Adventure Series
By Vasily Mahanenko

Reality Benders
a LitRPG series by Michael Atamanov

The Dark Herbalist
a LitRPG series by Michael Atamanov

Perimeter Defense
a LitRPG series by Michael Atamanov

League of Losers
a LitRPG series by Michael Atamanov

Chaos' Game
a LitRPG series by Alexey Svadkovsky

The Way of the Shaman
a LitRPG series by Vasily Mahanenko

The Alchemist
a LitRPG series by Vasily Mahanenko

Dark Paladin
a LitRPG series by Vasily Mahanenko

Galactogon
a LitRPG series by Vasily Mahanenko

Invasion
a LitRPG series by Vasily Mahanenko

World of the Changed
a LitRPG series by Vasily Mahanenko

The Bear Clan
a LitRPG series by Vasily Mahanenko

Starting Point
a LitRPG series by Vasily Mahanenko

The Bard from Barliona
a LitRPG series
by Eugenia Dmitrieva and Vasily Mahanenko

Condemned
(Lord Valevsky: Last of The Line)
a Progression Fantasy series
by Vasily Mahanenko

Loner
a LitRPG series by Alex Kosh

A Buccaneer's Due
a LitRPG series by Igor Knox

A Student Wants to Live
a LitRPG series by Boris Romanovsky

The Goldenblood Heir
a LitRPG series by Boris Romanovsky

Level Up
a LitRPG series by Dan Sugralinov

Level Up: The Knockout
a LitRPG series by Dan Sugralinov and Max Lagno

Adam Online
a LitRPG Series by Max Lagno

World 99
a LitRPG series by Dan Sugralinov

Disgardium
a LitRPG series by Dan Sugralinov

Nullform
a RealRPG Series by Dem Mikhailov

Clan Dominance: The Sleepless Ones
a LitRPG series by Dem Mikhailov

Heroes of the Final Frontier
a LitRPG series by Dem Mikhailov

The Crow Cycle
a LitRPG series by Dem Mikhailov

Interworld Network
a LitRPG series by Dmitry Bilik

Rogue Merchant
a LitRPG series by Roman Prokofiev

Project Stellar
a LitRPG series by Roman Prokofiev

In the System
a LitRPG series by Petr Zhgulyov

The Crow Cycle
a LitRPG series by Dem Mikhailov

Unfrozen
a LitRPG series by Anton Tekshin

The Neuro
a LitRPG series by Andrei Livadny

Phantom Server
a LitRPG series by Andrei Livadny

Respawn Trials
a LitRPG series by Andrei Livadny

The Expansion (The History of the Galaxy)
a Space Exploration Saga by A. Livadny

The Range
a LitRPG series by Yuri Ulengov

Point Apocalypse
a near-future action thriller by Alex Bobl

Moskau
a dystopian thriller by G. Zotov

El Diablo
a supernatural thriller by G.Zotov

Mirror World
a LitRPG series by Alexey Osadchuk

Underdog
a LitRPG series by Alexey Osadchuk

Last Life
a Progression Fantasy series by Alexey Osadchuk

Alpha Rome
a LitRPG series by Ros Per

In order to have new books of the series translated faster, we need your help and support! Please consider leaving a review or spread the word by recommending *Condemned* to your friends and posting the link on social media. The more people buy the book, the sooner we'll be able to make new translations available.

Thank you!

Till next time!

www.ingramcontent.com/pod-product-compliance
Lightning Source LLC
LaVergne TN
LVHW051253200726
843510LV00010B/1112